BEOWULF

BEO

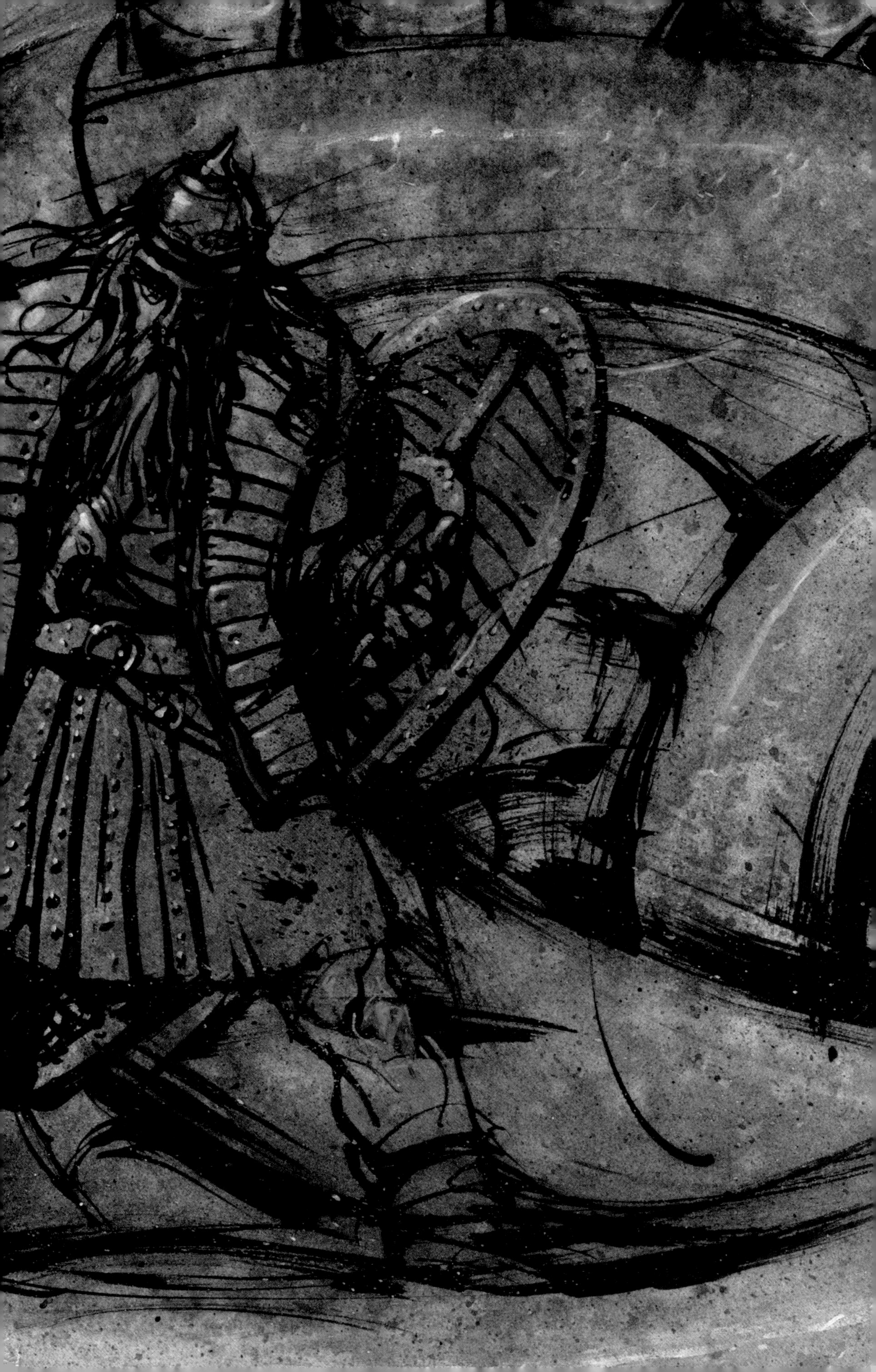

WULF

adapted and illustrated by Gareth Hinds

CANDLEWICK PRESS
CAMBRIDGE, MASSACHUSETTS

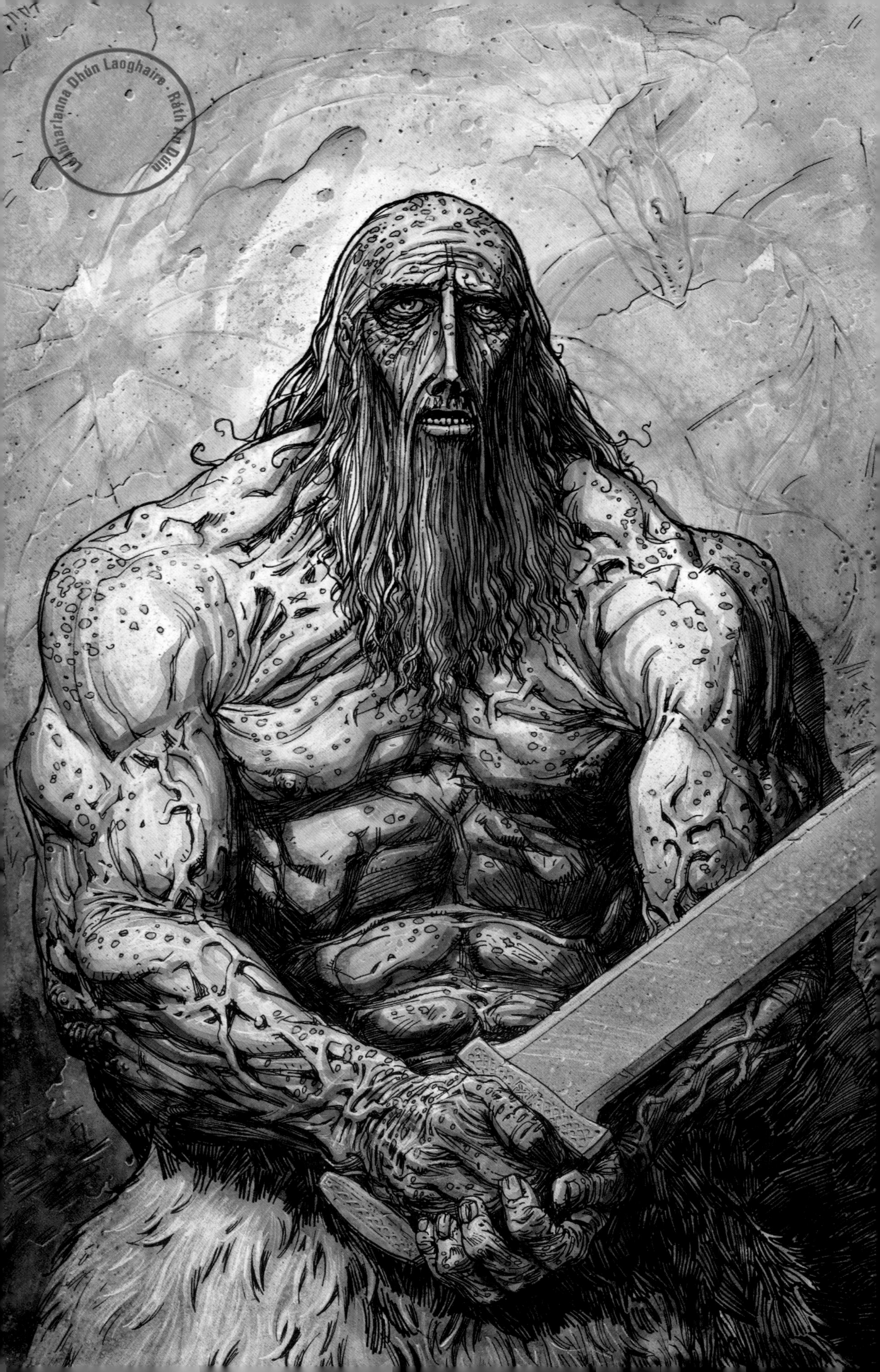

AUTHOR'S NOTE

The exact date of the composition of *Beowulf* is not known. It is an epic poem that was passed down orally for many generations before it was recorded. The first existing manuscript dates to around 1000 AD. The death of Hygelac, Beowulf's lord, is recorded in 521 AD in the Frankish annals. The most probable date of *Beowulf*'s composition, then, is thought to be around 700 to 850 AD. And yet it still resonates today, and indeed has much in common with our modern superhero stories.

For this edition, the author and editors have prepared a new text, based on the translation by A. J. Church published by Seeley & Co. in 1904. This is a colloquial translation, and we have attempted to strike a balance between easy readability and the poetic drama found in our favorite verse translations (particularly that of Francis Gummere, which appeared in the original, self-published edition of this book).

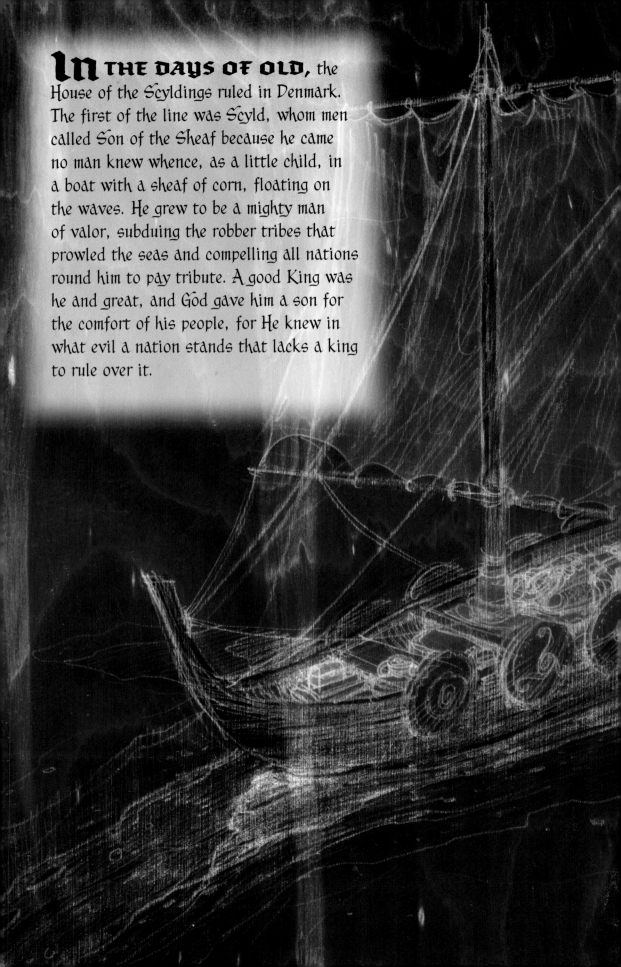

IN THE DAYS OF OLD, the House of the Scyldings ruled in Denmark. The first of the line was Scyld, whom men called Son of the Sheaf because he came no man knew whence, as a little child, in a boat with a sheaf of corn, floating on the waves. He grew to be a mighty man of valor, subduing the robber tribes that prowled the seas and compelling all nations round him to pay tribute. A good King was he and great, and God gave him a son for the comfort of his people, for He knew in what evil a nation stands that lacks a king to rule over it.

Now, the time came that King Scyld must die, for he had grown old and feeble. So they carried him to the sea, and there stood his ship, newly adorned, with sails set as for a voyage. There in the middle, hard by the mast, did the comrades of Scyld the King lay down their dead lord with many precious things. Never was a ship adorned in more comely fashion, with warriors' gear and weapons of war, battle-axes and coats of mail. With empty hands he had come into this world, but he departed into the land of the waters with a king's treasure. And the helm they left free, so that the sea might take him wheresoever it would.

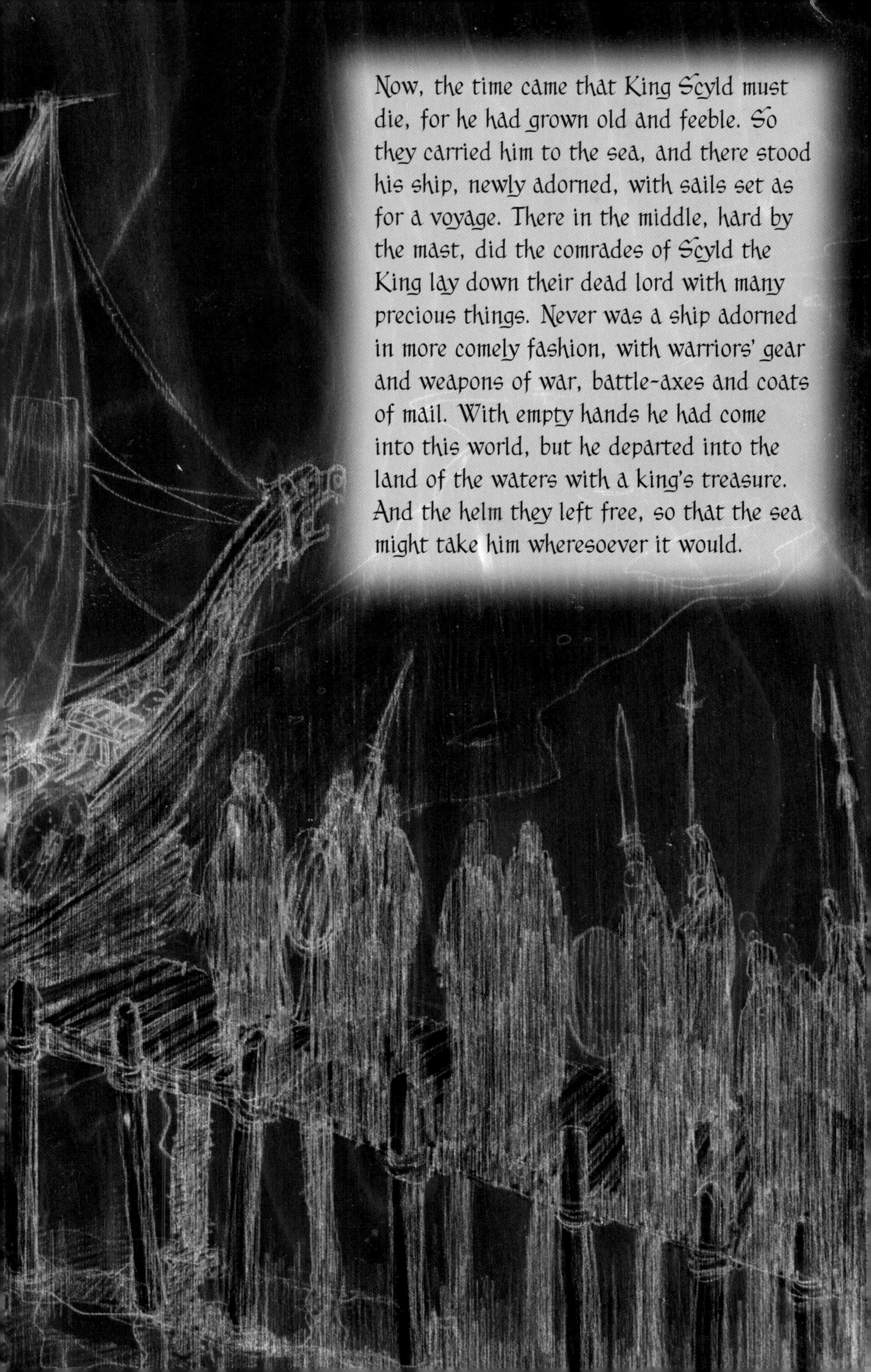

King Scyld having thus gone to his place, Beow his son reigned in his stead for many years even unto old age and was followed in turn by his son, Healfdane the Great. To him were granted four strong children, Heorogar, Hrothgar, Halga, and Yrse.

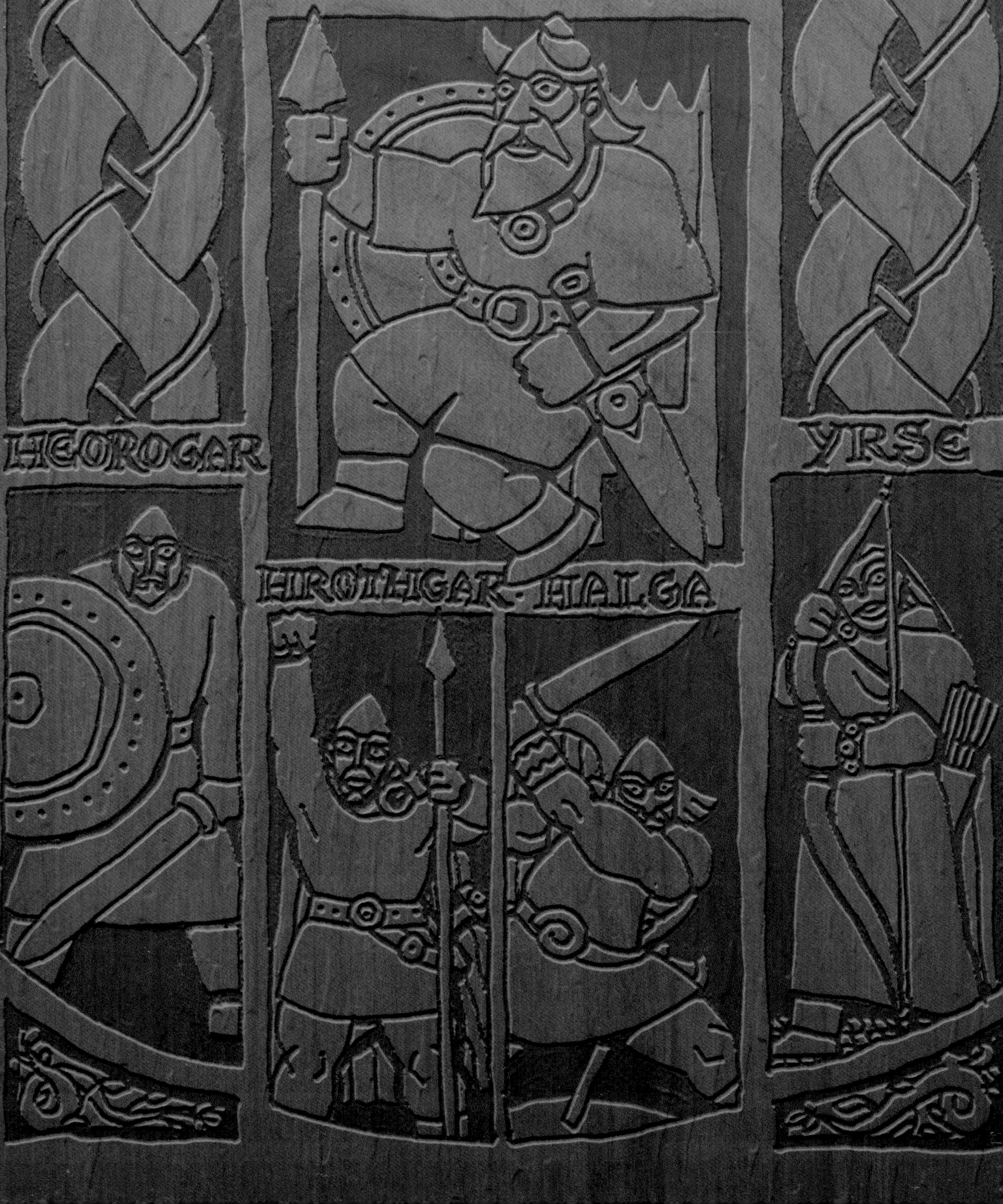
HEOROGAR
YRSE
HROTHGAR
HALGA

BOOK ONE

HROTHGAR excelled all that had gone before him in valiant deeds. It came into his mind that he would build a banquet hall greater than man had ever heard tell of. And as he purposed, so he did. Quickly was the hall set up, and when it was finished, it was the stateliest in all the lands of men, a home of peace, towering high. Nor did any that beheld it dream that there should ever be strife within.

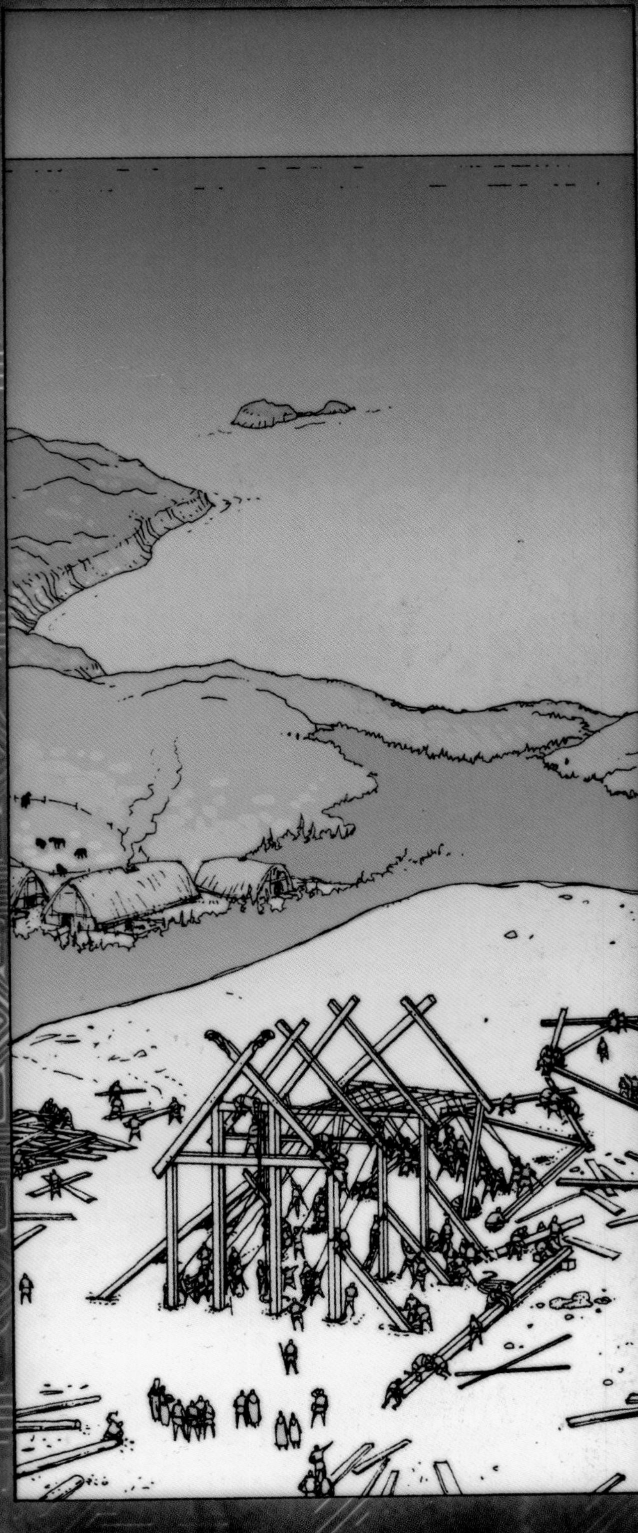

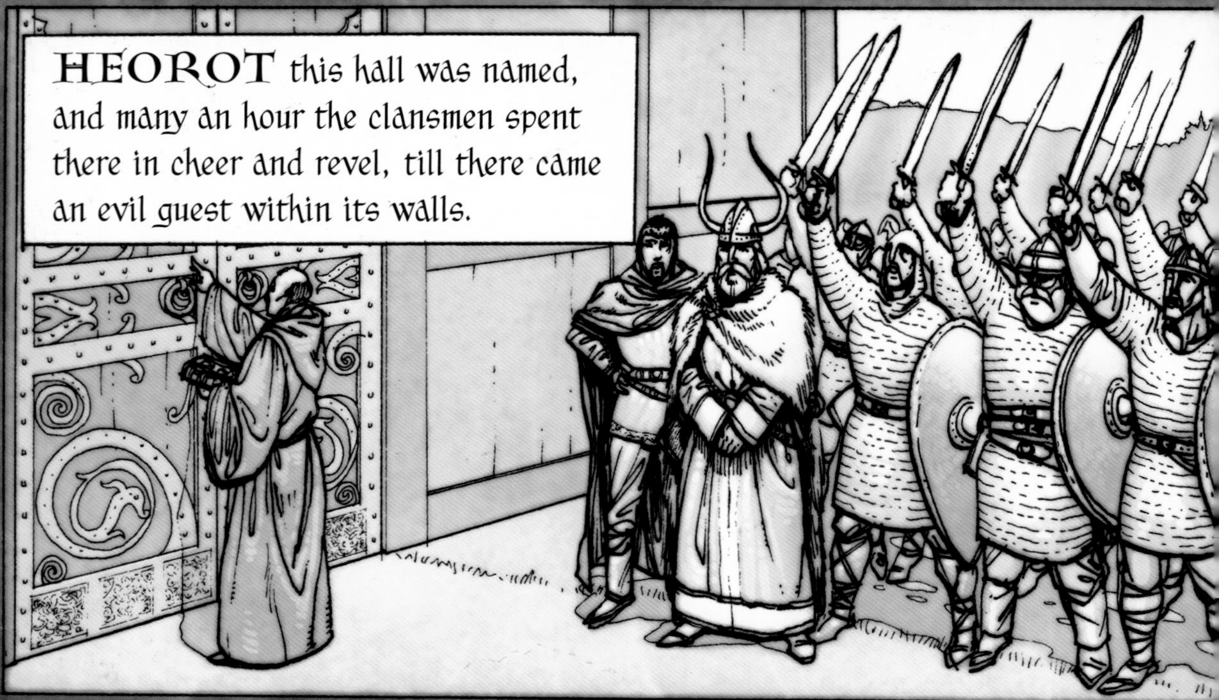
HEOROT this hall was named, and many an hour the clansmen spent there in cheer and revel, till there came an evil guest within its walls.

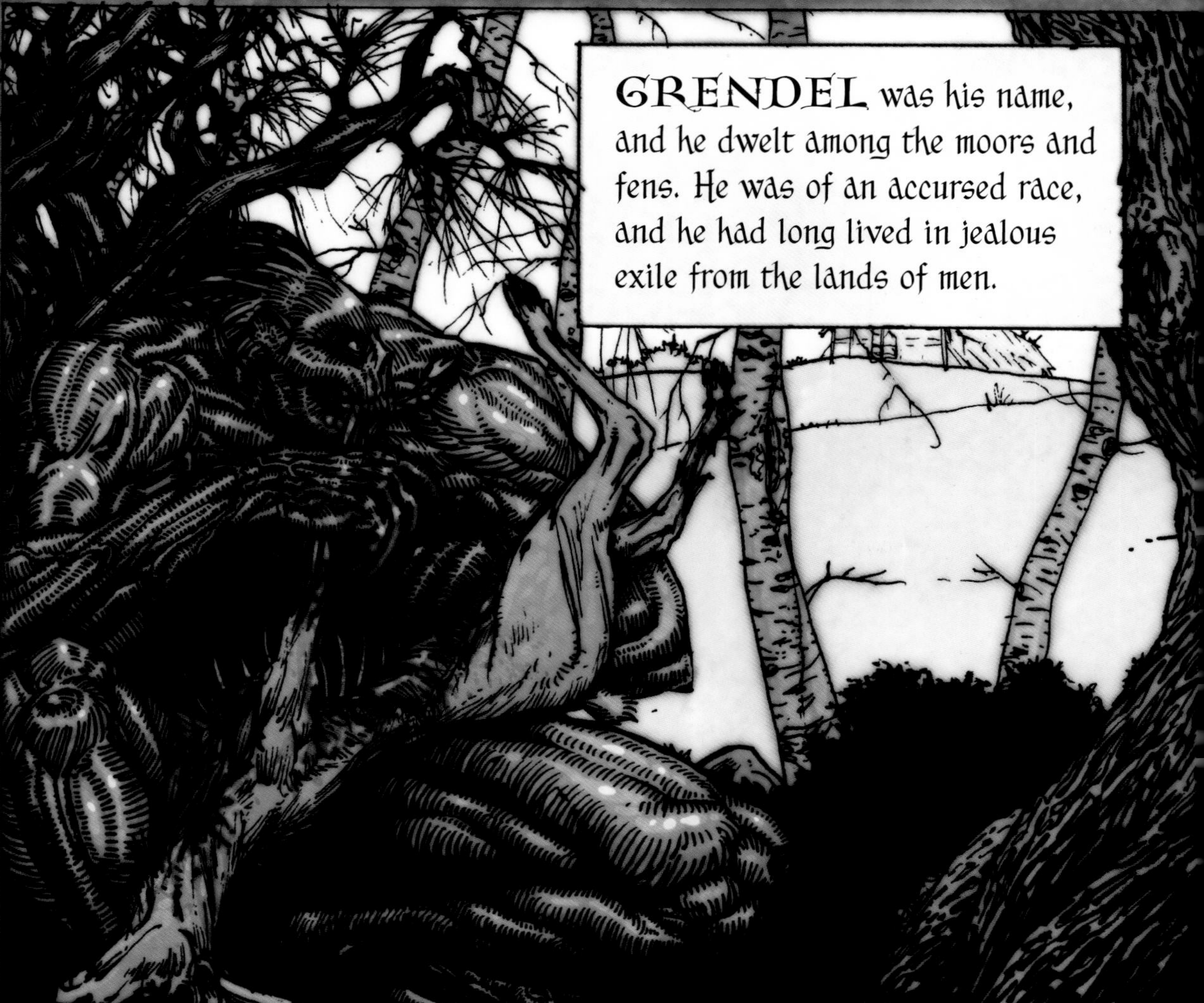
GRENDEL was his name, and he dwelt among the moors and fens. He was of an accursed race, and he had long lived in jealous exile from the lands of men.

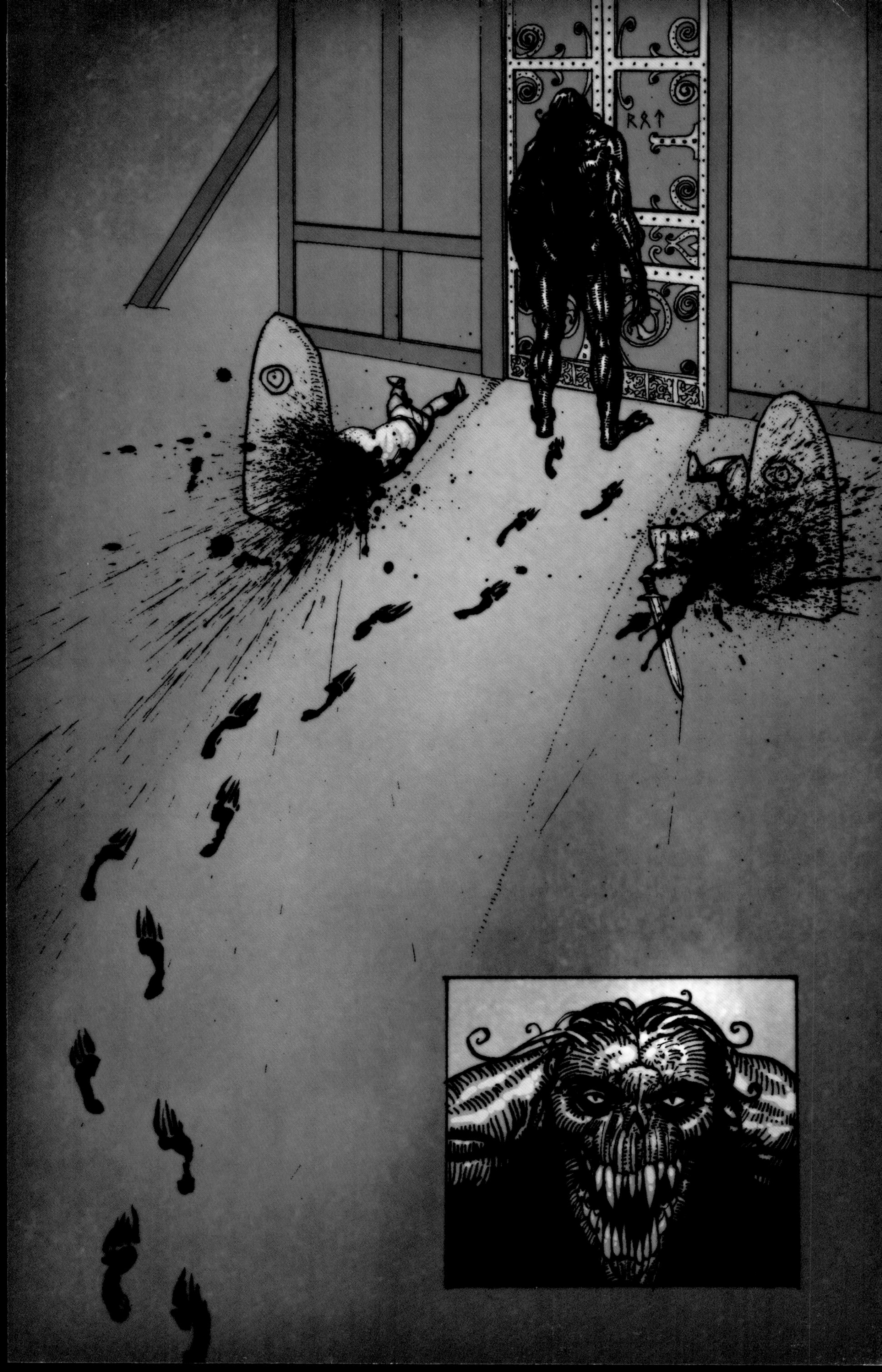

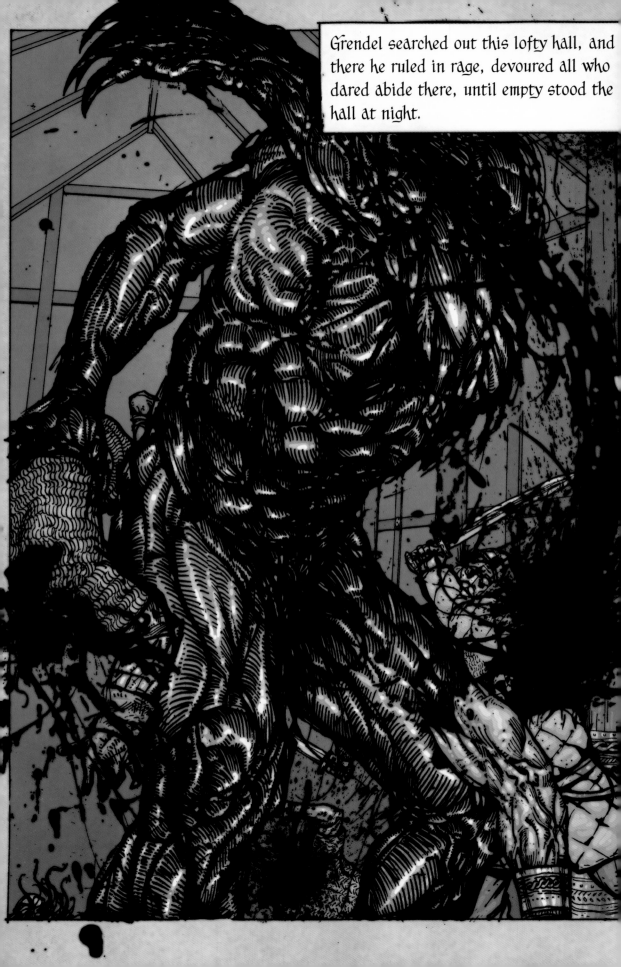

Grendel searched out this lofty hall, and there he ruled in rage, devoured all who dared abide there, until empty stood the hall at night.

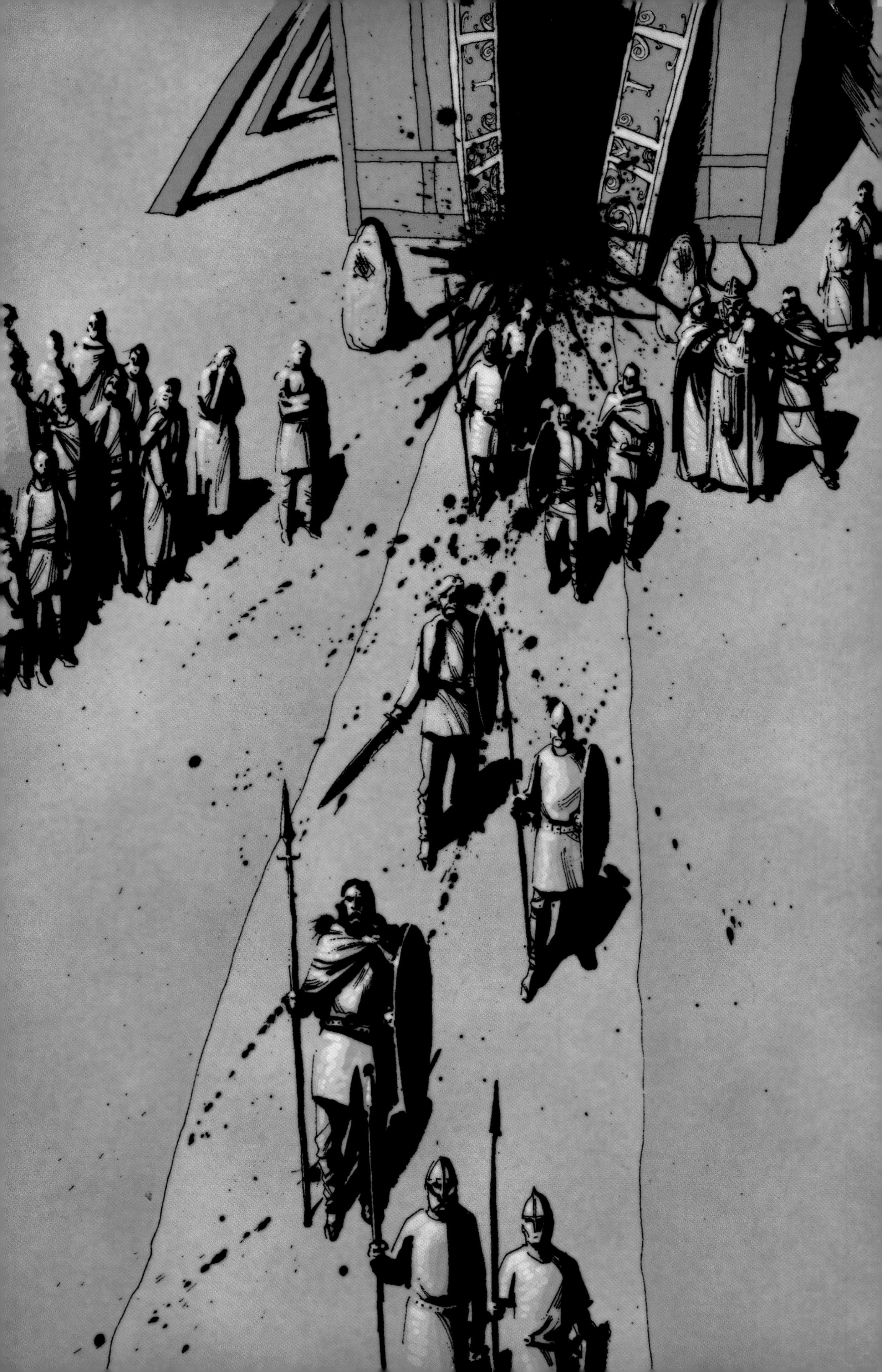

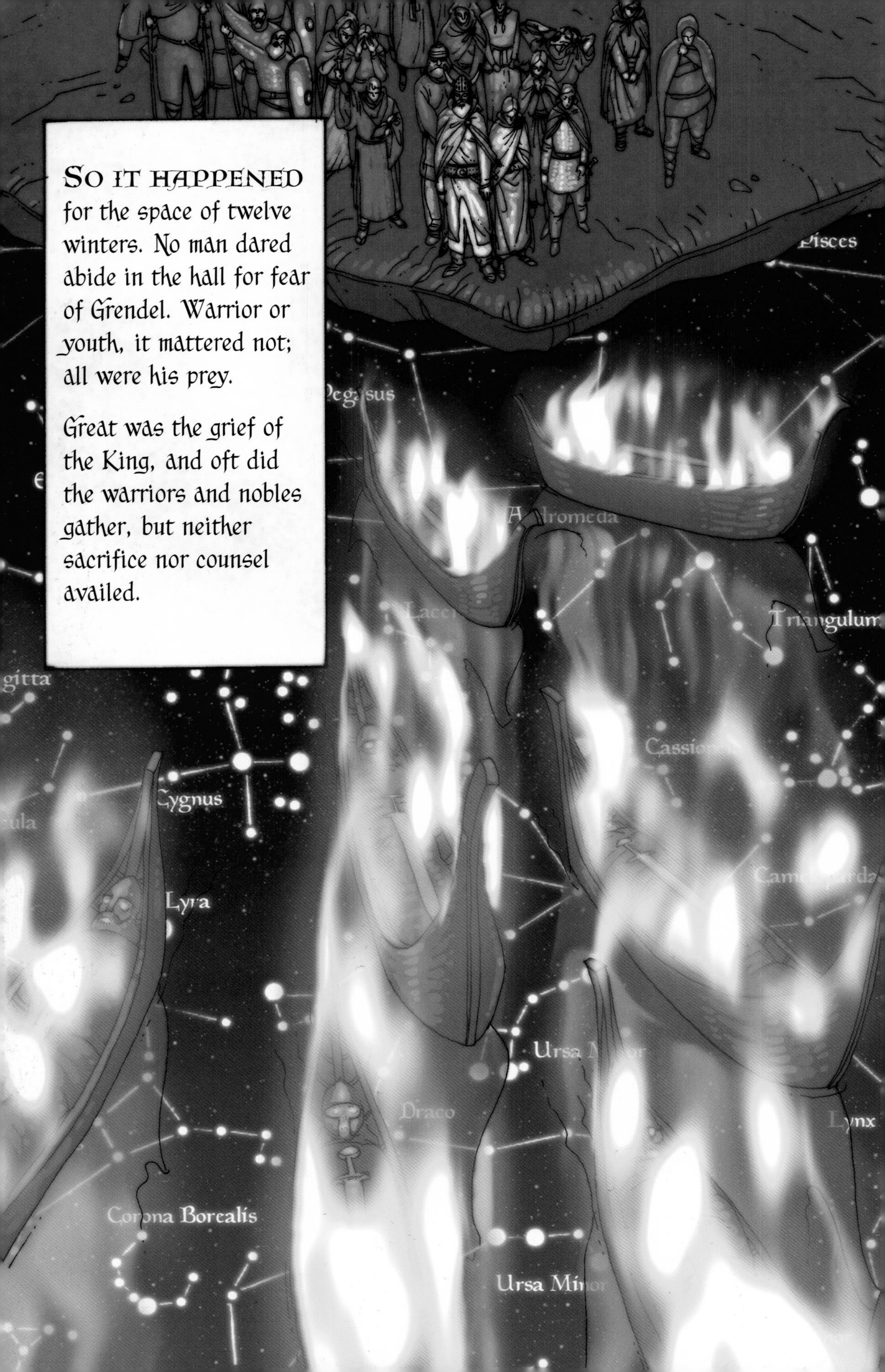
SO IT HAPPENED for the space of twelve winters. No man dared abide in the hall for fear of Grendel. Warrior or youth, it mattered not; all were his prey.
Great was the grief of the King, and oft did the warriors and nobles gather, but neither sacrifice nor counsel availed.
Cygnus
Lyra
Draco
Lynx
Corona Borealis

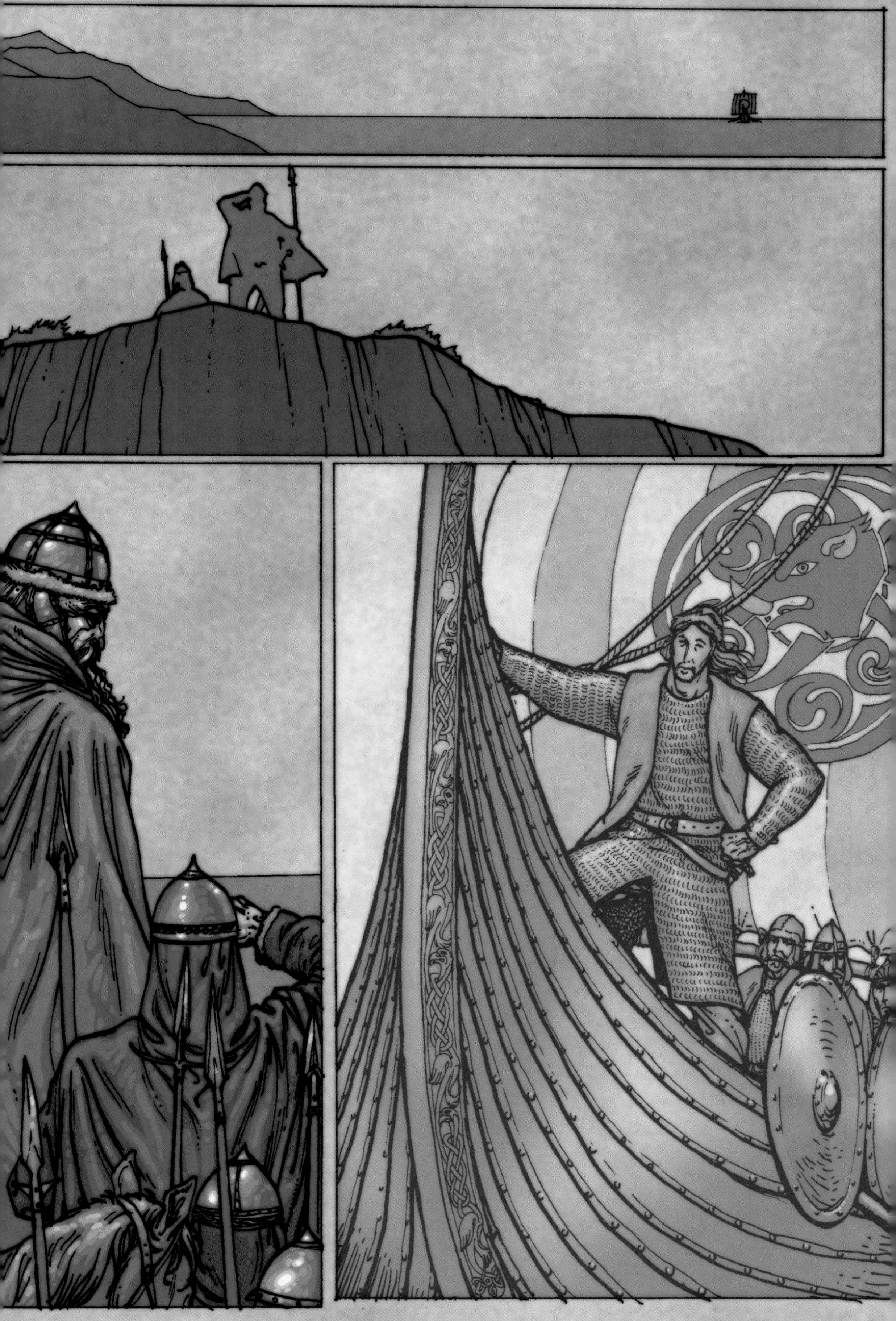

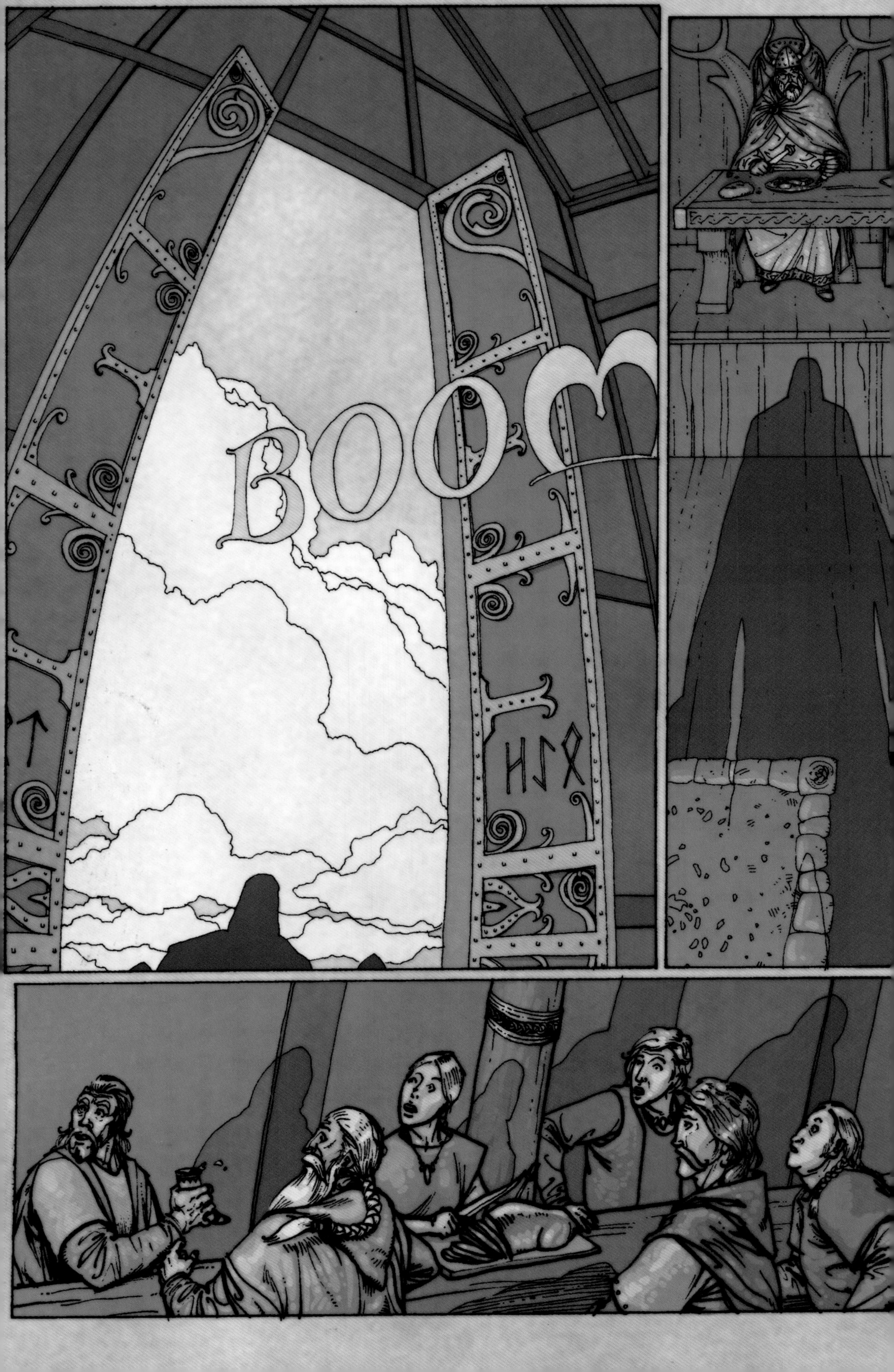
BOOM

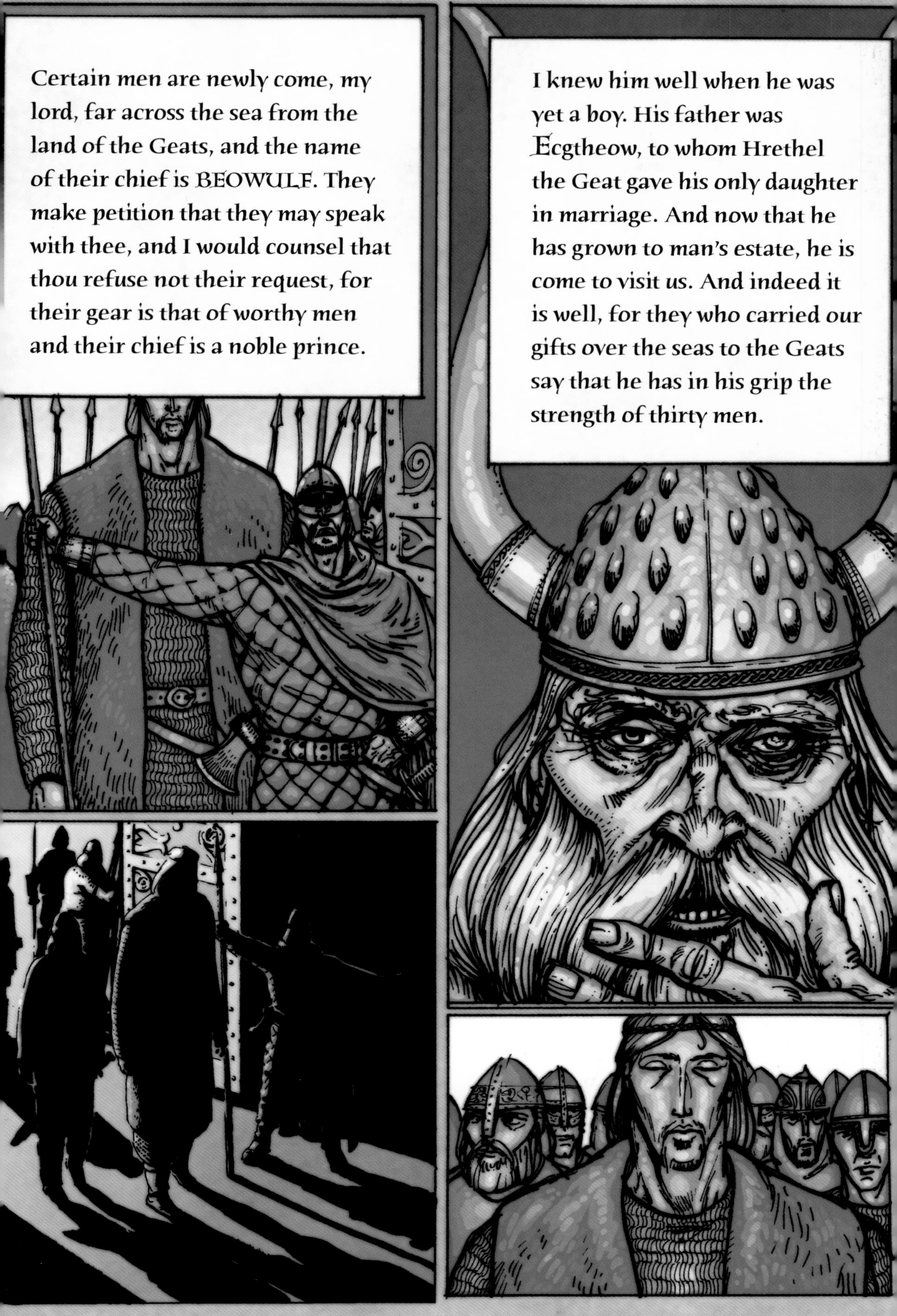
Certain men are newly come, my lord, far across the sea from the land of the Geats, and the name of their chief is BEOWULF. They make petition that they may speak with thee, and I would counsel that thou refuse not their request, for their gear is that of worthy men and their chief is a noble prince.
I knew him well when he was yet a boy. His father was Ecgtheow, to whom Hrethel the Geat gave his only daughter in marriage. And now that he has grown to man's estate, he is come to visit us. And indeed it is well, for they who carried our gifts over the seas to the Geats say that he has in his grip the strength of thirty men.

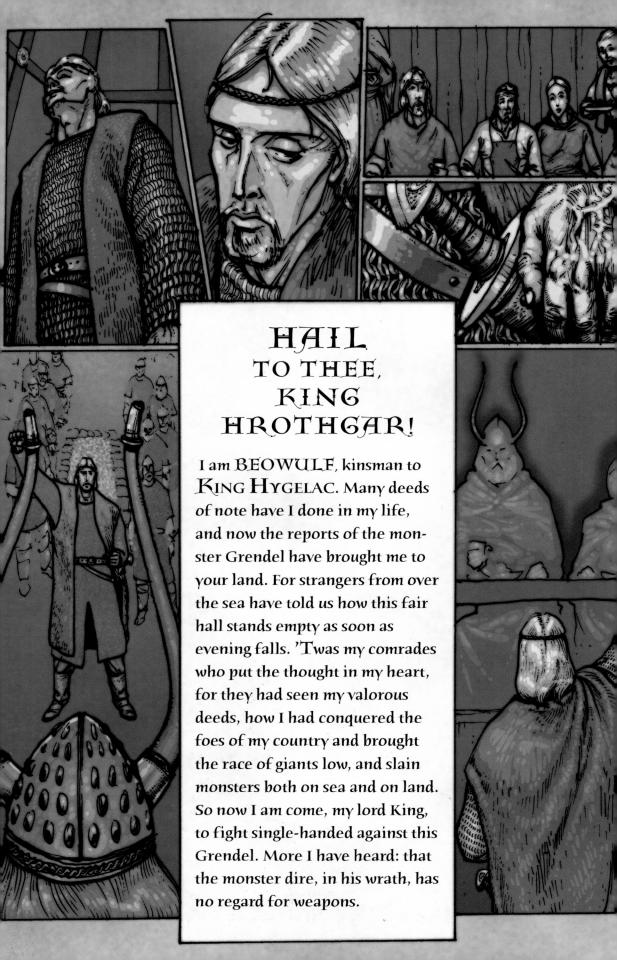

HAIL TO THEE, KING HROTHGAR!

I am BEOWULF, kinsman to KING HYGELAC. Many deeds of note have I done in my life, and now the reports of the monster Grendel have brought me to your land. For strangers from over the sea have told us how this fair hall stands empty as soon as evening falls. 'Twas my comrades who put the thought in my heart, for they had seen my valorous deeds, how I had conquered the foes of my country and brought the race of giants low, and slain monsters both on sea and on land. So now I am come, my lord King, to fight single-handed against this Grendel. More I have heard: that the monster dire, in his wrath, has no regard for weapons.

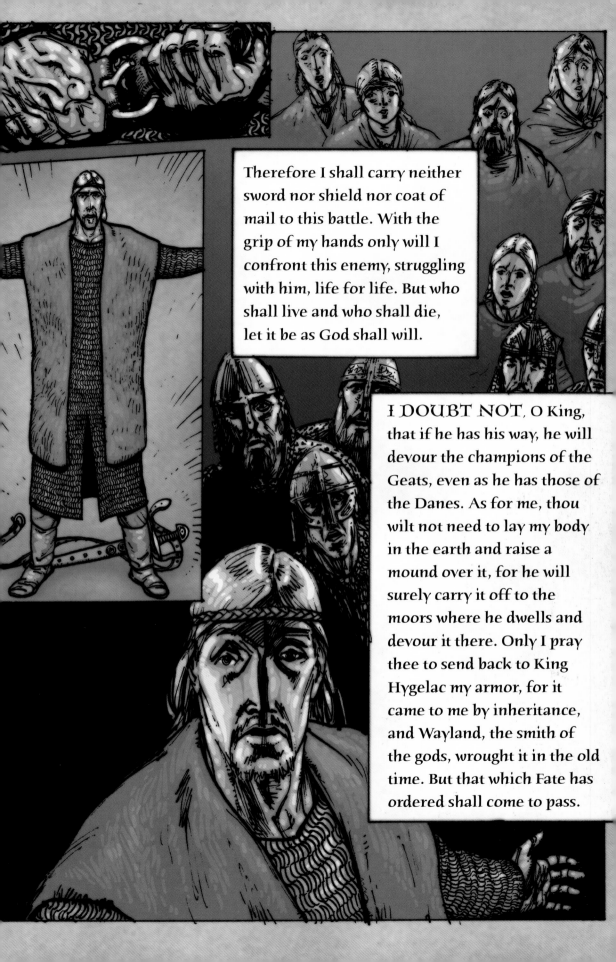

Therefore I shall carry neither sword nor shield nor coat of mail to this battle. With the grip of my hands only will I confront this enemy, struggling with him, life for life. But who shall live and who shall die, let it be as God shall will.

I DOUBT NOT, O King, that if he has his way, he will devour the champions of the Geats, even as he has those of the Danes. As for me, thou wilt not need to lay my body in the earth and raise a mound over it, for he will surely carry it off to the moors where he dwells and devour it there. Only I pray thee to send back to King Hygelac my armor, for it came to me by inheritance, and Wayland, the smith of the gods, wrought it in the old time. But that which Fate has ordered shall come to pass.

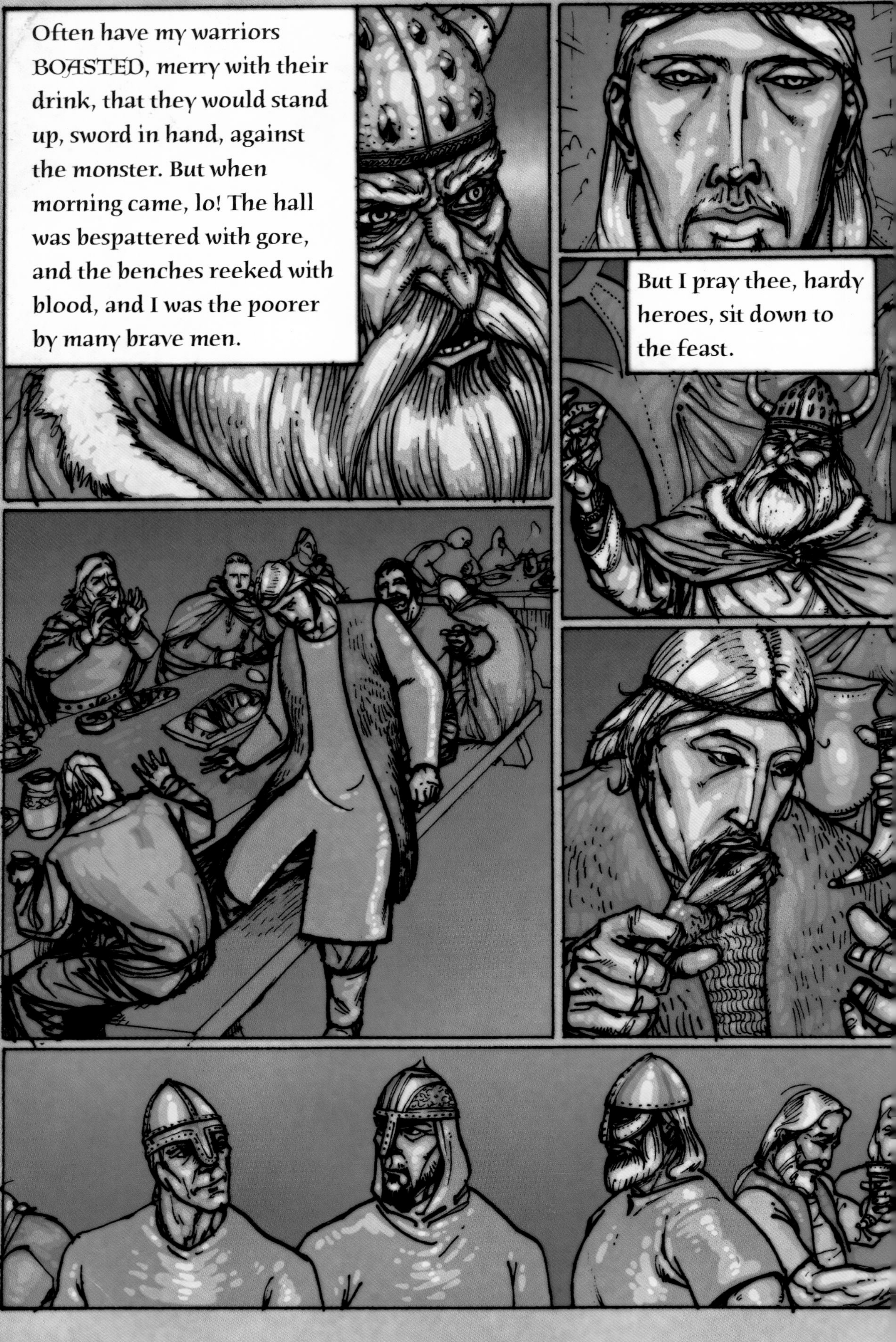
Often have my warriors BOASTED, merry with their drink, that they would stand up, sword in hand, against the monster. But when morning came, lo! The hall was bespattered with gore, and the benches reeked with blood, and I was the poorer by many brave men.
But I pray thee, hardy heroes, sit down to the feast.

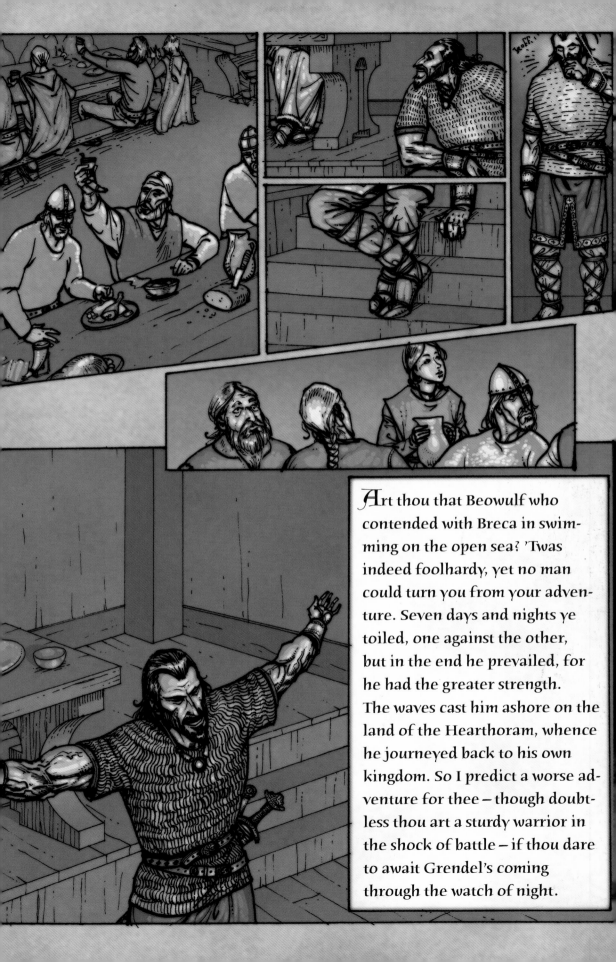

Art thou that Beowulf who contended with Breca in swimming on the open sea? 'Twas indeed foolhardy, yet no man could turn you from your adventure. Seven days and nights ye toiled, one against the other, but in the end he prevailed, for he had the greater strength. The waves cast him ashore on the land of the Hearthoram, whence he journeyed back to his own kingdom. So I predict a worse adventure for thee — though doubtless thou art a sturdy warrior in the shock of battle — if thou dare to await Grendel's coming through the watch of night.

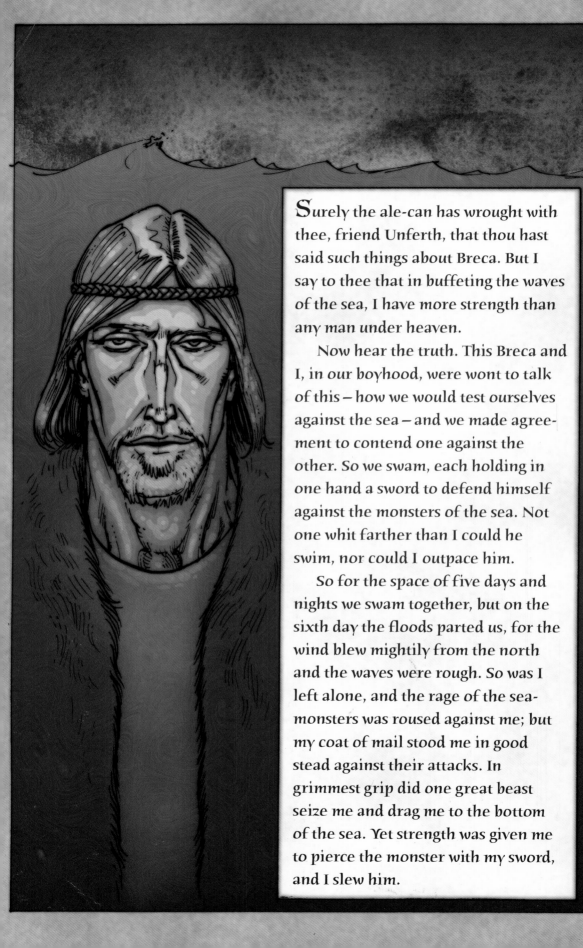

Surely the ale-can has wrought with thee, friend Unferth, that thou hast said such things about Breca. But I say to thee that in buffeting the waves of the sea, I have more strength than any man under heaven.

Now hear the truth. This Breca and I, in our boyhood, were wont to talk of this — how we would test ourselves against the sea — and we made agreement to contend one against the other. So we swam, each holding in one hand a sword to defend himself against the monsters of the sea. Not one whit farther than I could he swim, nor could I outpace him.

So for the space of five days and nights we swam together, but on the sixth day the floods parted us, for the wind blew mightily from the north and the waves were rough. So was I left alone, and the rage of the sea-monsters was roused against me; but my coat of mail stood me in good stead against their attacks. In grimmest grip did one great beast seize me and drag me to the bottom of the sea. Yet strength was given me to pierce the monster with my sword, and I slew him.

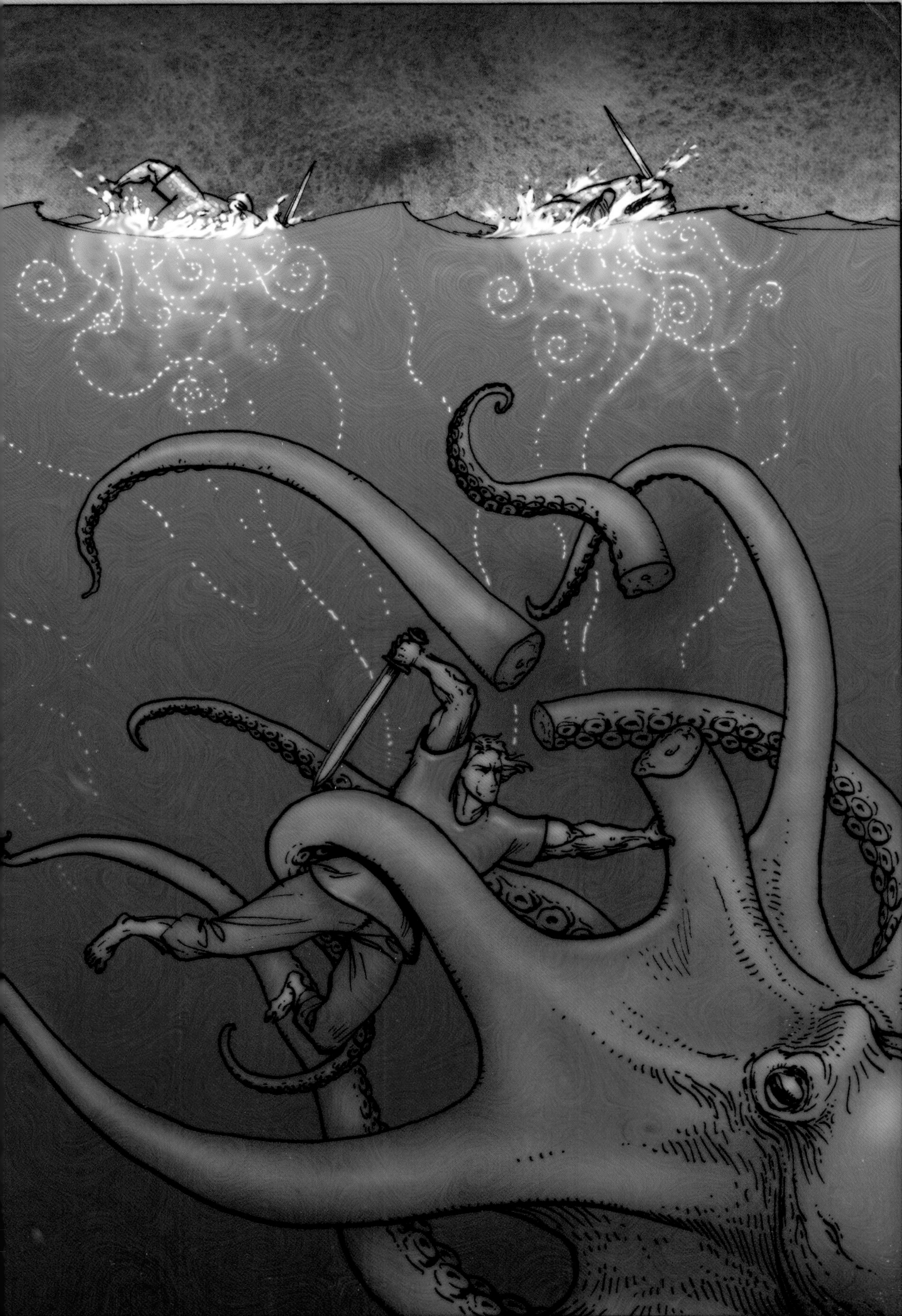

And so it came that I slew with my sword nine monsters of the deep and escaped with my life. Never was a man more hardly pressed by the waves of the sea or put into greater peril of death. Spent with swimming, I was finally cast up by the tide upon the land of the Finns. I have heard of no such deeds as done by thee, Unferth, son of Ecglaf.

THONK!

HaHaHaHaHaHa

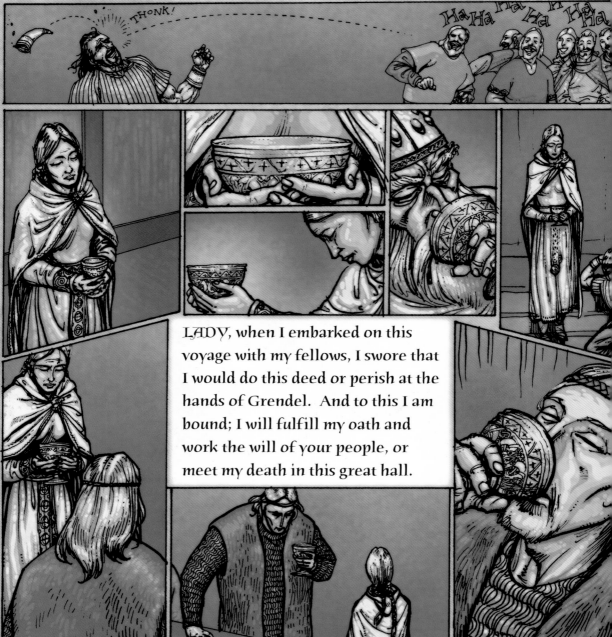

LADY, when I embarked on this voyage with my fellows, I swore that I would do this deed or perish at the hands of Grendel. And to this I am bound; I will fulfill my oath and work the will of your people, or meet my death in this great hall.

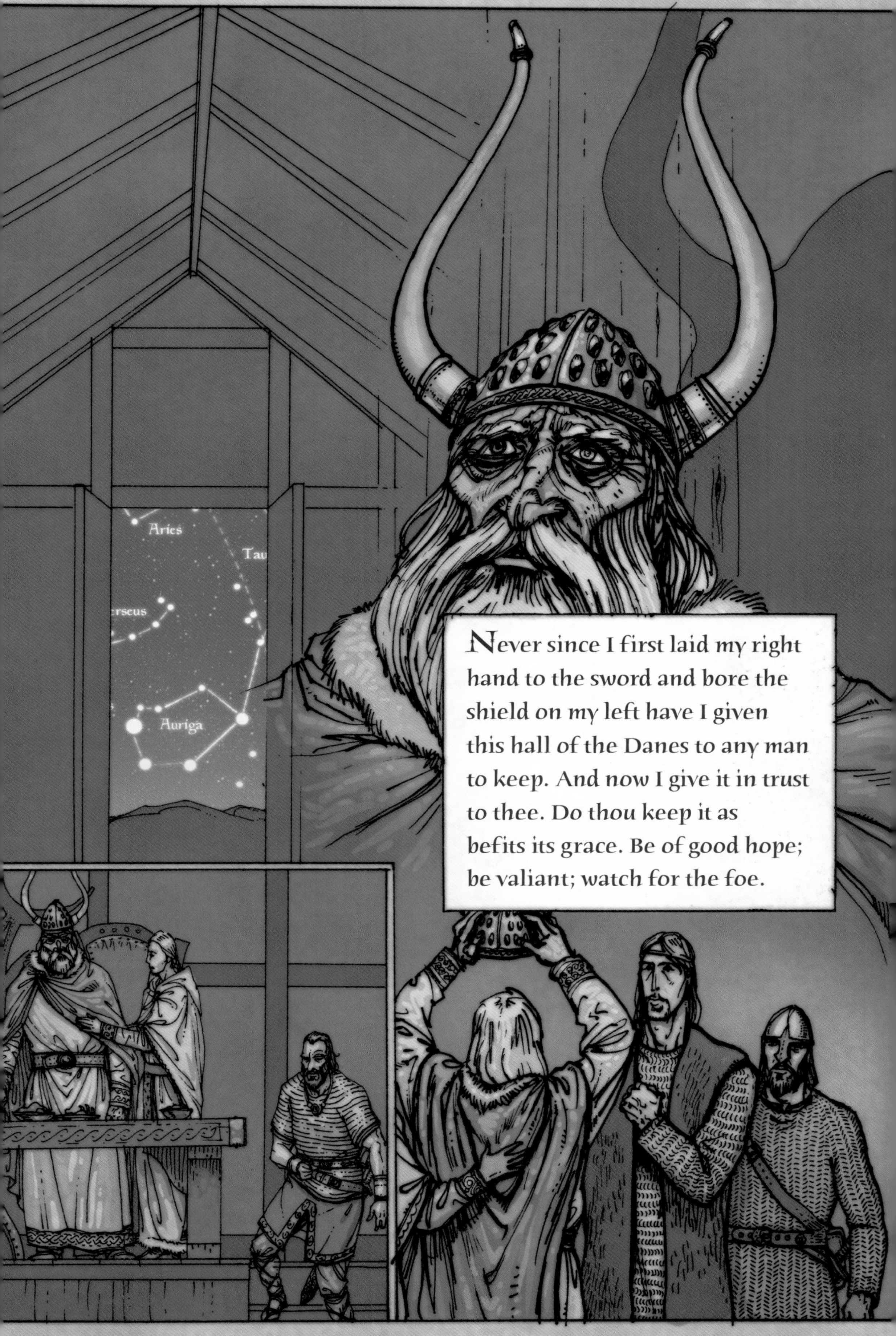
Aries
Perseus
Auriga
Never since I first laid my right hand to the sword and bore the shield on my left have I given this hall of the Danes to any man to keep. And now I give it in trust to thee. Do thou keep it as befits its grace. Be of good hope; be valiant; watch for the foe.

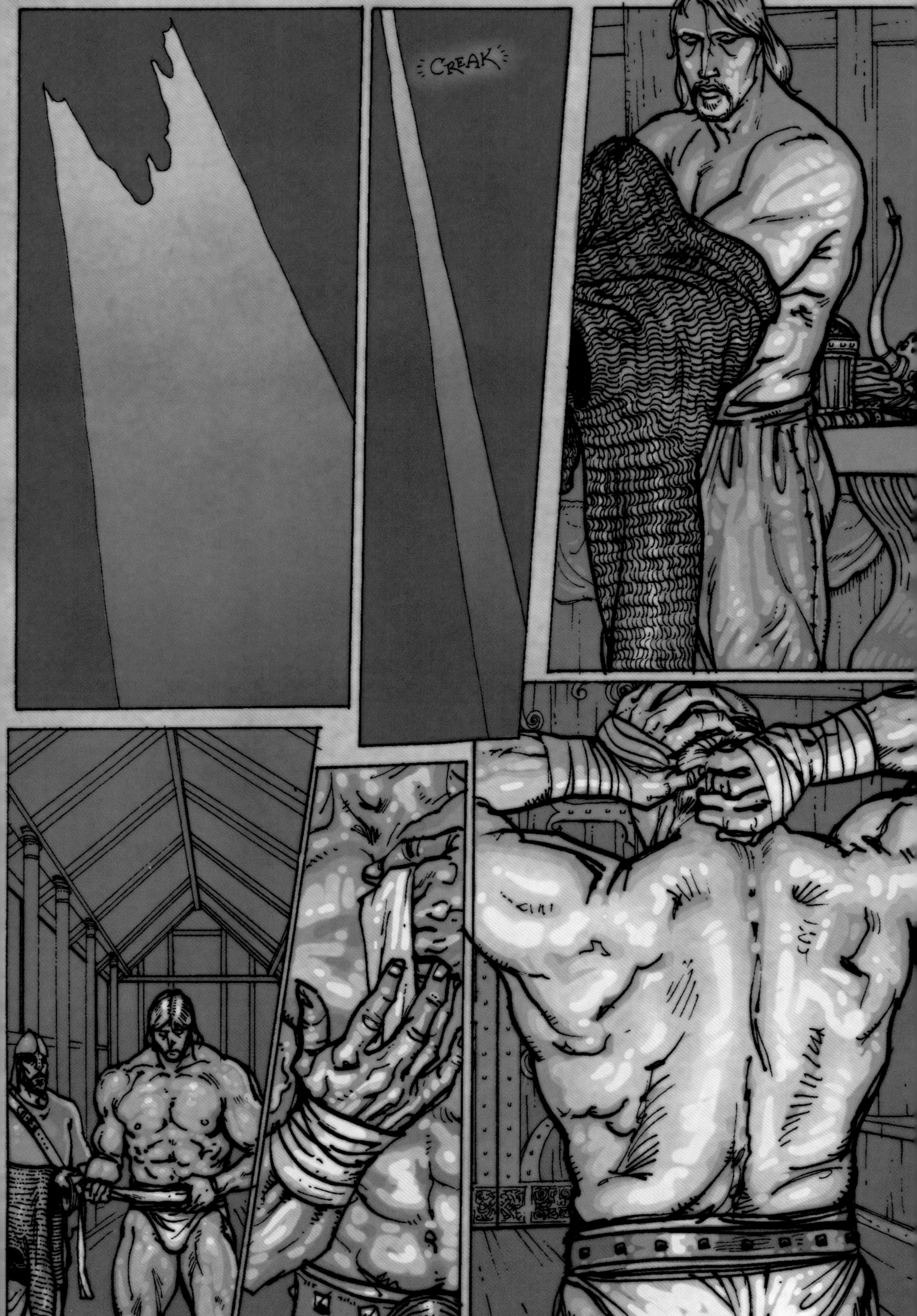
CREAK

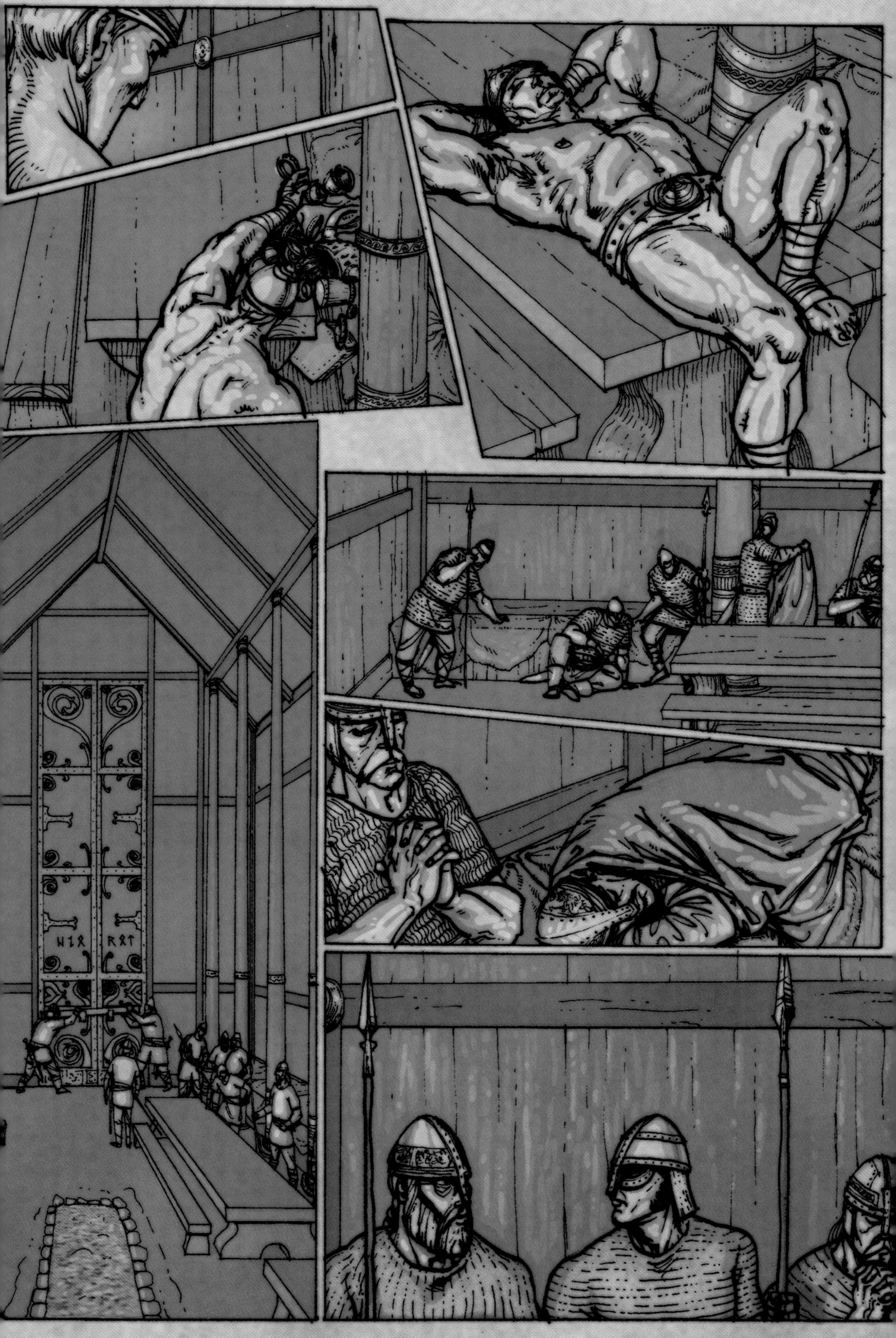

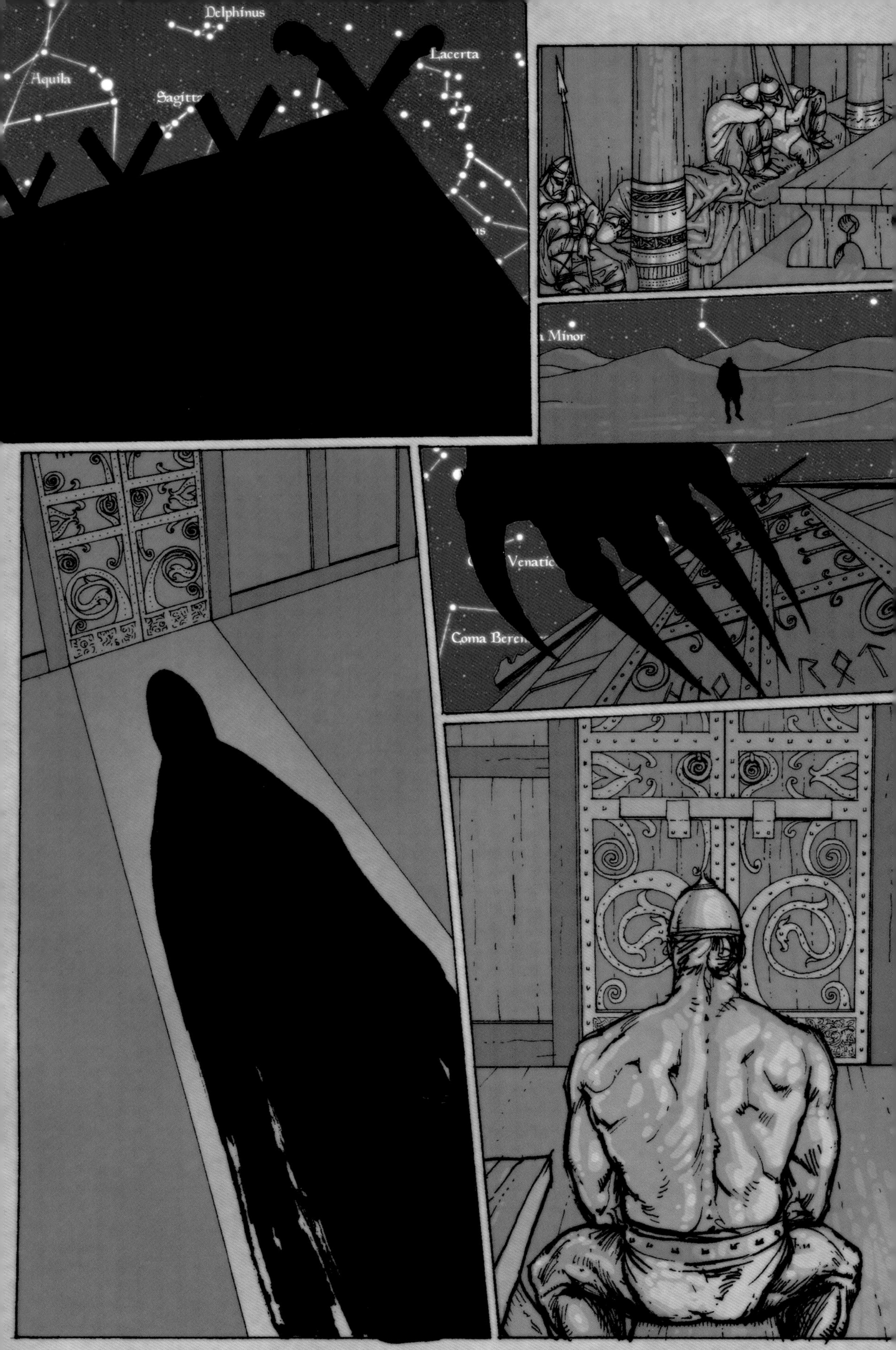
Delphinus
Aquila
Lacerta

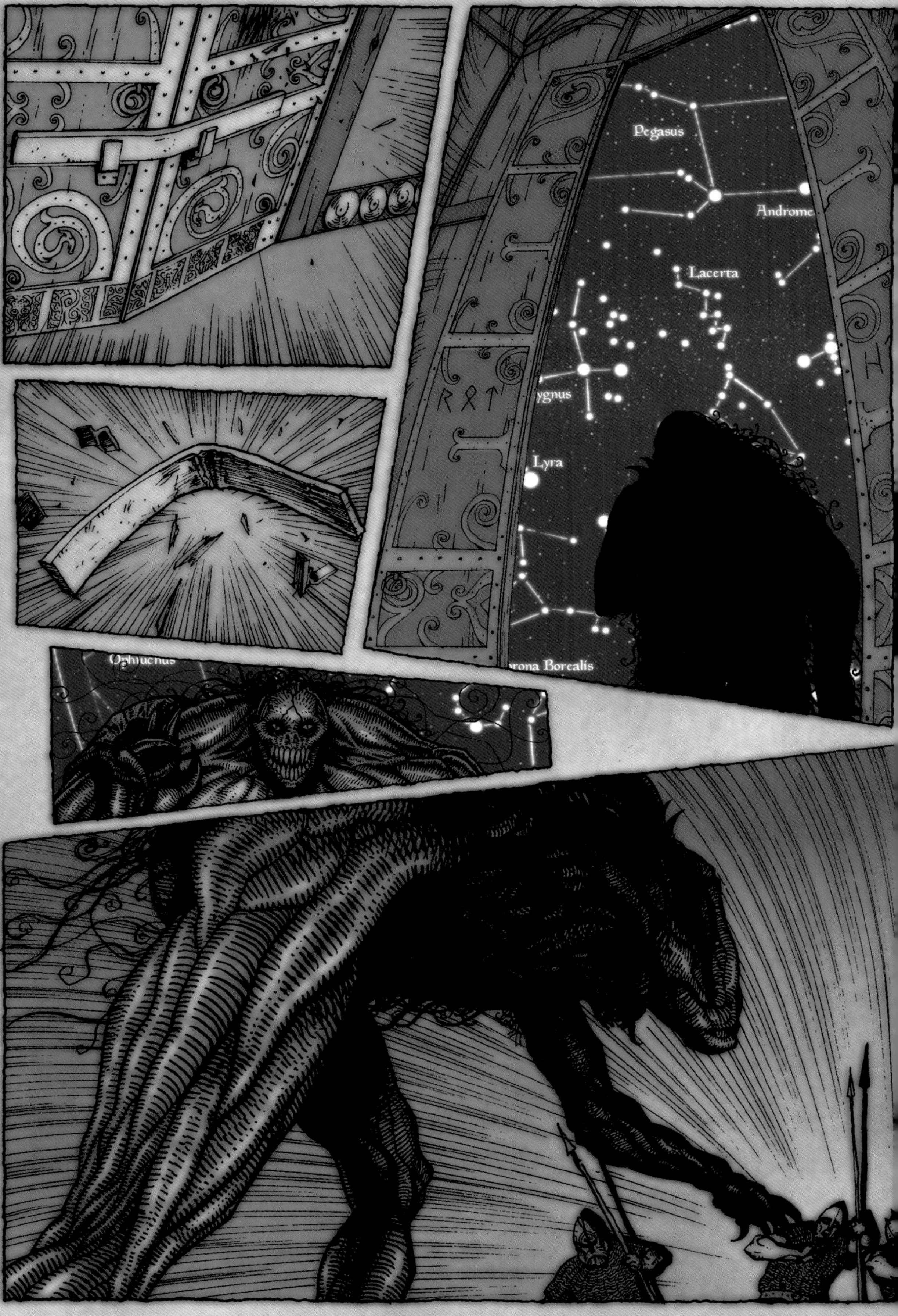

Pegasus
Androme
Lacerta
ygnus
Lyra
rona Borealis
Ophiuchus

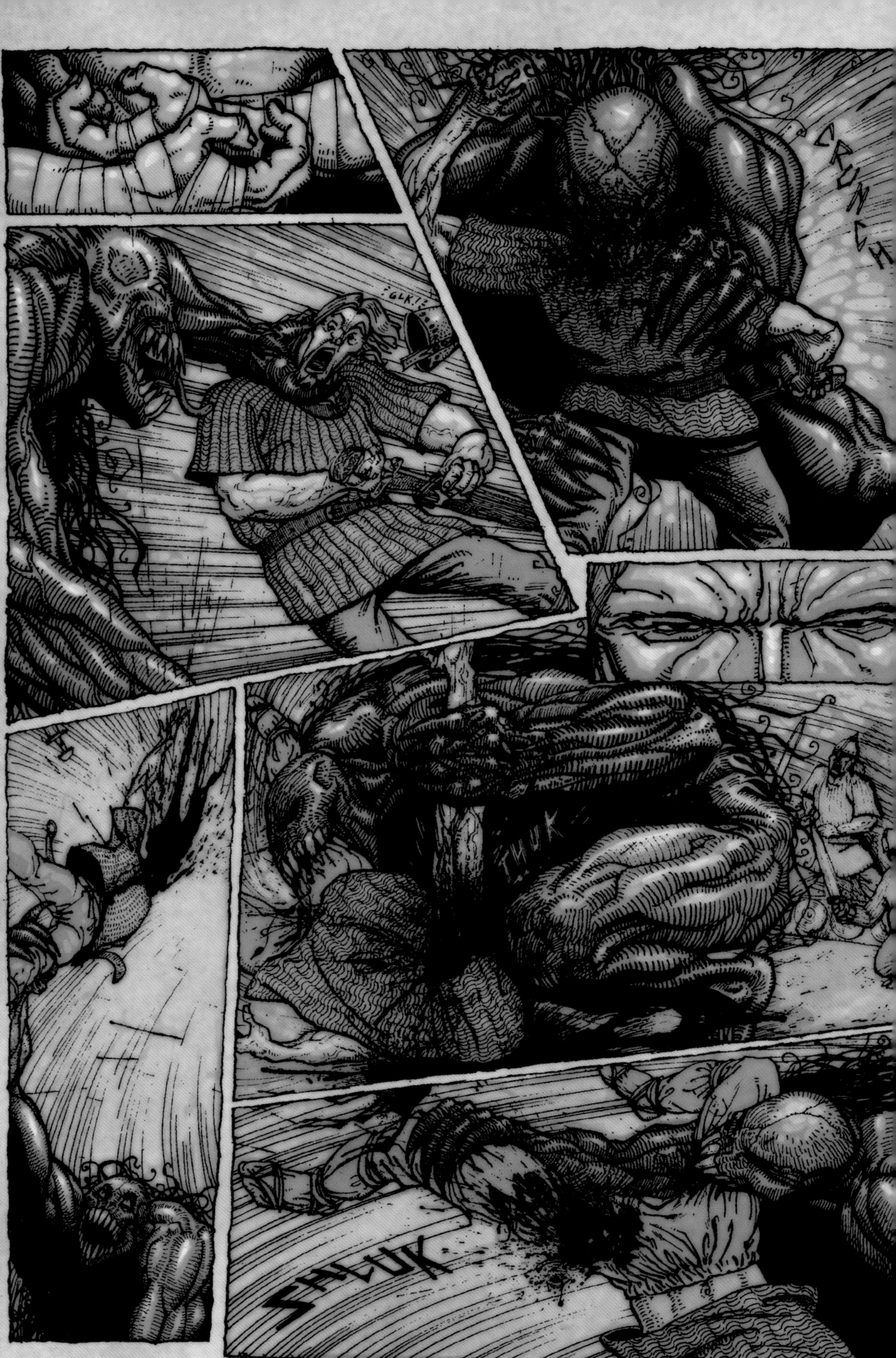
CRUNCH
GLK!?
THUK
SHLUK

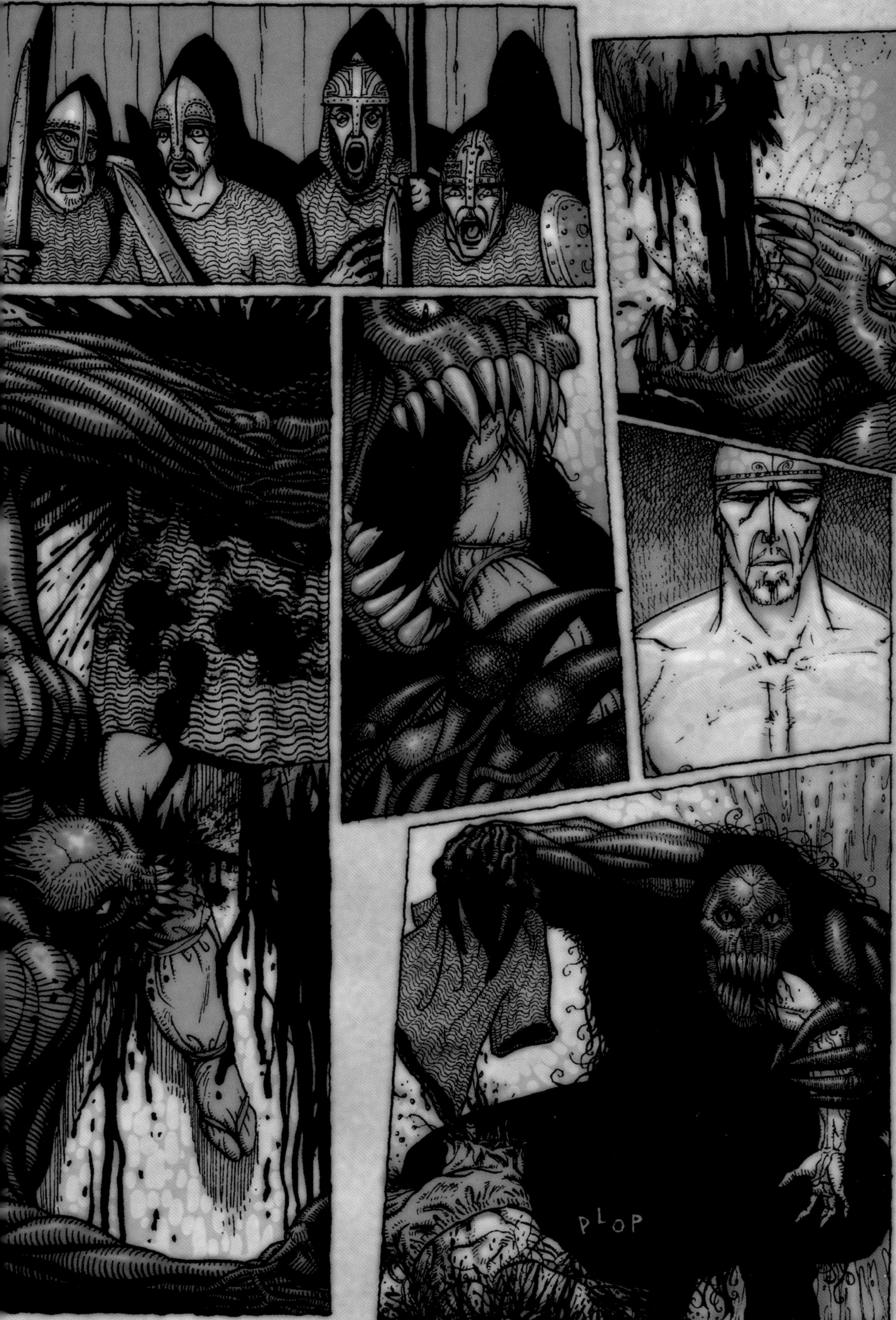
PLOP

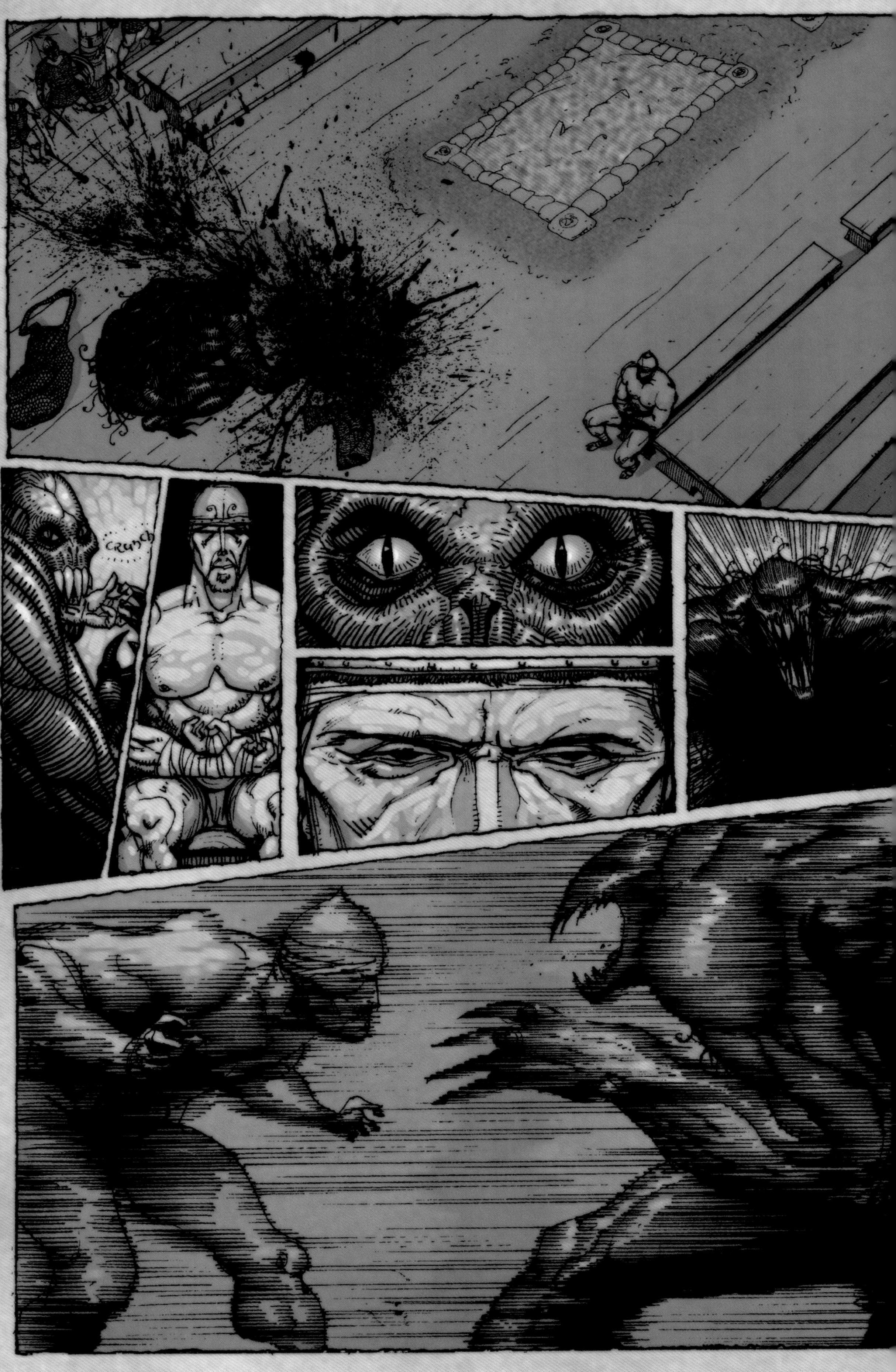
CRUNCH

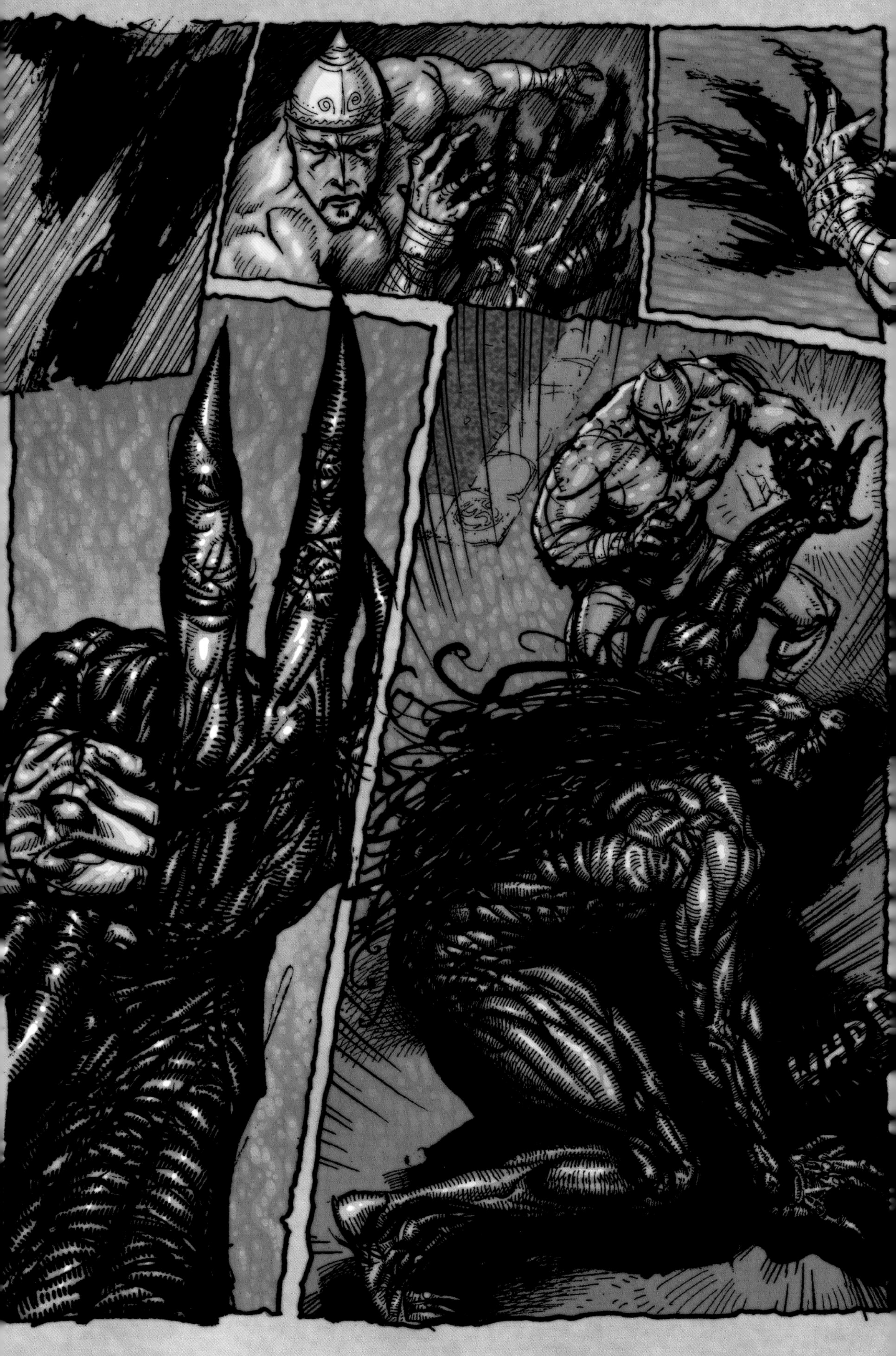

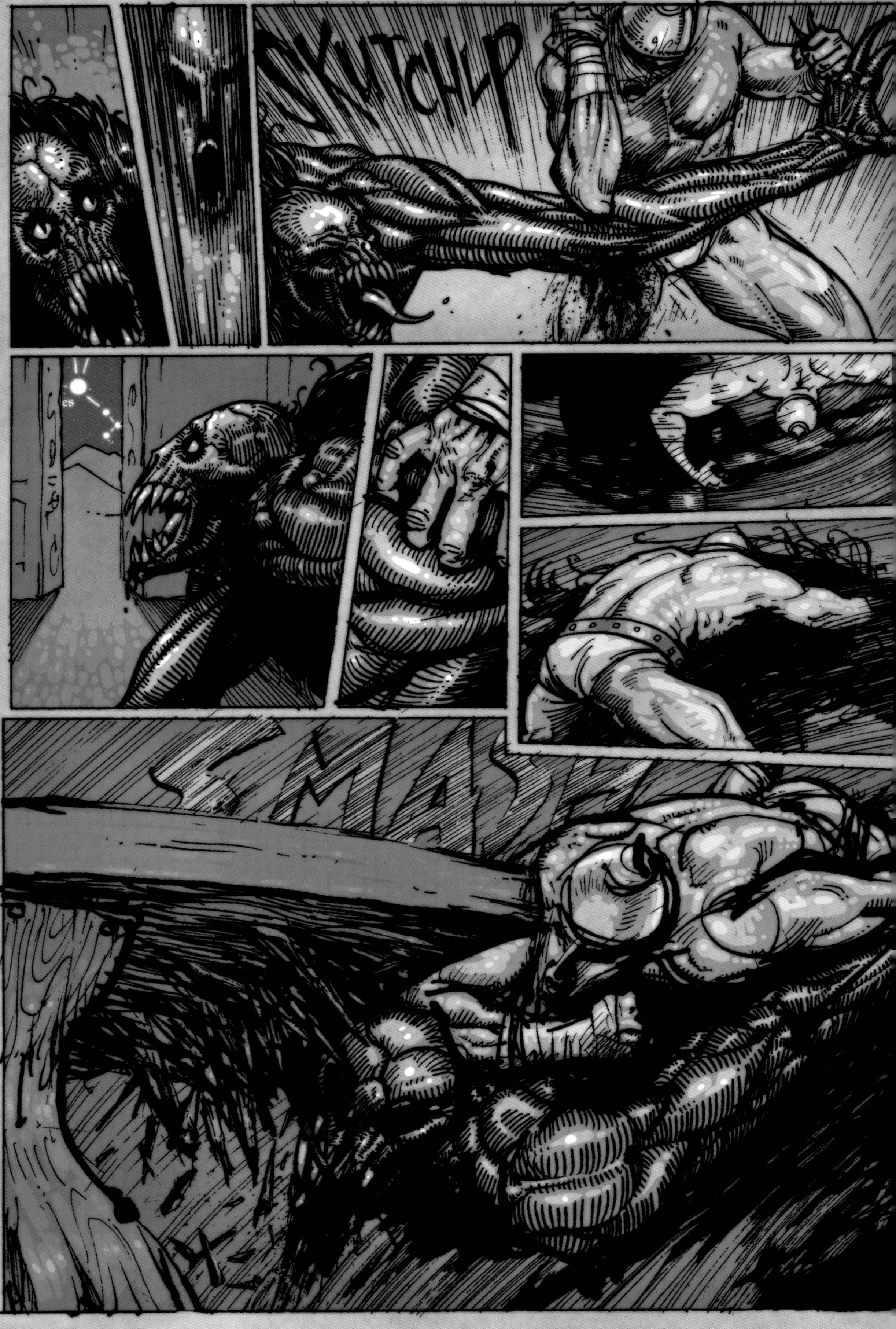
SKUTCHLP
SMASH

Sagitta

Cygnus

Vulpecula

Lyra

Cassiopeia

Camel

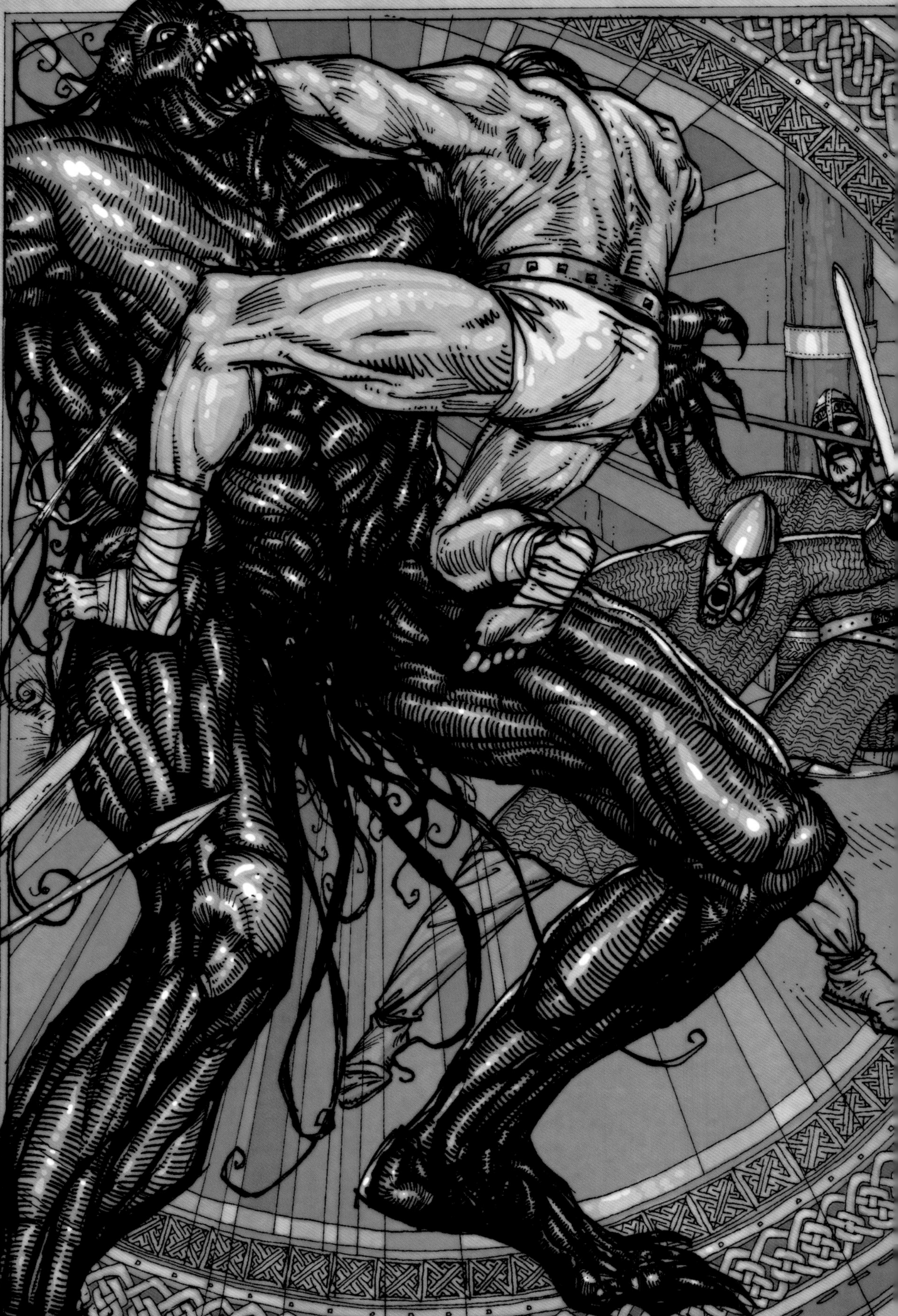

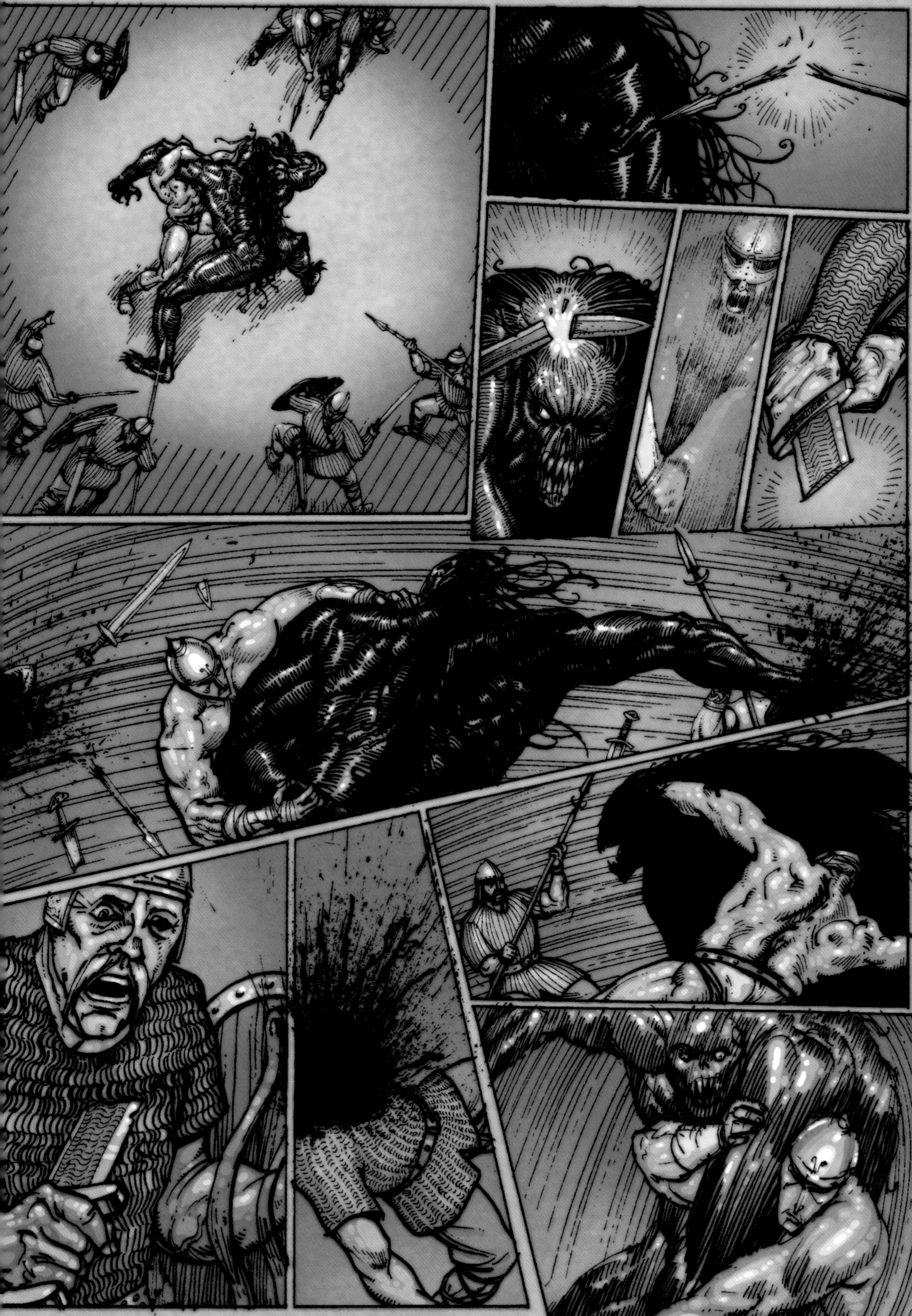

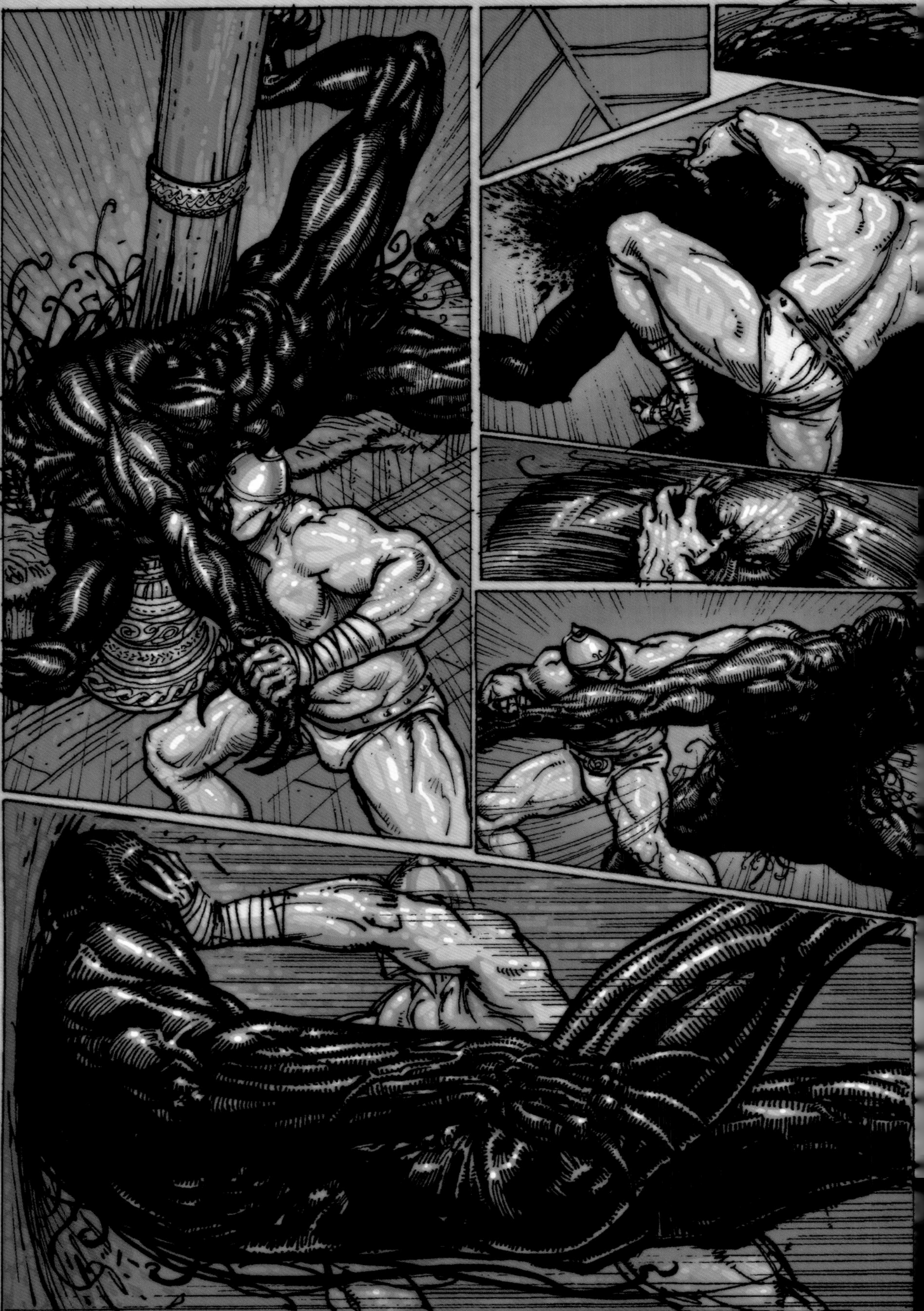

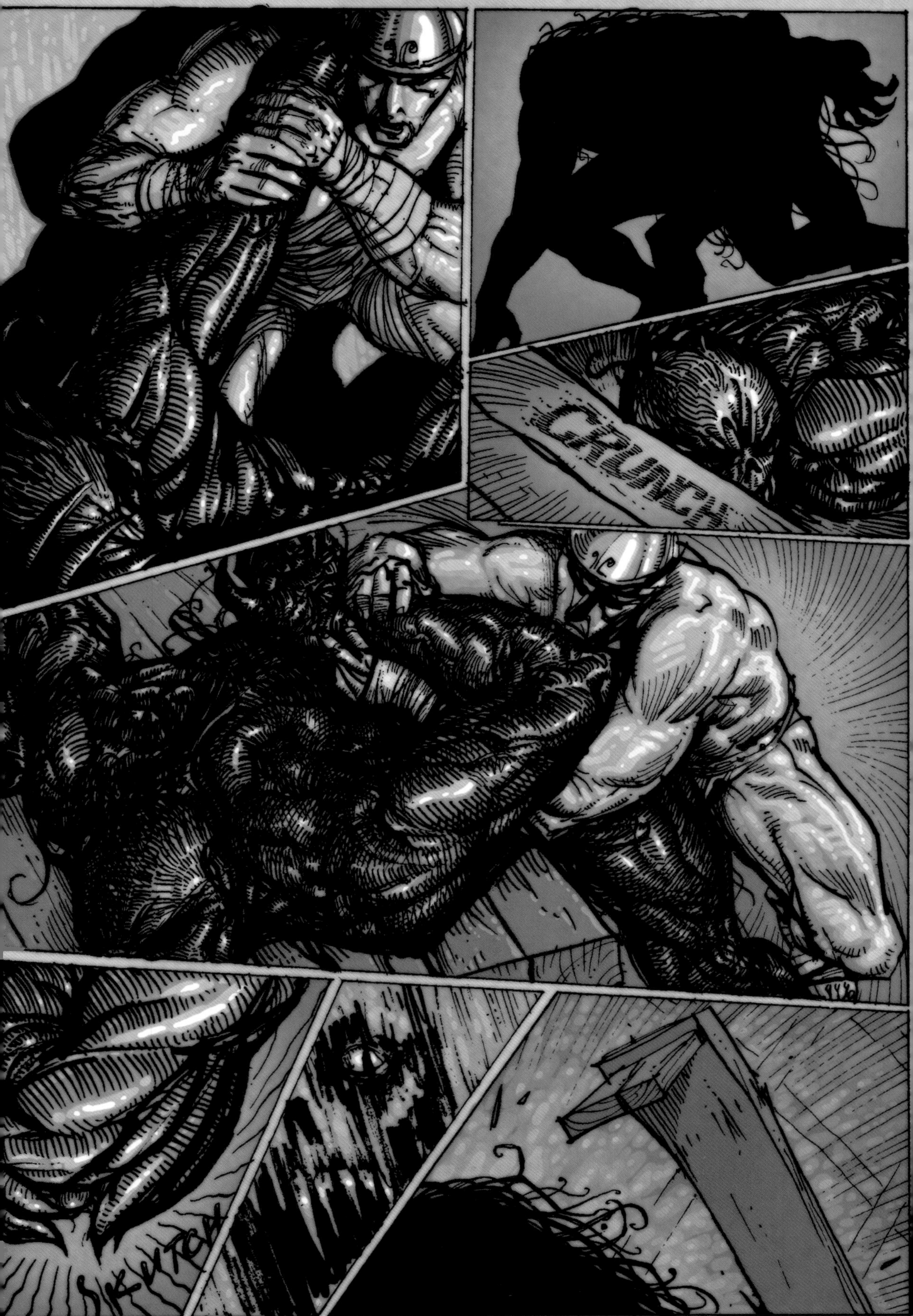
CRUNCH

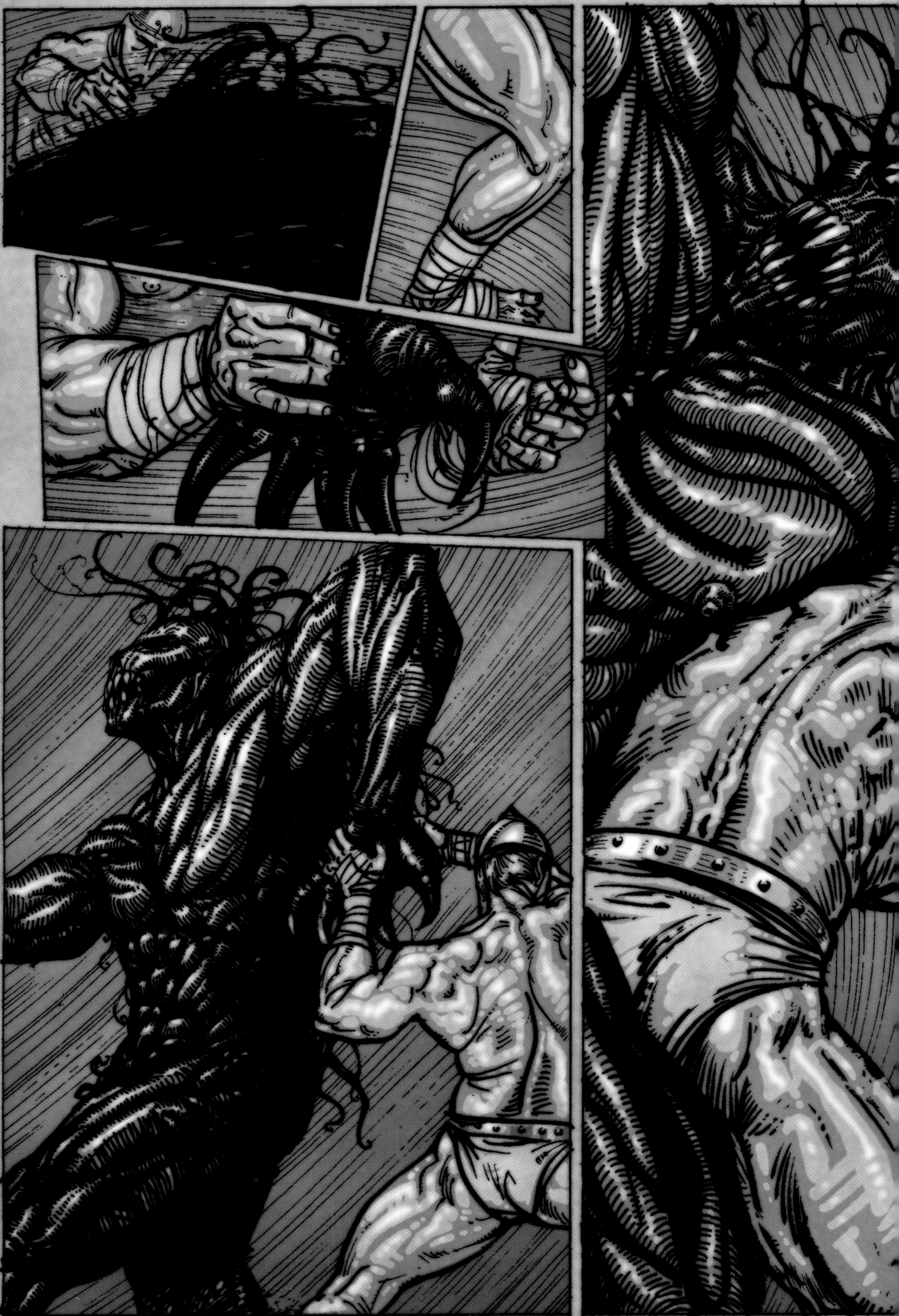

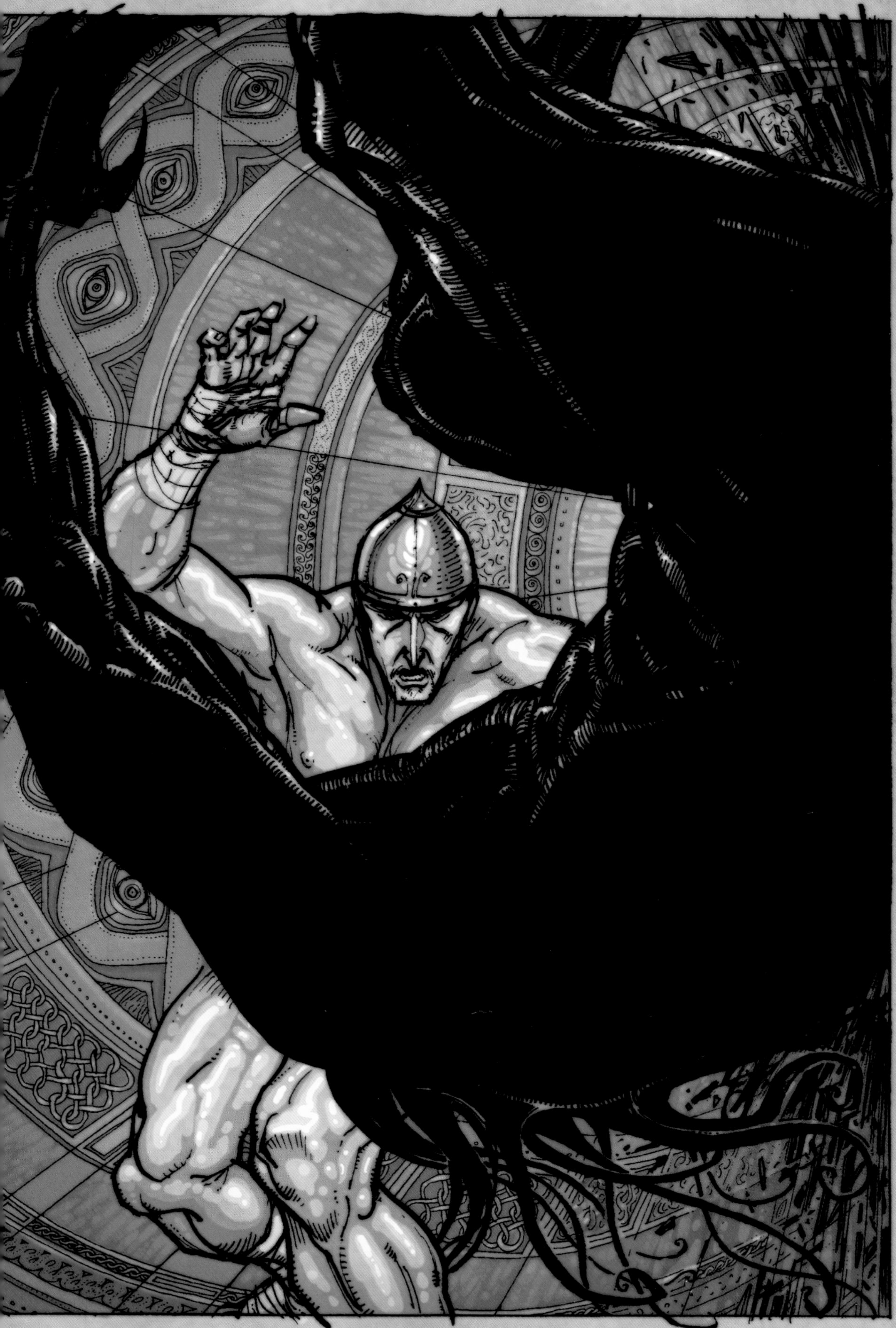

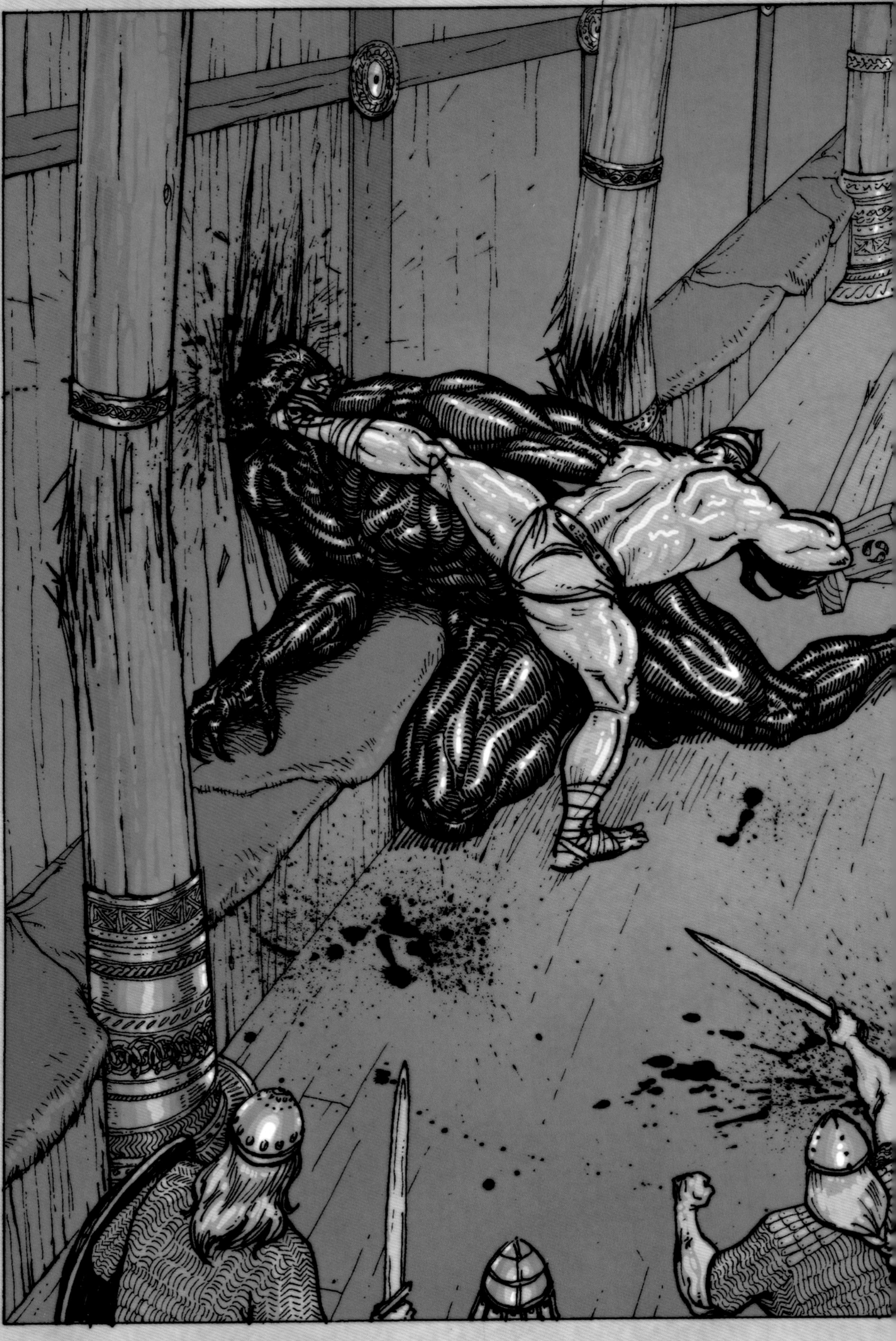

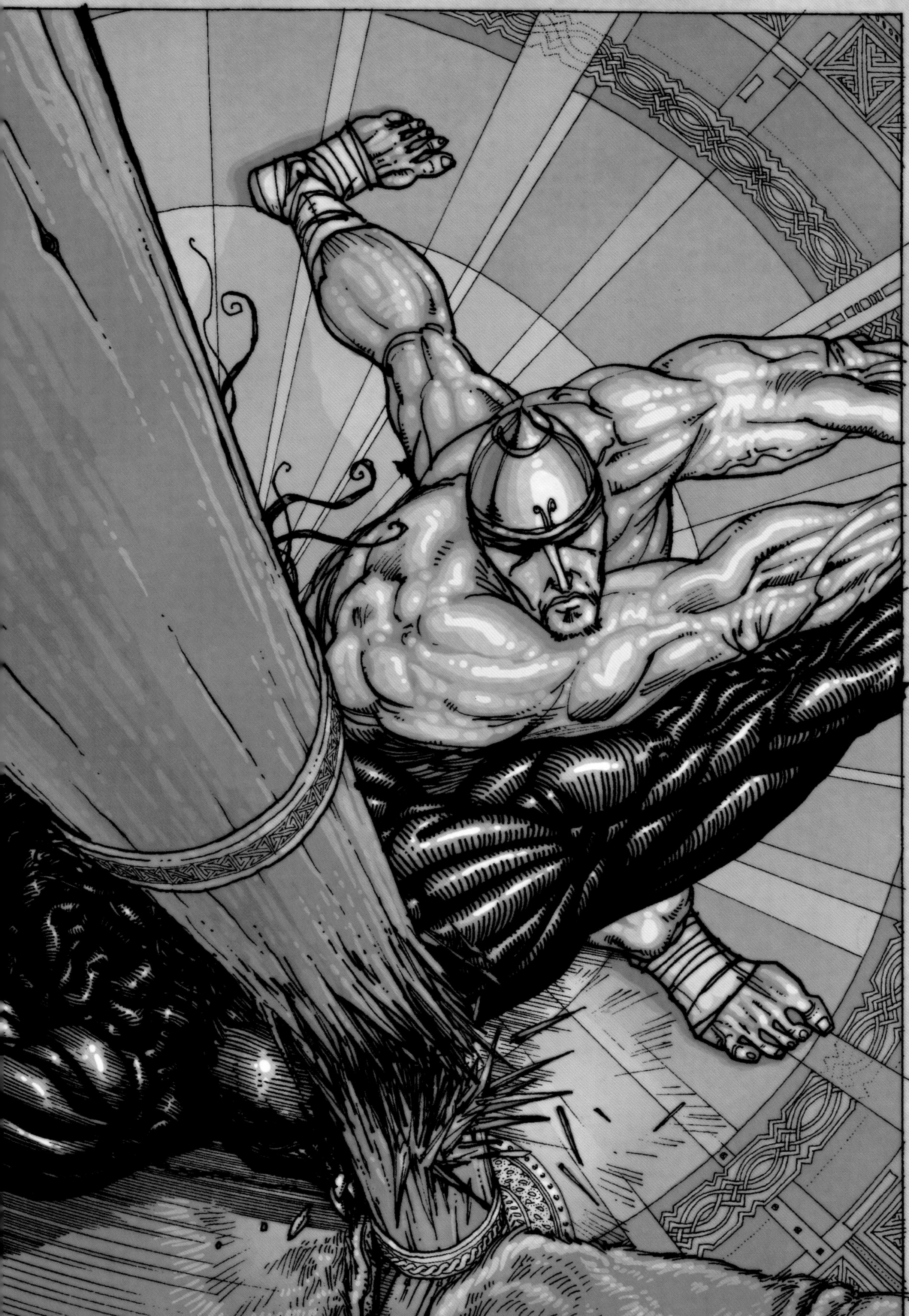

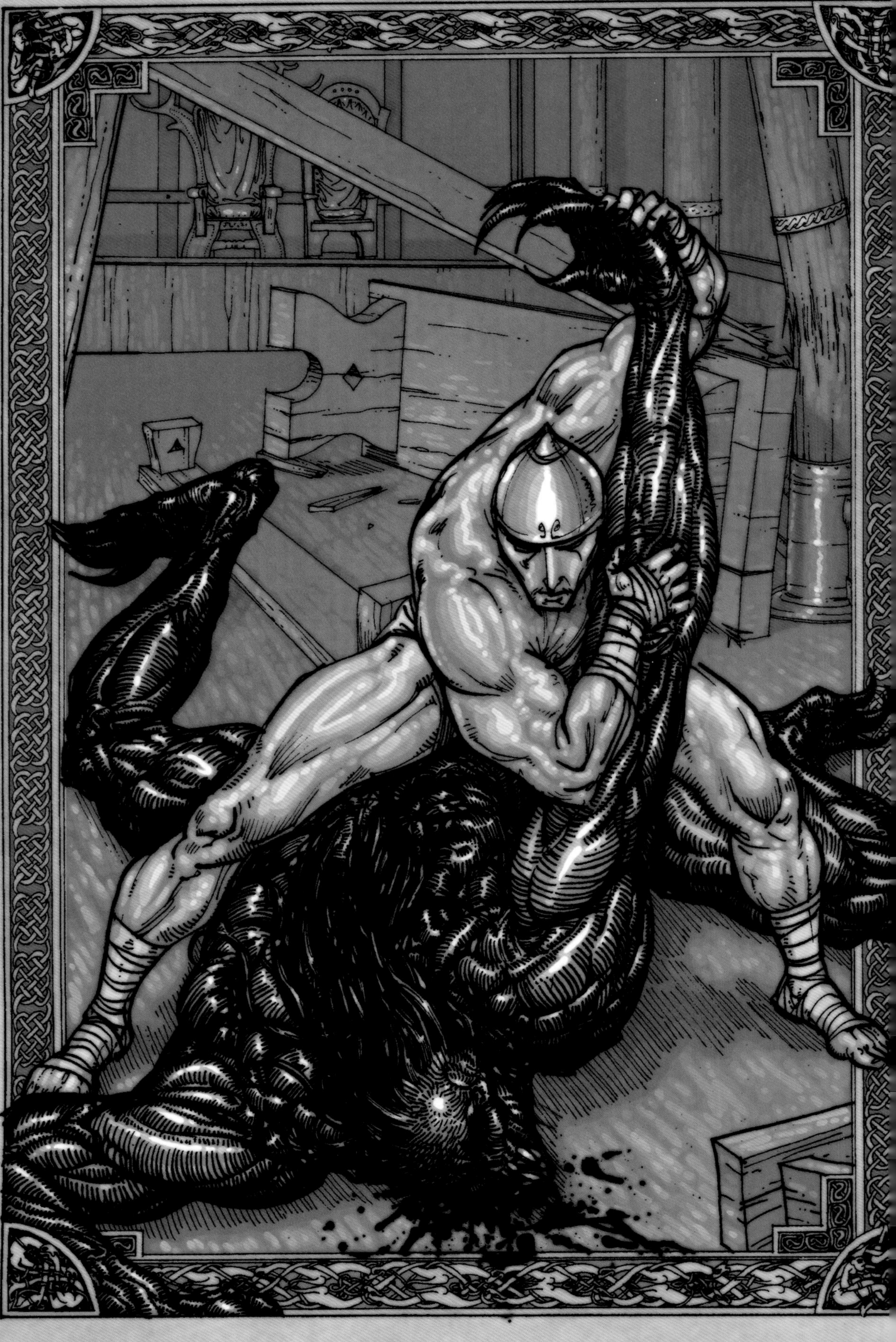

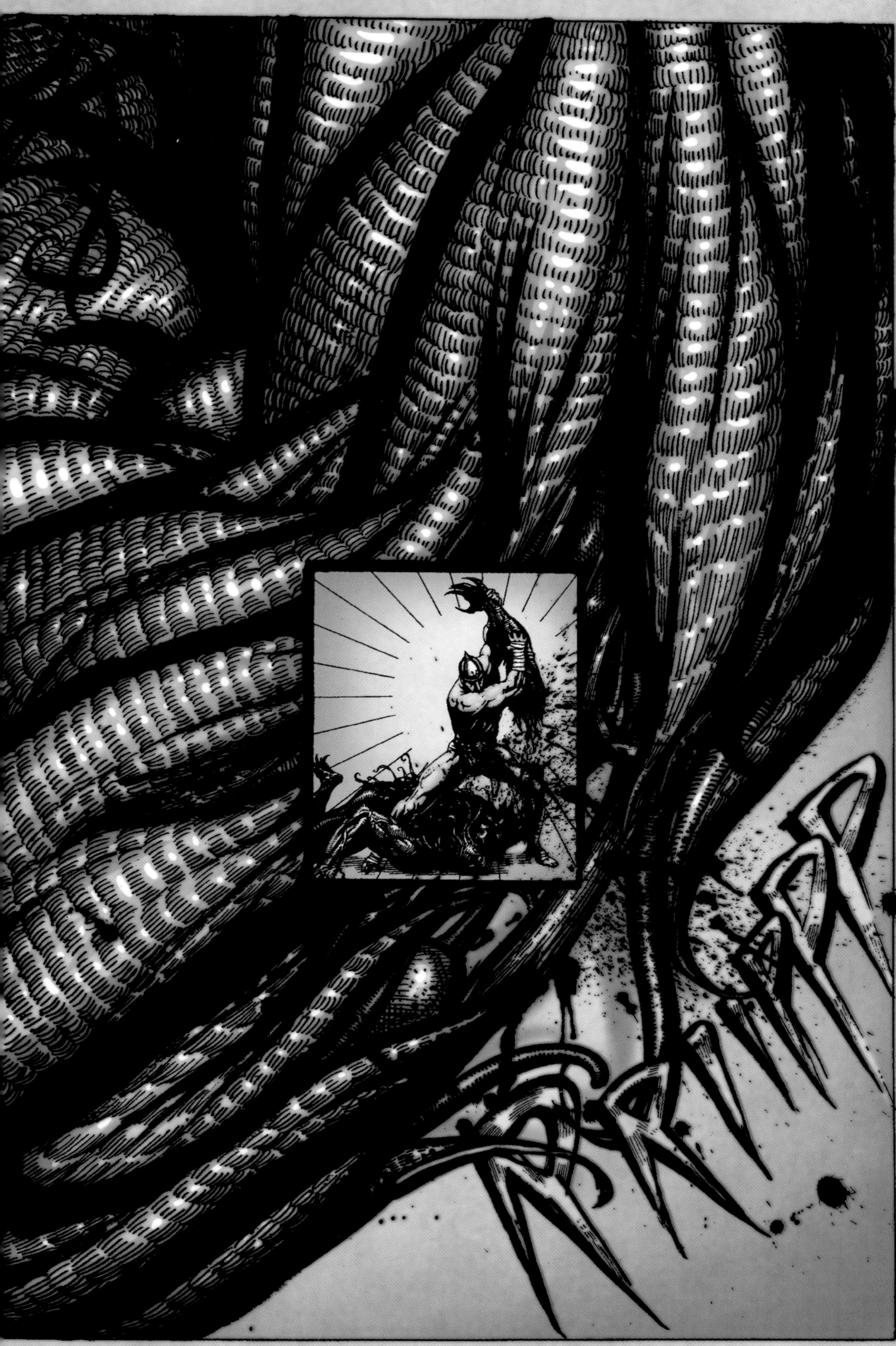

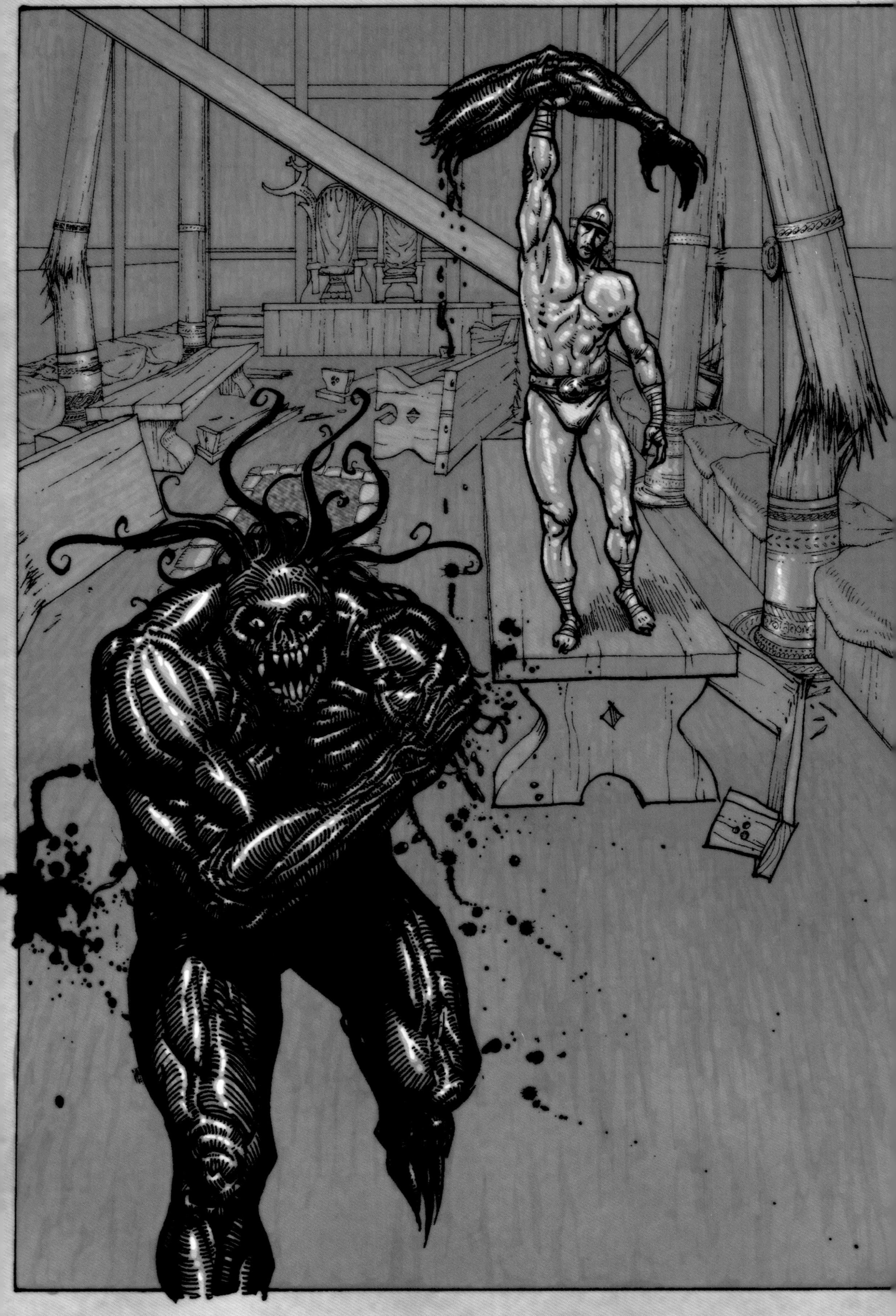

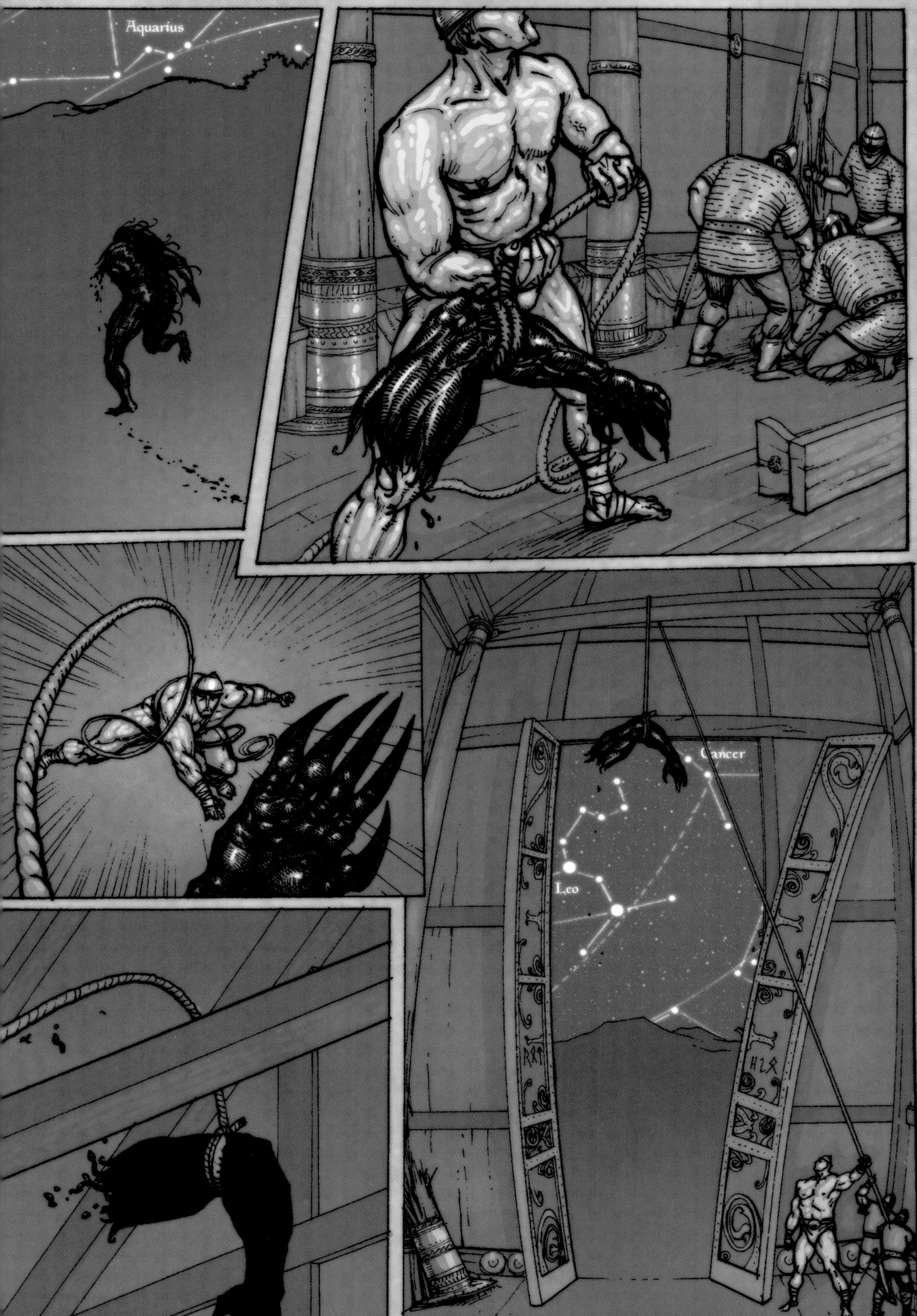
Aquarius
Cancer
Leo

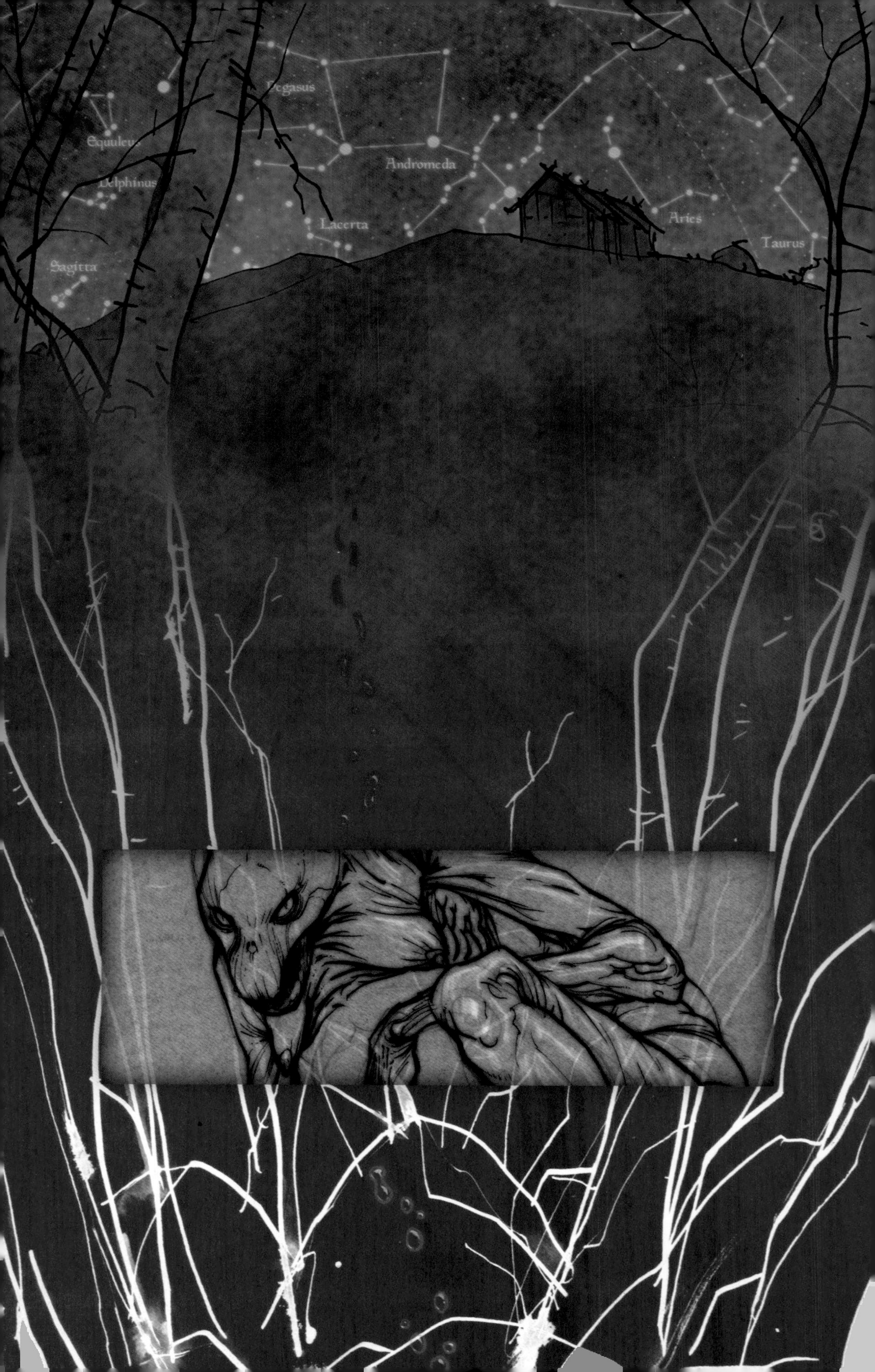
Pegasus
Equuleus
Delphinus
Andromeda
Lacerta
Aries
Sagitta
Taurus

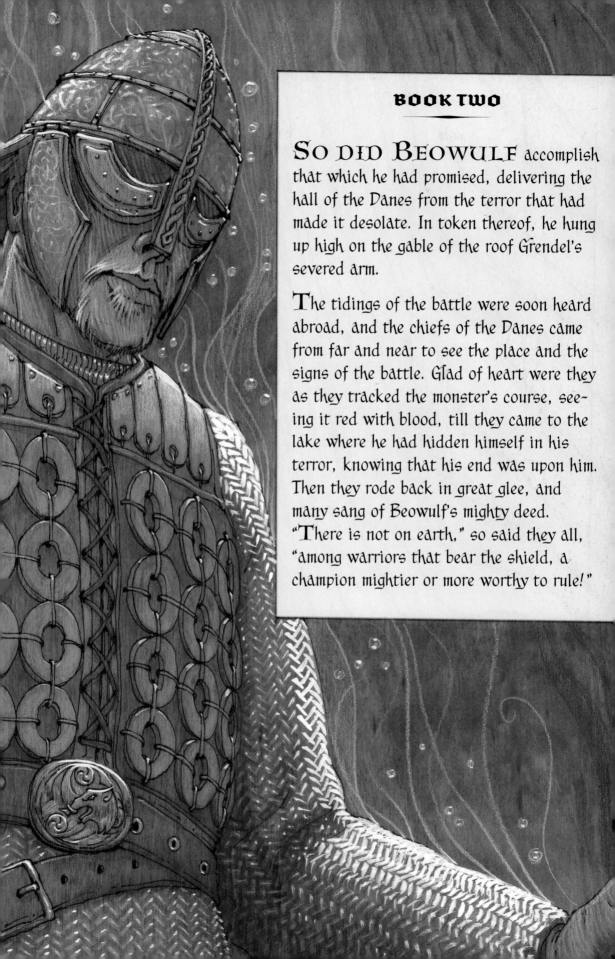

BOOK TWO

SO DID BEOWULF accomplish that which he had promised, delivering the hall of the Danes from the terror that had made it desolate. In token thereof, he hung up high on the gable of the roof Grendel's severed arm.

The tidings of the battle were soon heard abroad, and the chiefs of the Danes came from far and near to see the place and the signs of the battle. Glad of heart were they as they tracked the monster's course, seeing it red with blood, till they came to the lake where he had hidden himself in his terror, knowing that his end was upon him. Then they rode back in great glee, and many sang of Beowulf's mighty deed. "There is not on earth," so said they all, "among warriors that bear the shield, a champion mightier or more worthy to rule!"

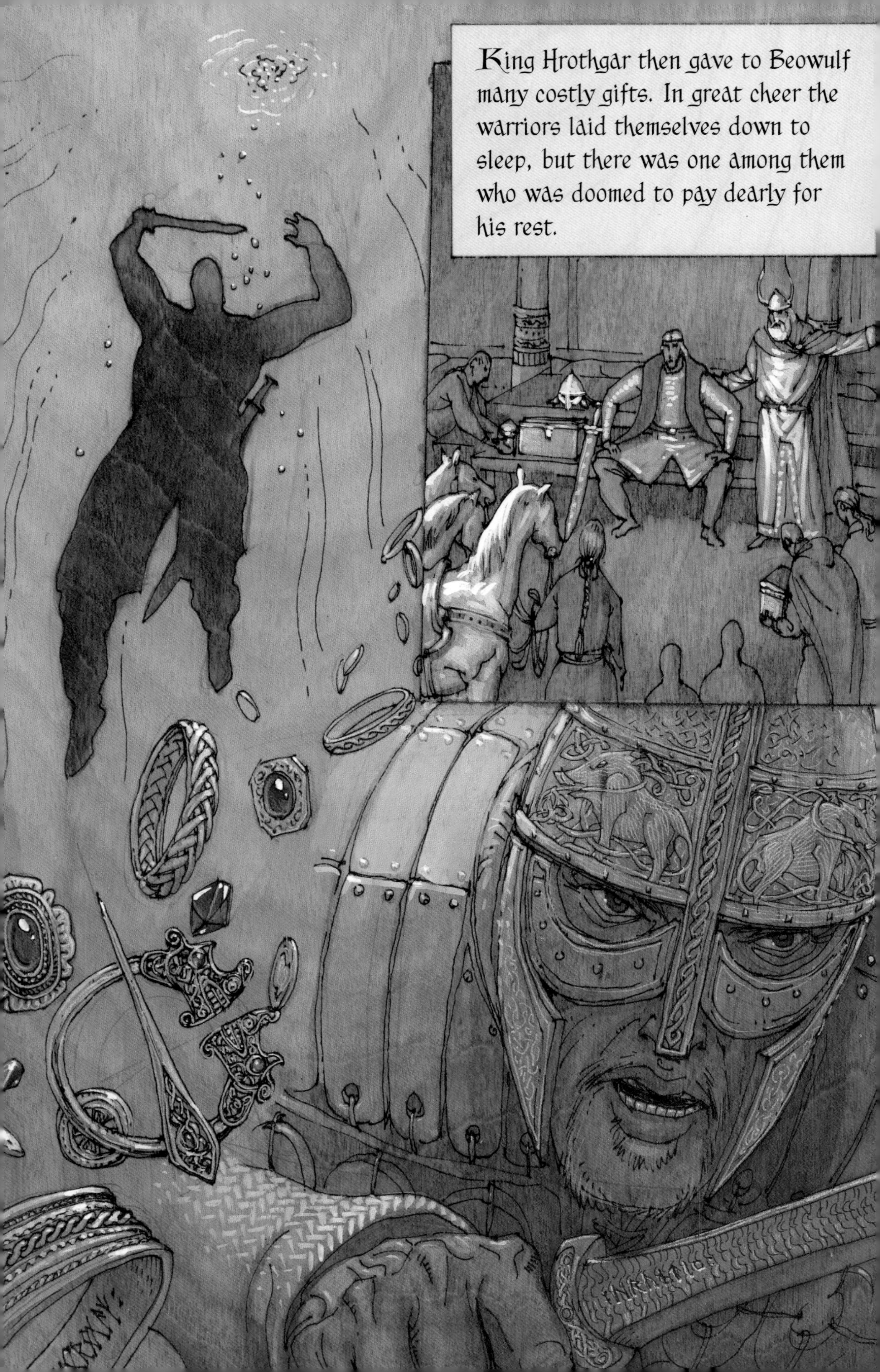
King Hrothgar then gave to Beowulf many costly gifts. In great cheer the warriors laid themselves down to sleep, but there was one among them who was doomed to pay dearly for his rest.

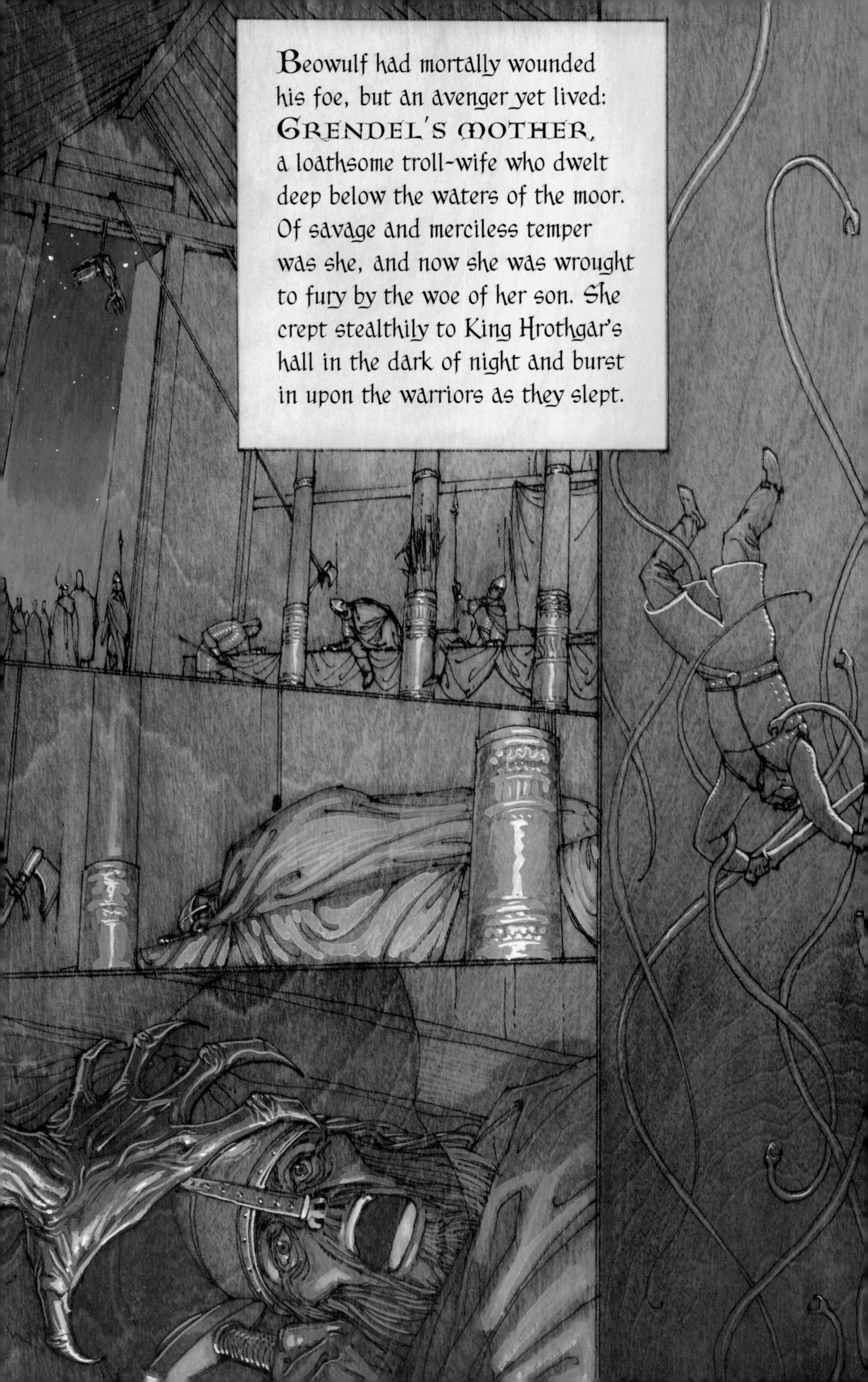
Beowulf had mortally wounded his foe, but an avenger yet lived: GRENDEL'S MOTHER, a loathsome troll-wife who dwelt deep below the waters of the moor. Of savage and merciless temper was she, and now she was wrought to fury by the woe of her son. She crept stealthily to King Hrothgar's hall in the dark of night and burst in upon the warriors as they slept.

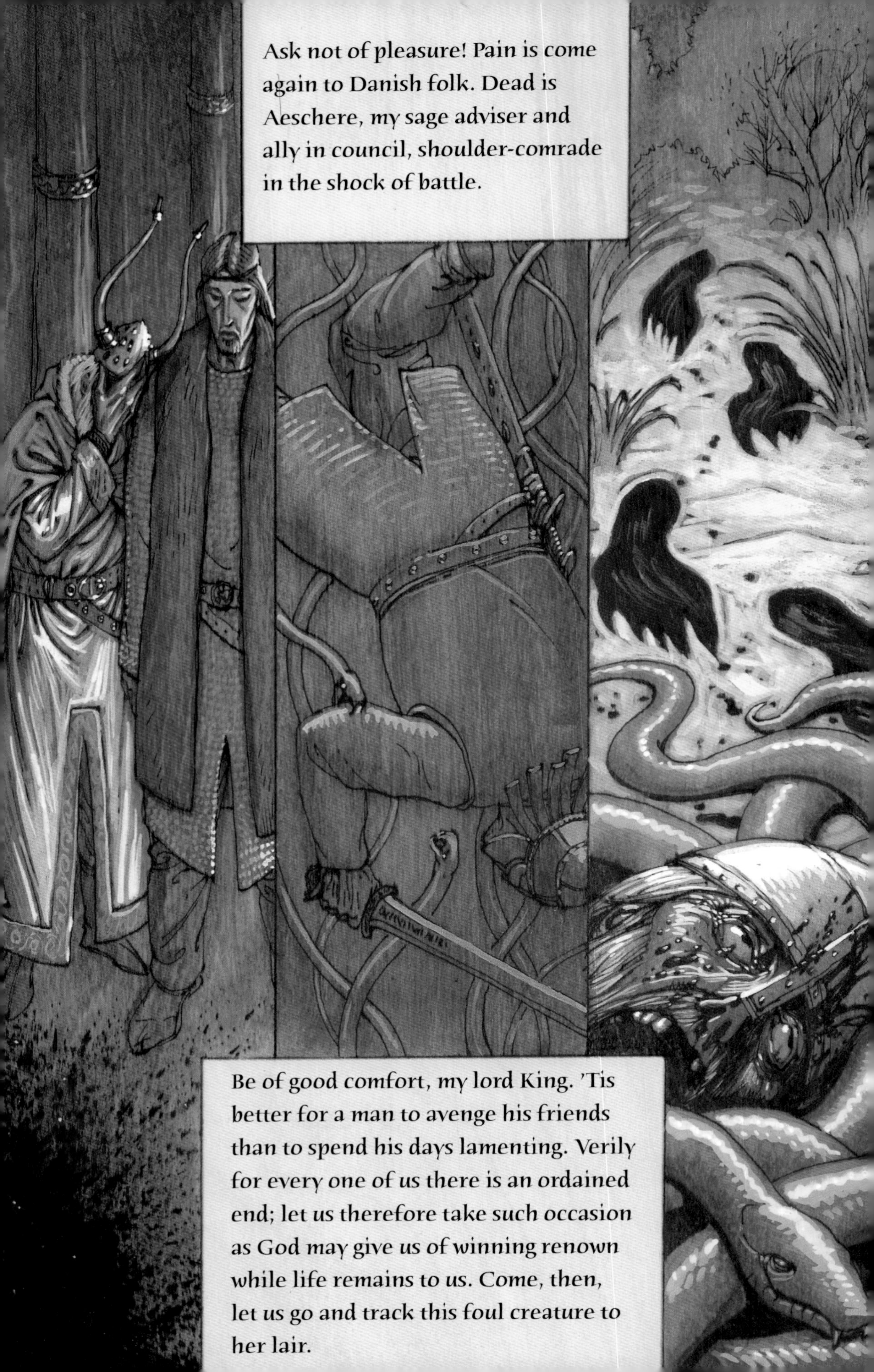
Ask not of pleasure! Pain is come again to Danish folk. Dead is Aeschere, my sage adviser and ally in council, shoulder-comrade in the shock of battle.
Be of good comfort, my lord King. 'Tis better for a man to avenge his friends than to spend his days lamenting. Verily for every one of us there is an ordained end; let us therefore take such occasion as God may give us of winning renown while life remains to us. Come, then, let us go and track this foul creature to her lair.

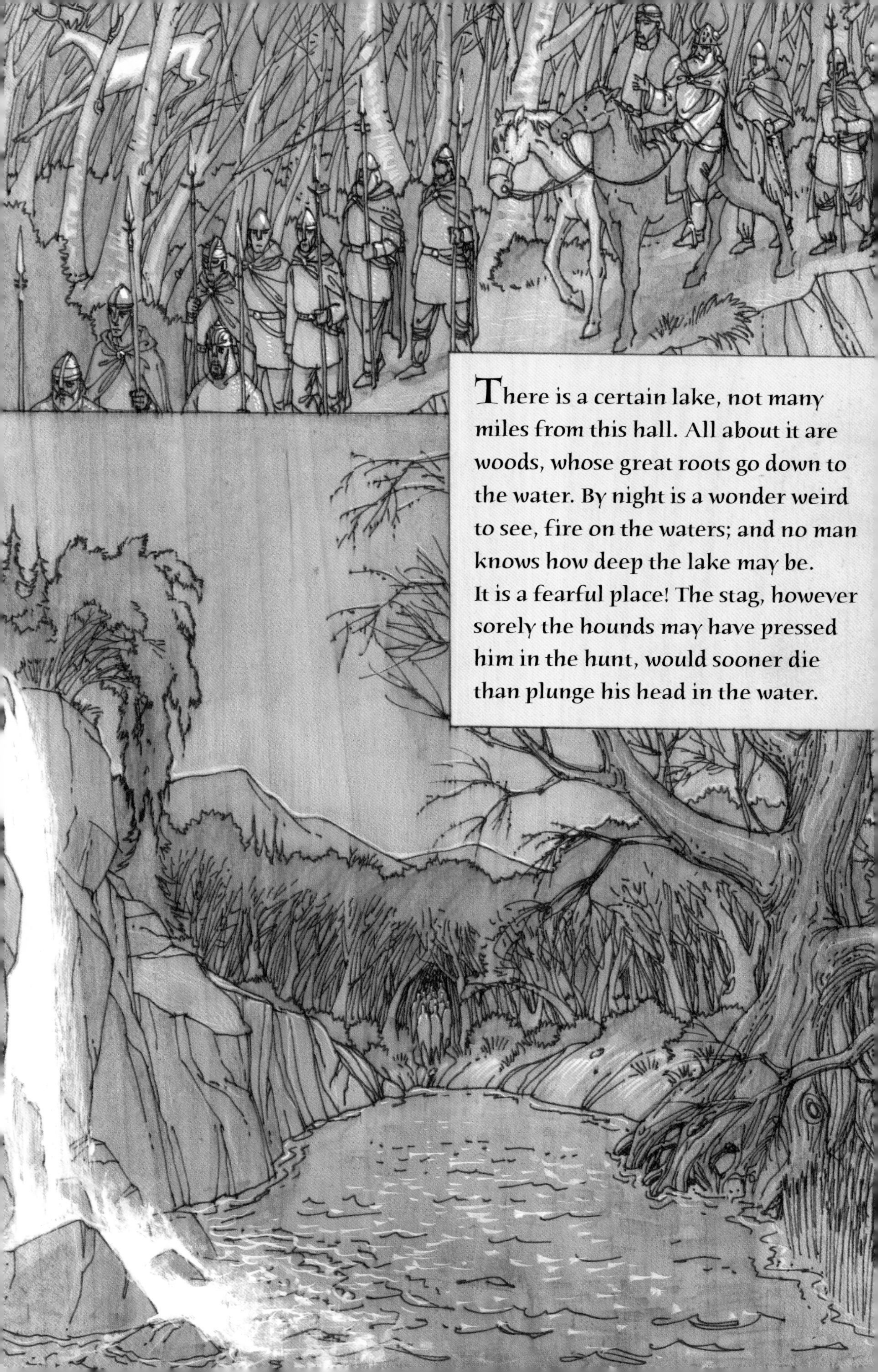

There is a certain lake, not many miles from this hall. All about it are woods, whose great roots go down to the water. By night is a wonder weird to see, fire on the waters; and no man knows how deep the lake may be. It is a fearful place! The stag, however sorely the hounds may have pressed him in the hunt, would sooner die than plunge his head in the water.

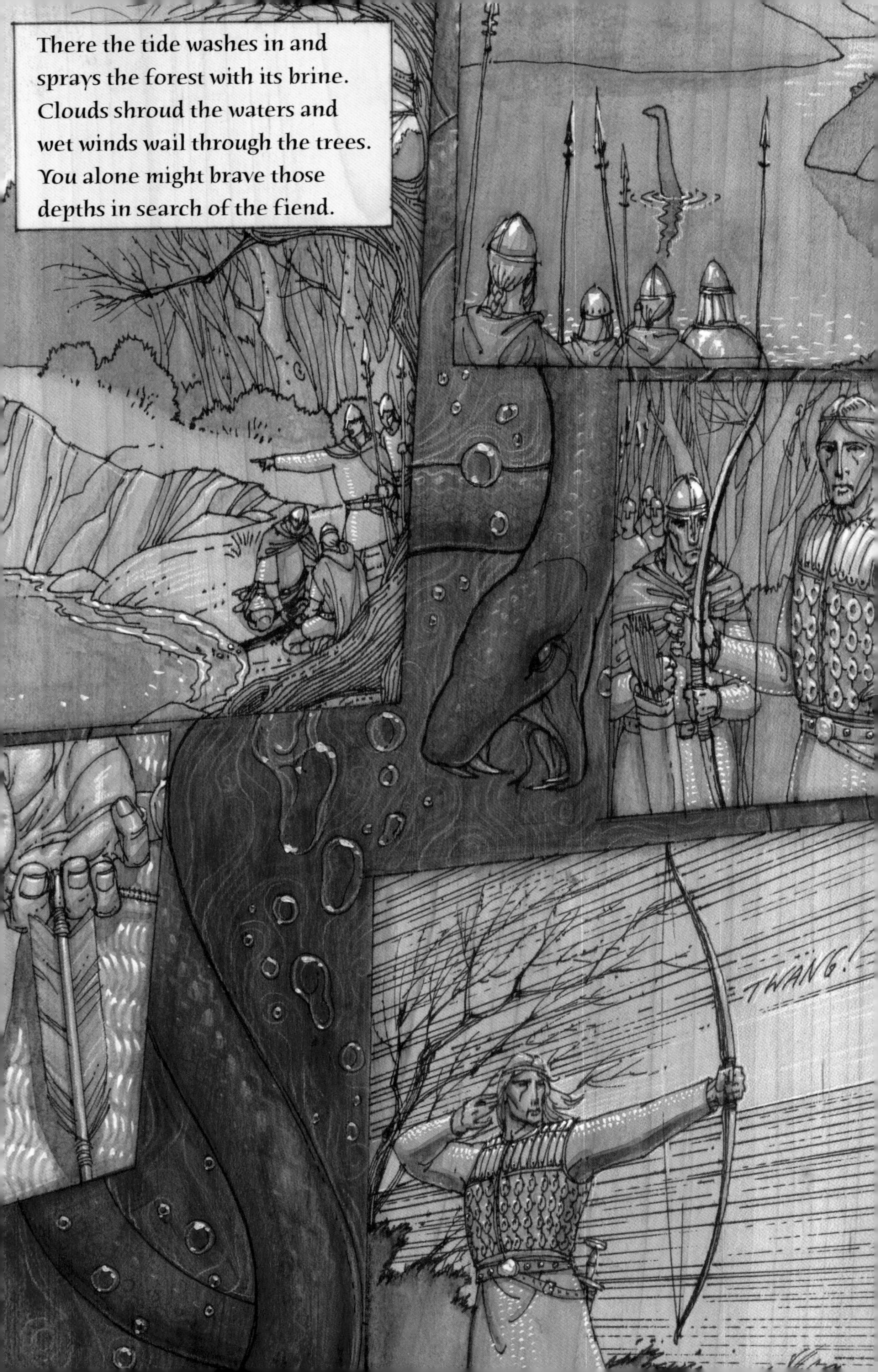
There the tide washes in and sprays the forest with its brine. Clouds shroud the waters and wet winds wail through the trees. You alone might brave those depths in search of the fiend.
TWANG!

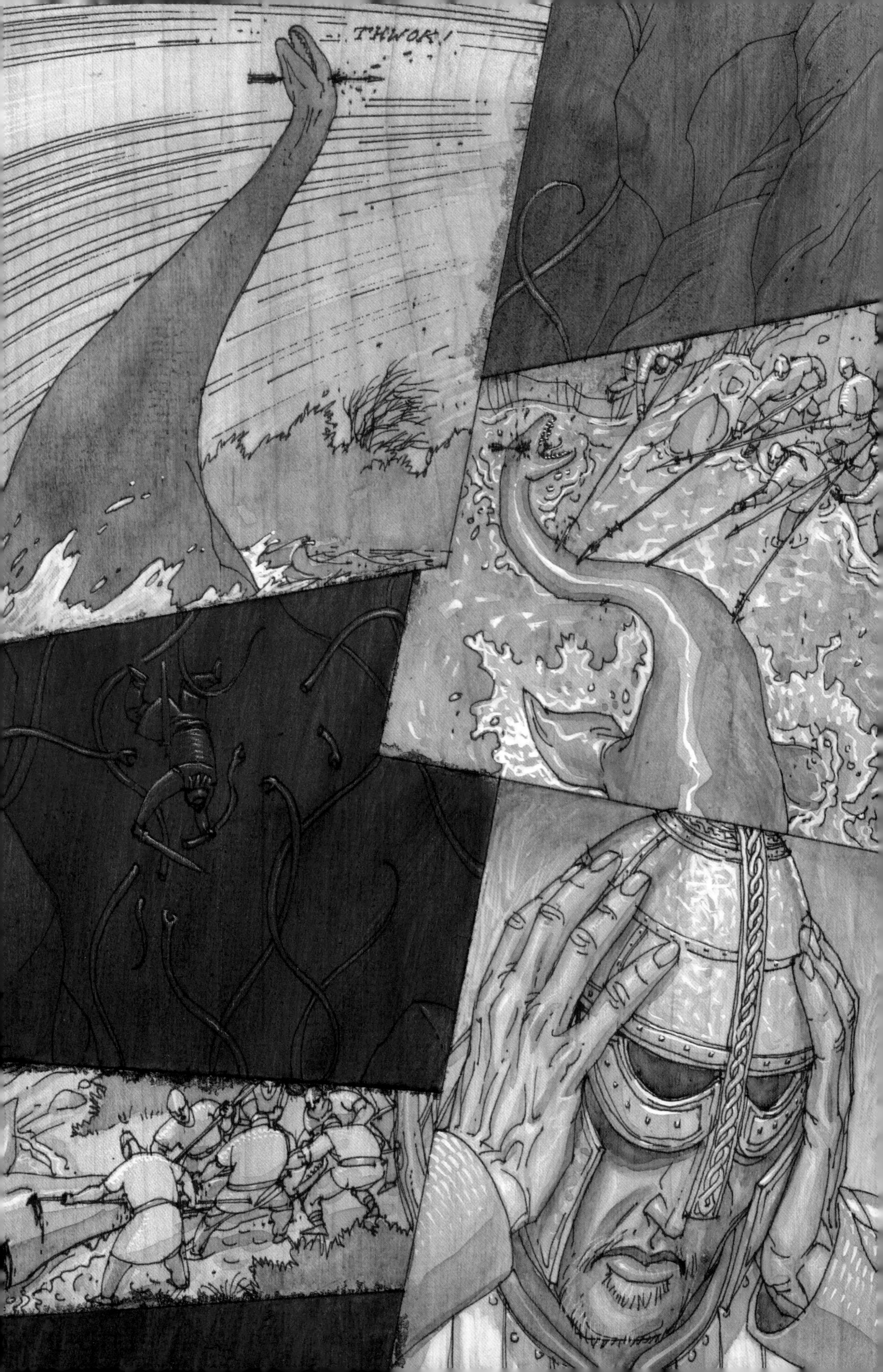
THWOK!

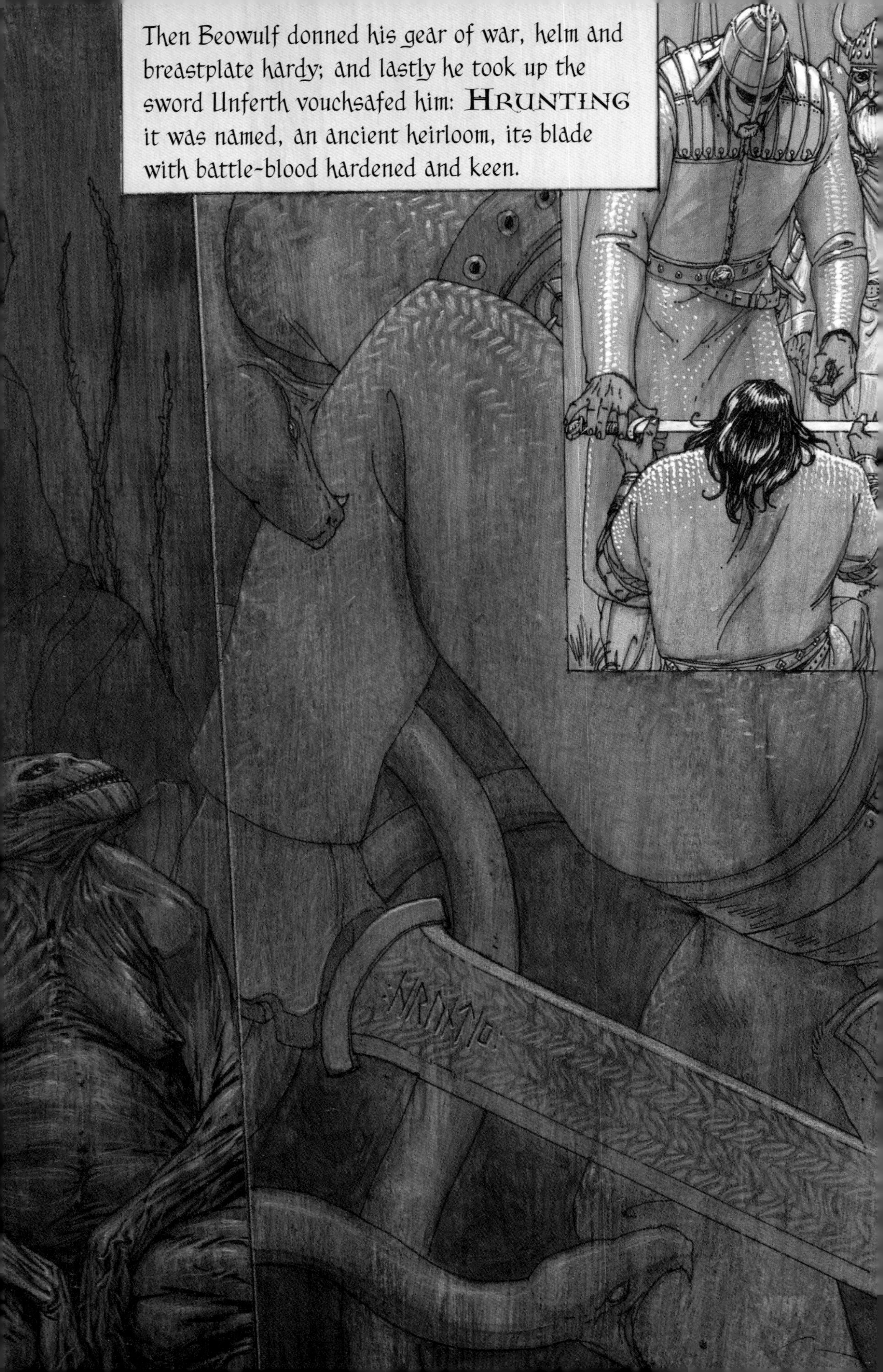
Then Beowulf donned his gear of war, helm and breastplate hardy; and lastly he took up the sword Unferth vouchsafed him: HRUNTING it was named, an ancient heirloom, its blade with battle-blood hardened and keen.

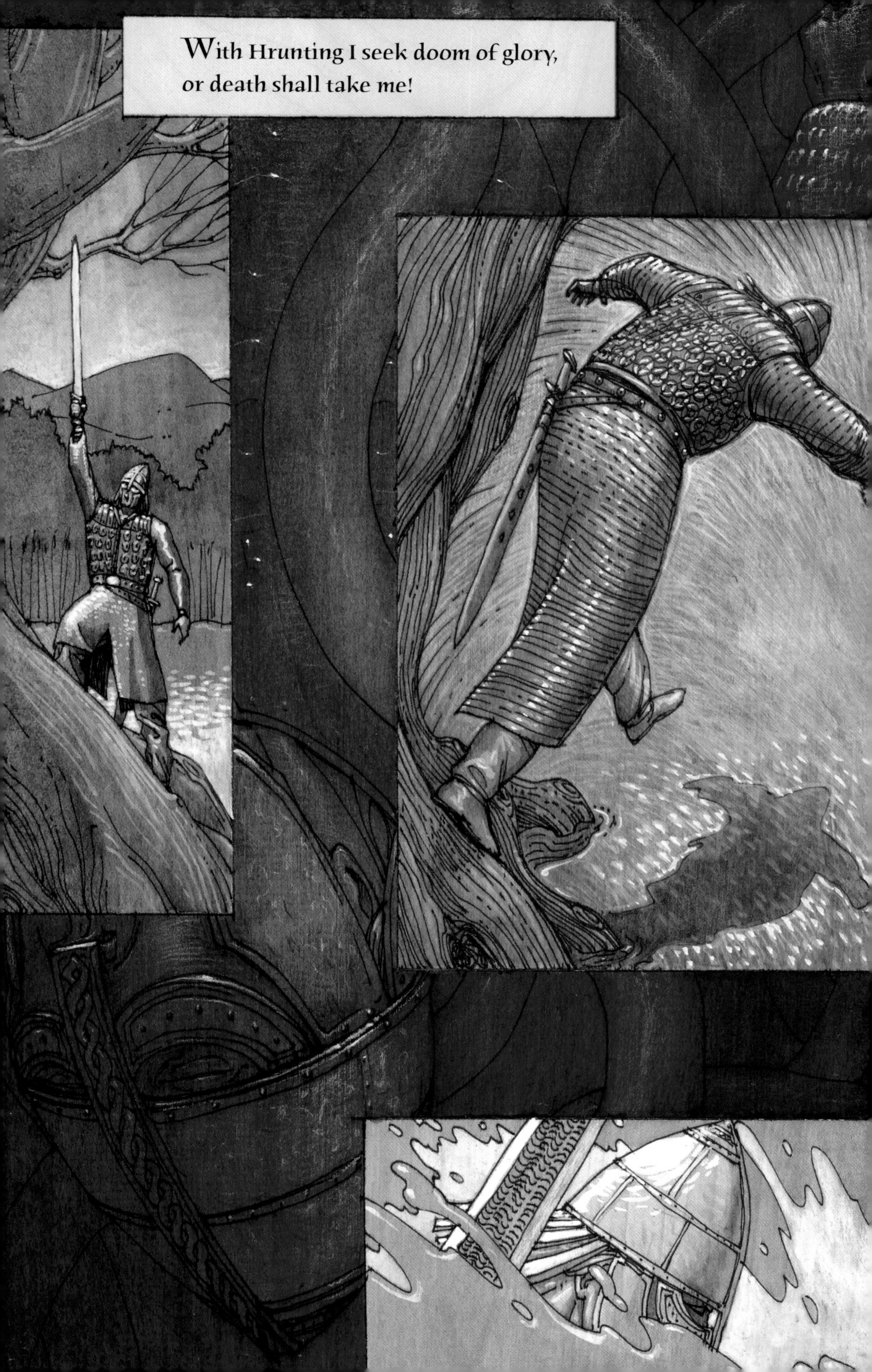
With Hrunting I seek doom of glory, or death shall take me!

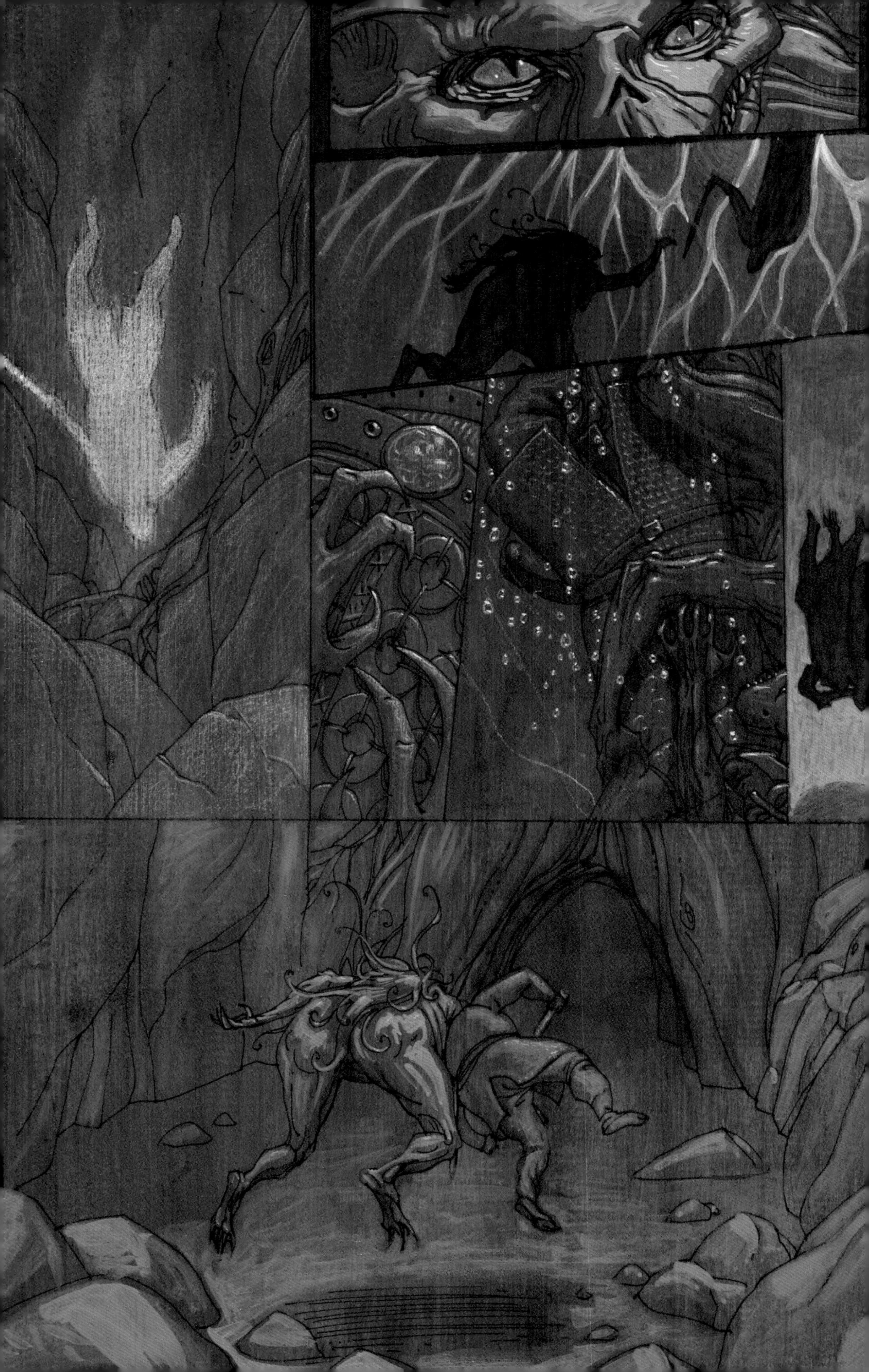

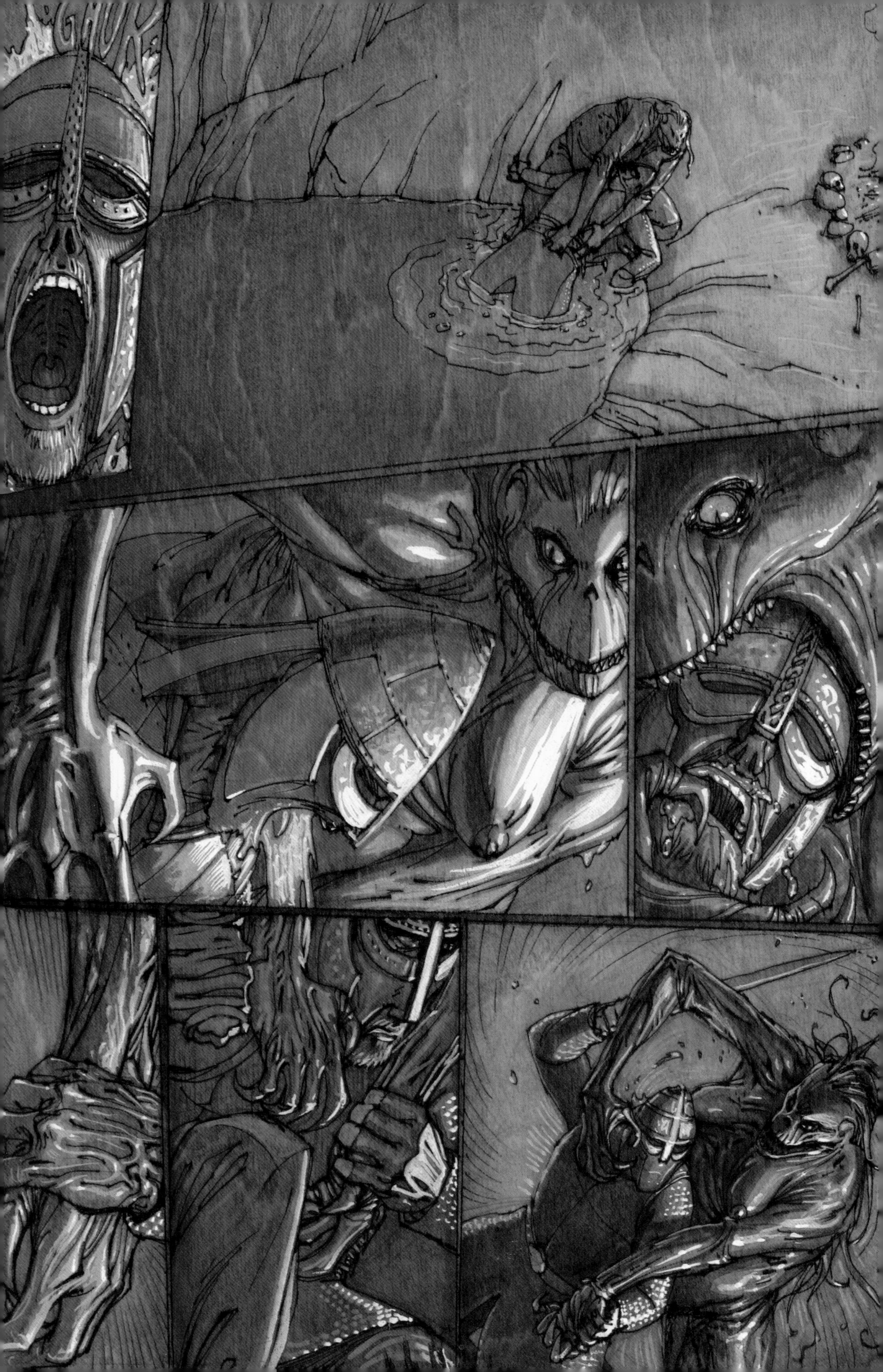
GHUK

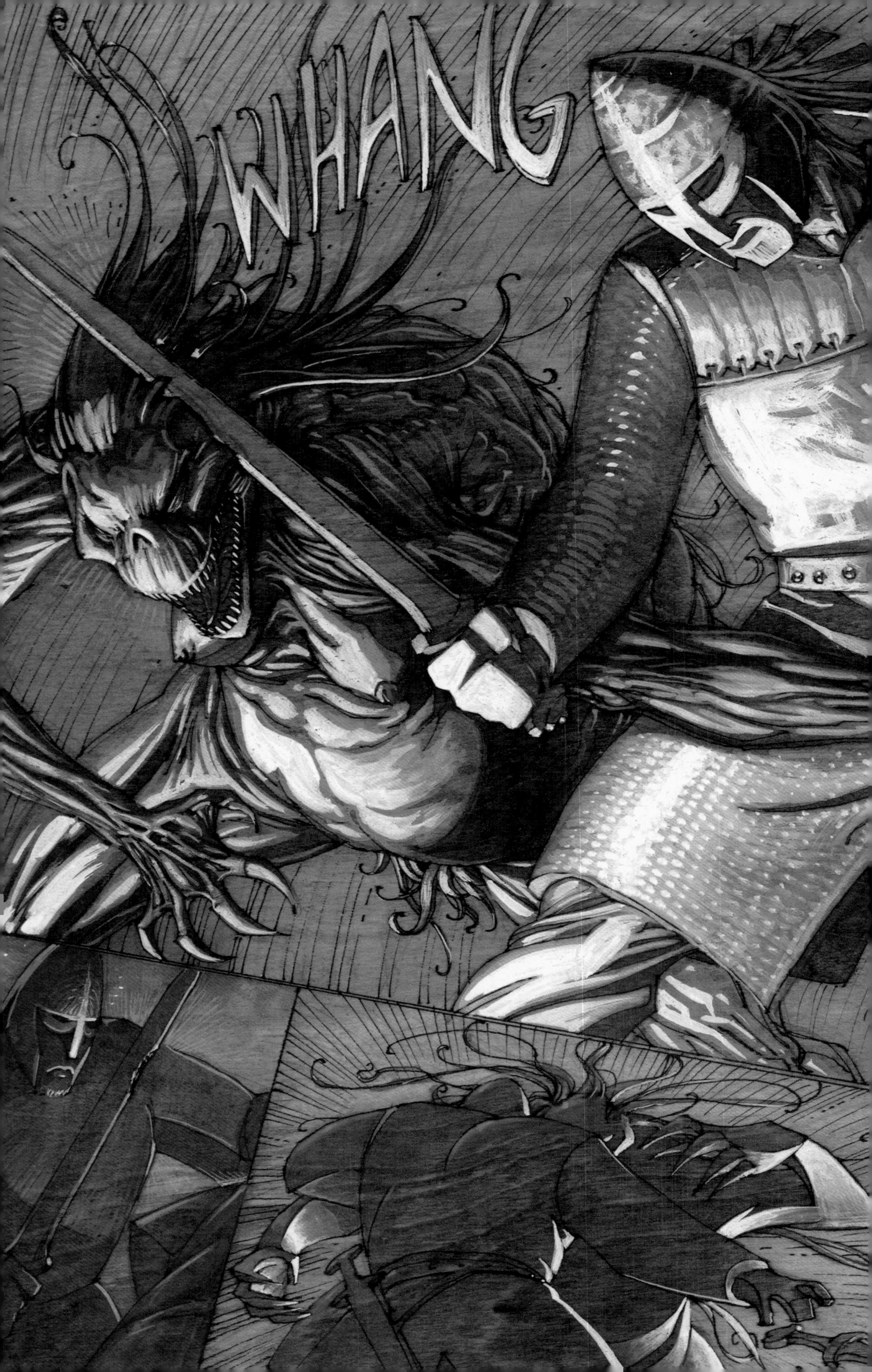
WHANG

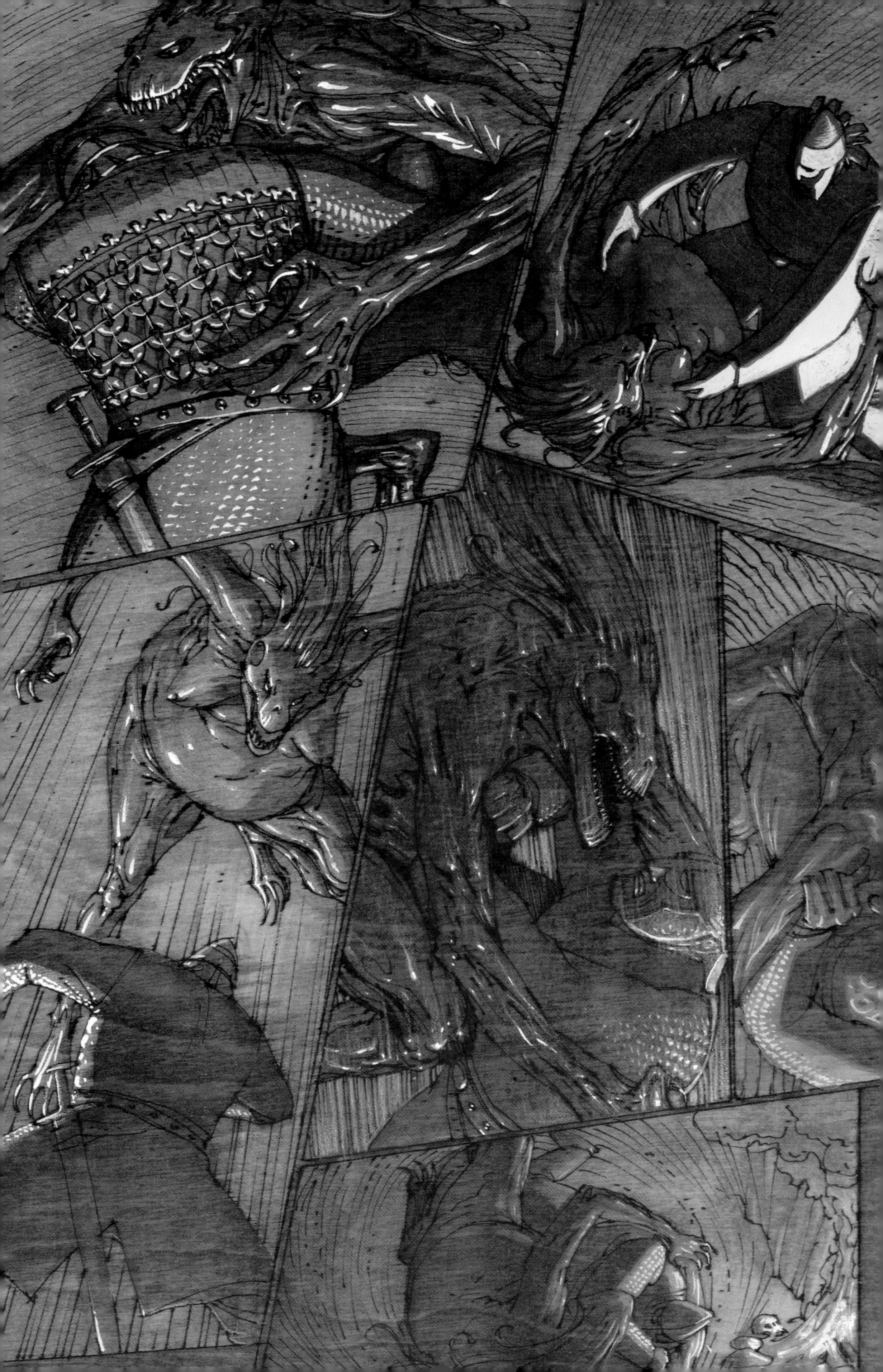

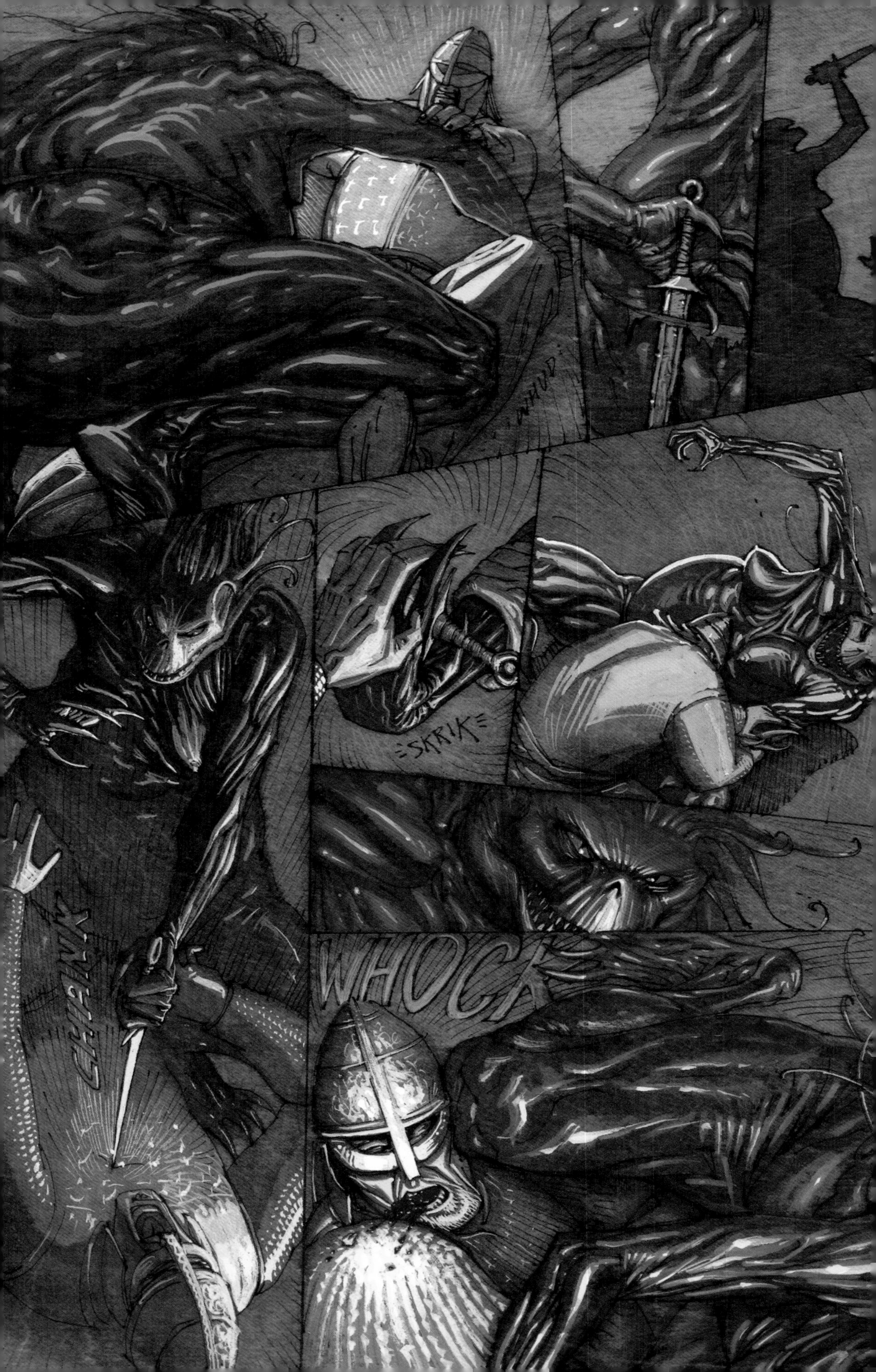
WHUD
SKRIK
CHHINK
WHOCK

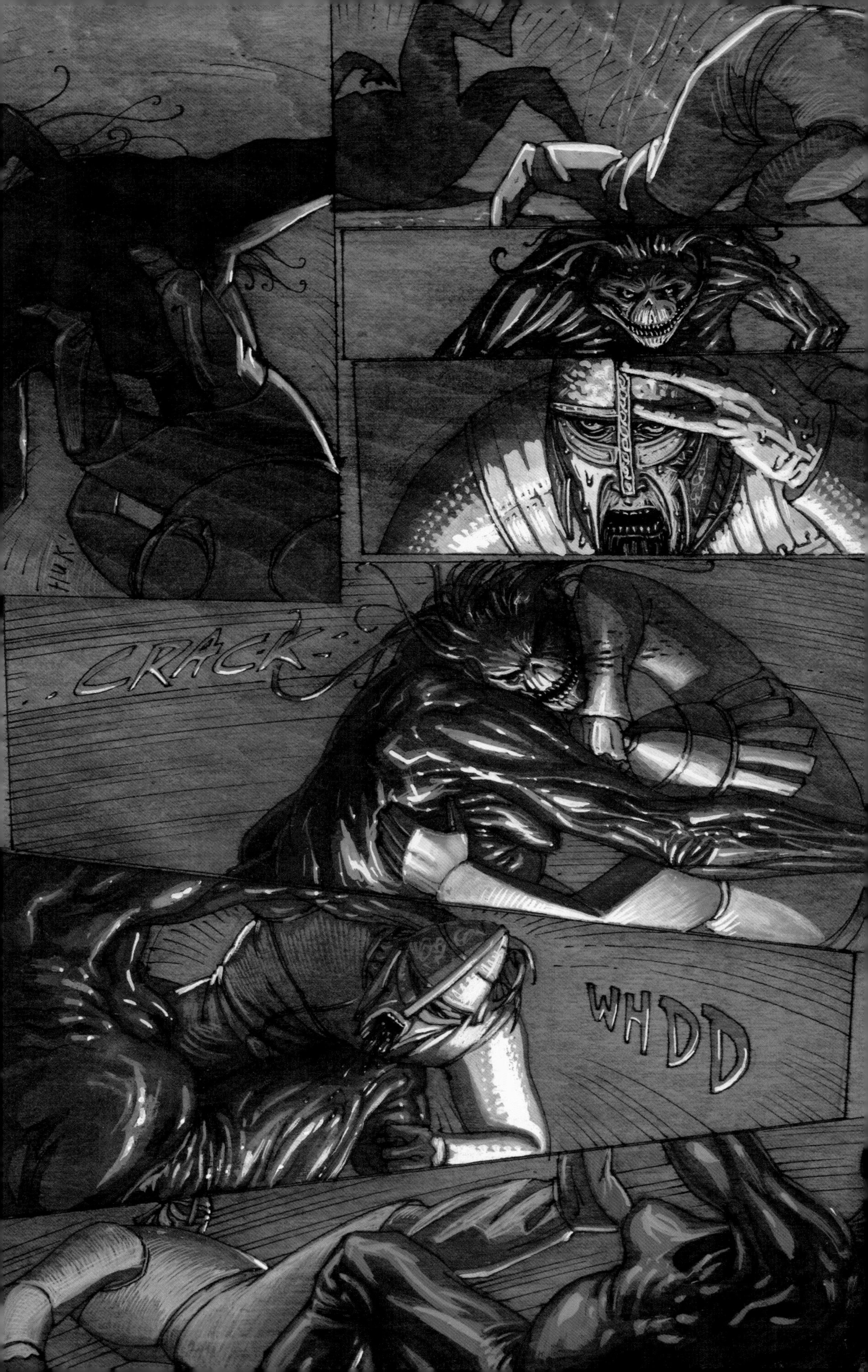
HUK
CRACK
WHDD

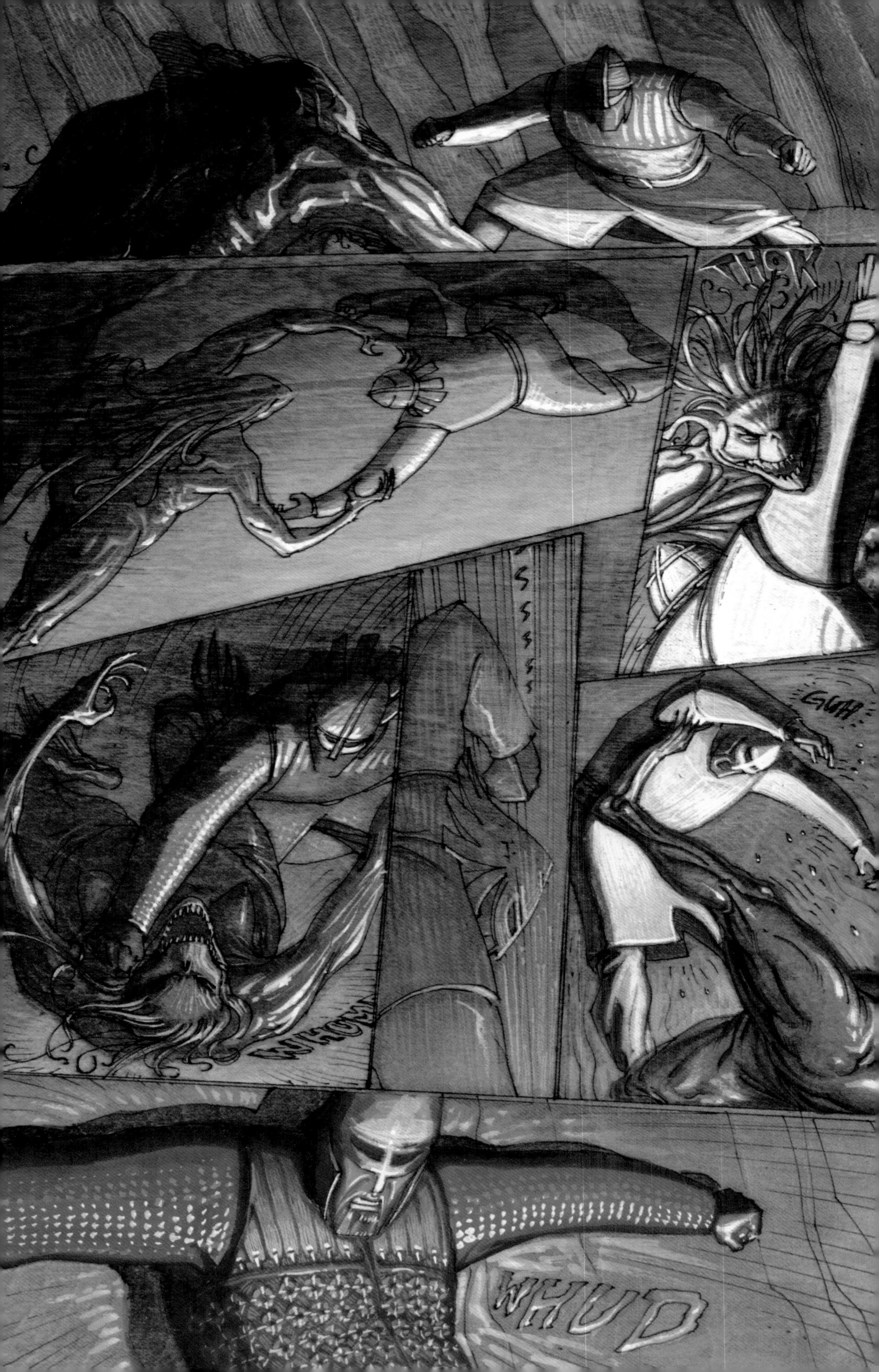
THOK
WHOOM
GUH
WHUD

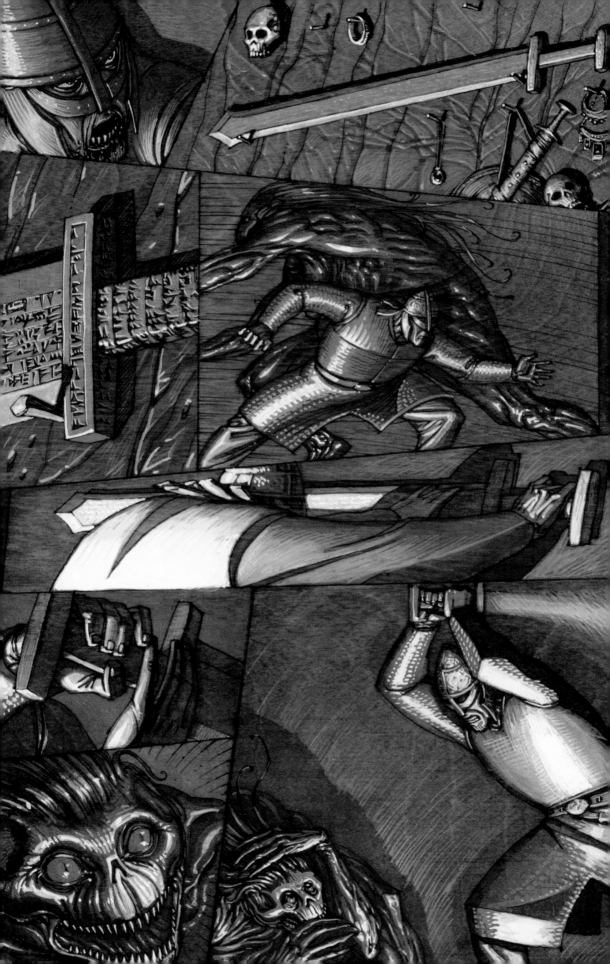

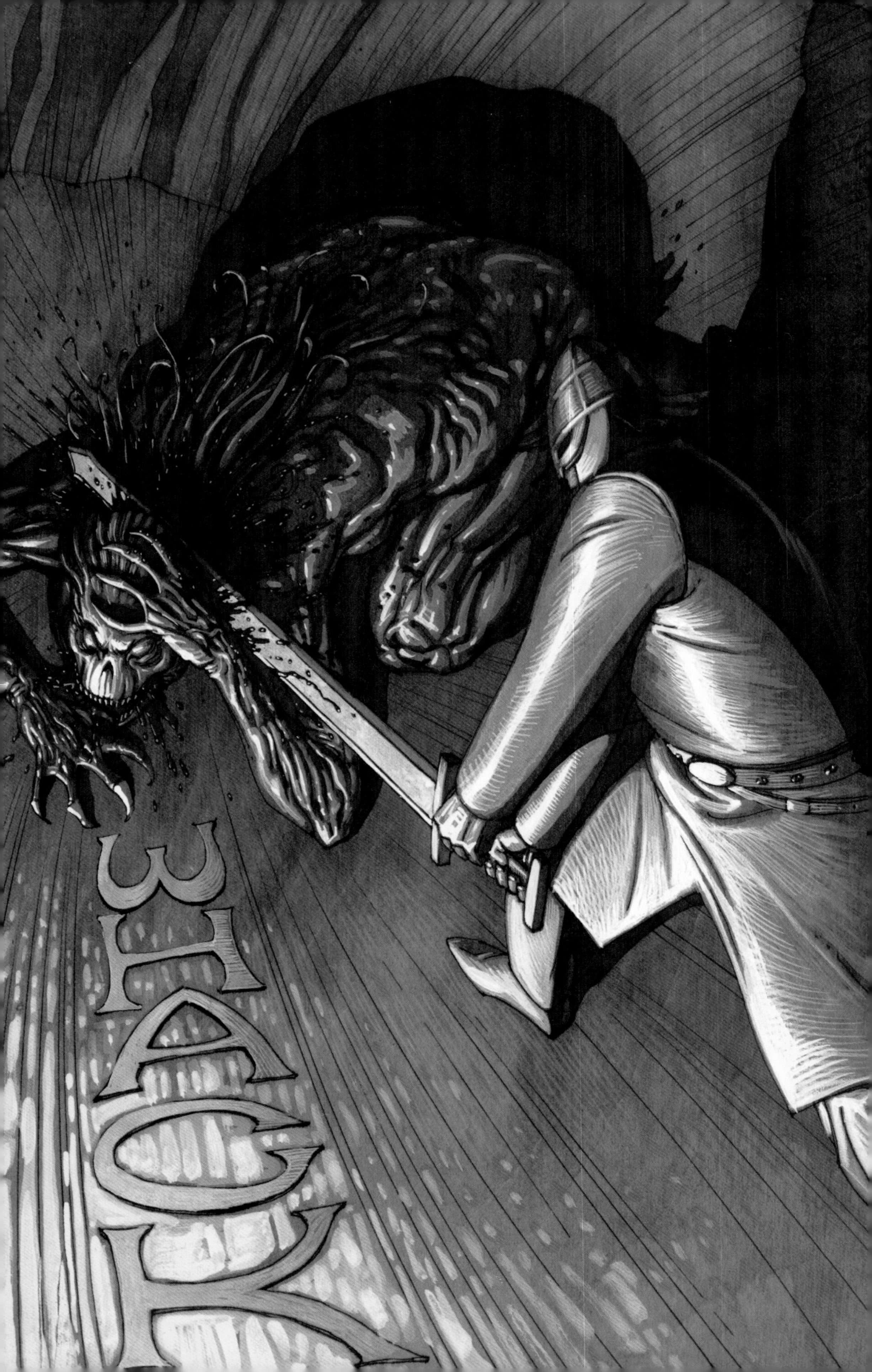
WHACK

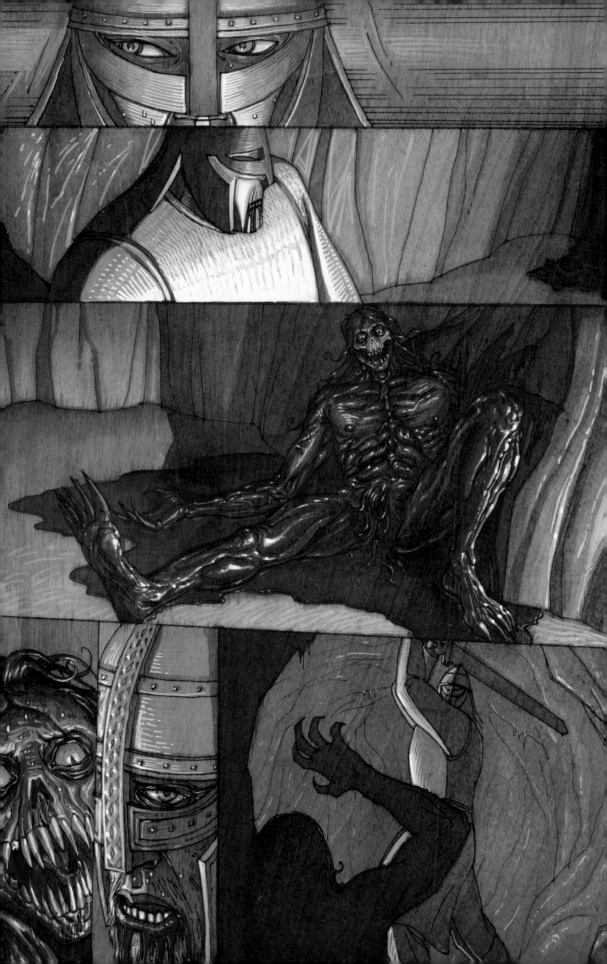

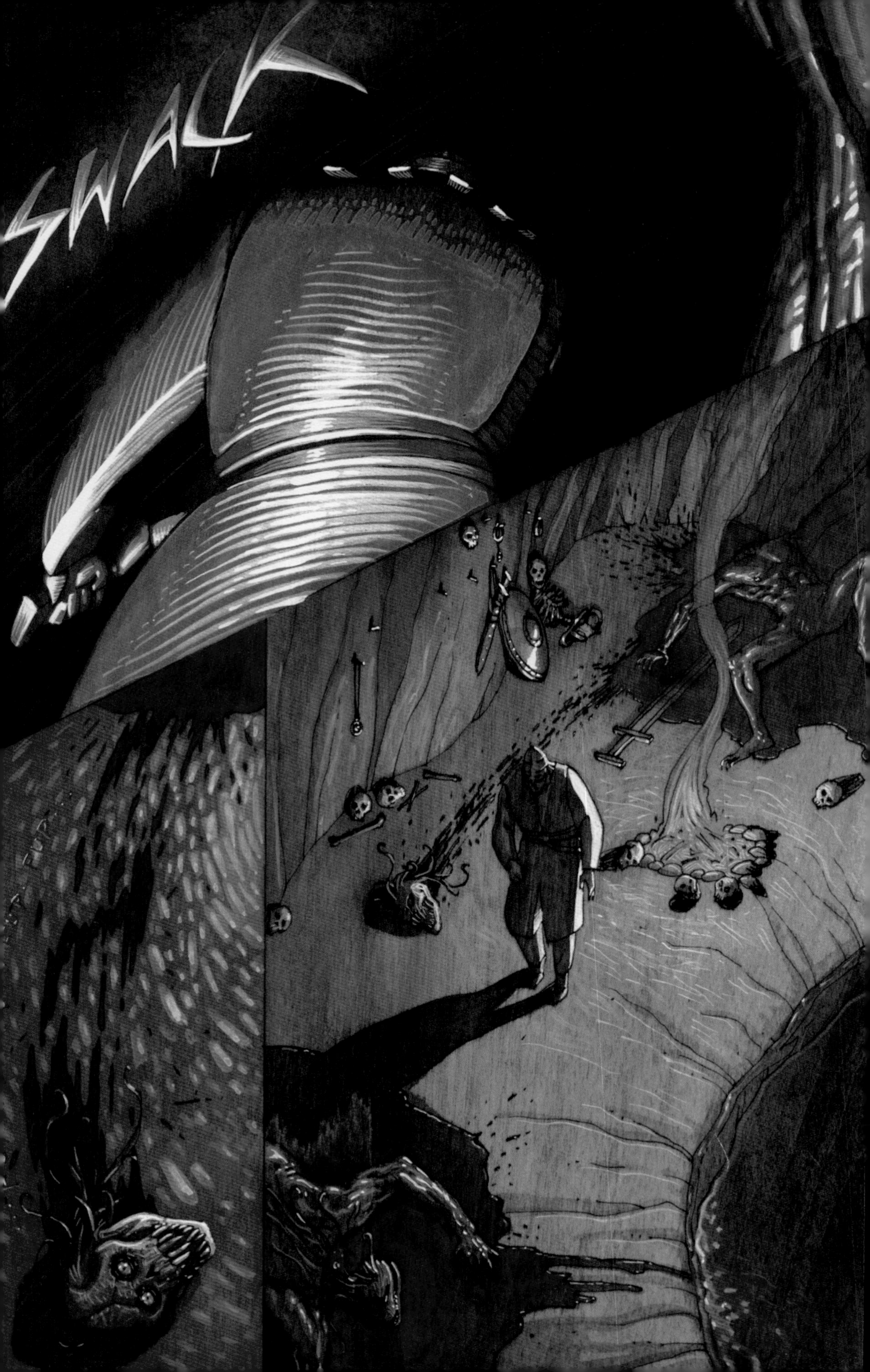
SWACK

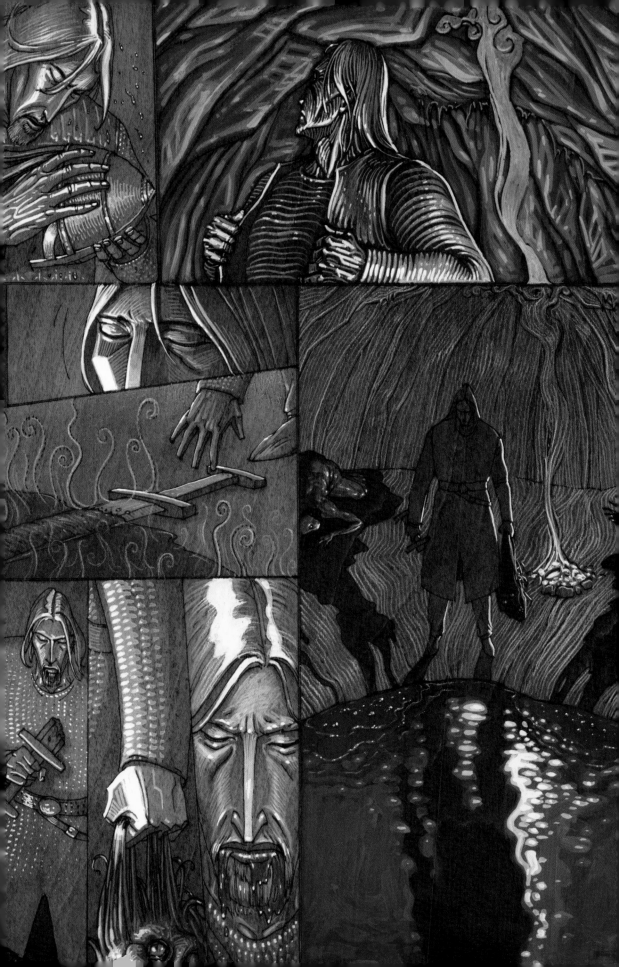

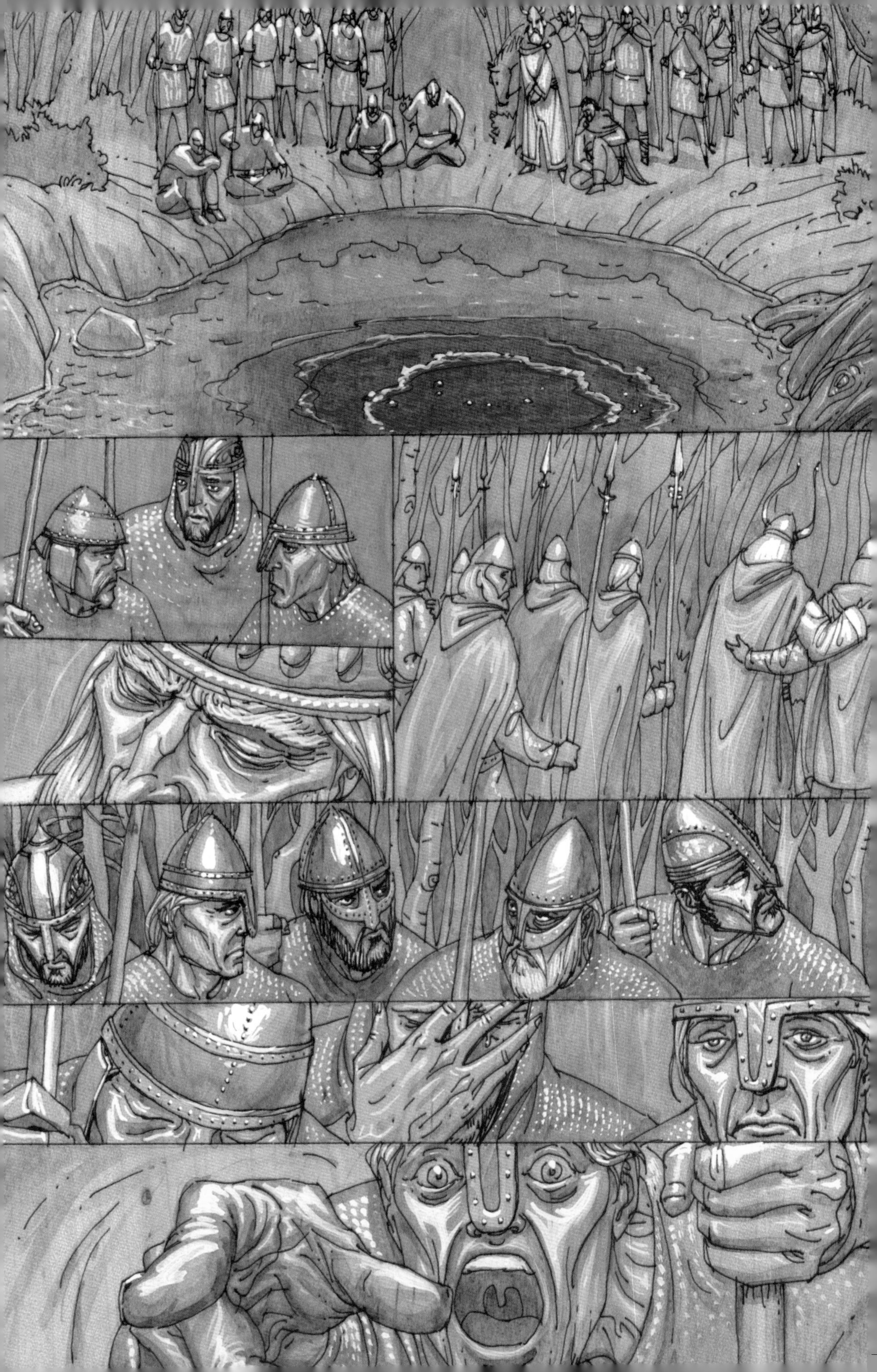

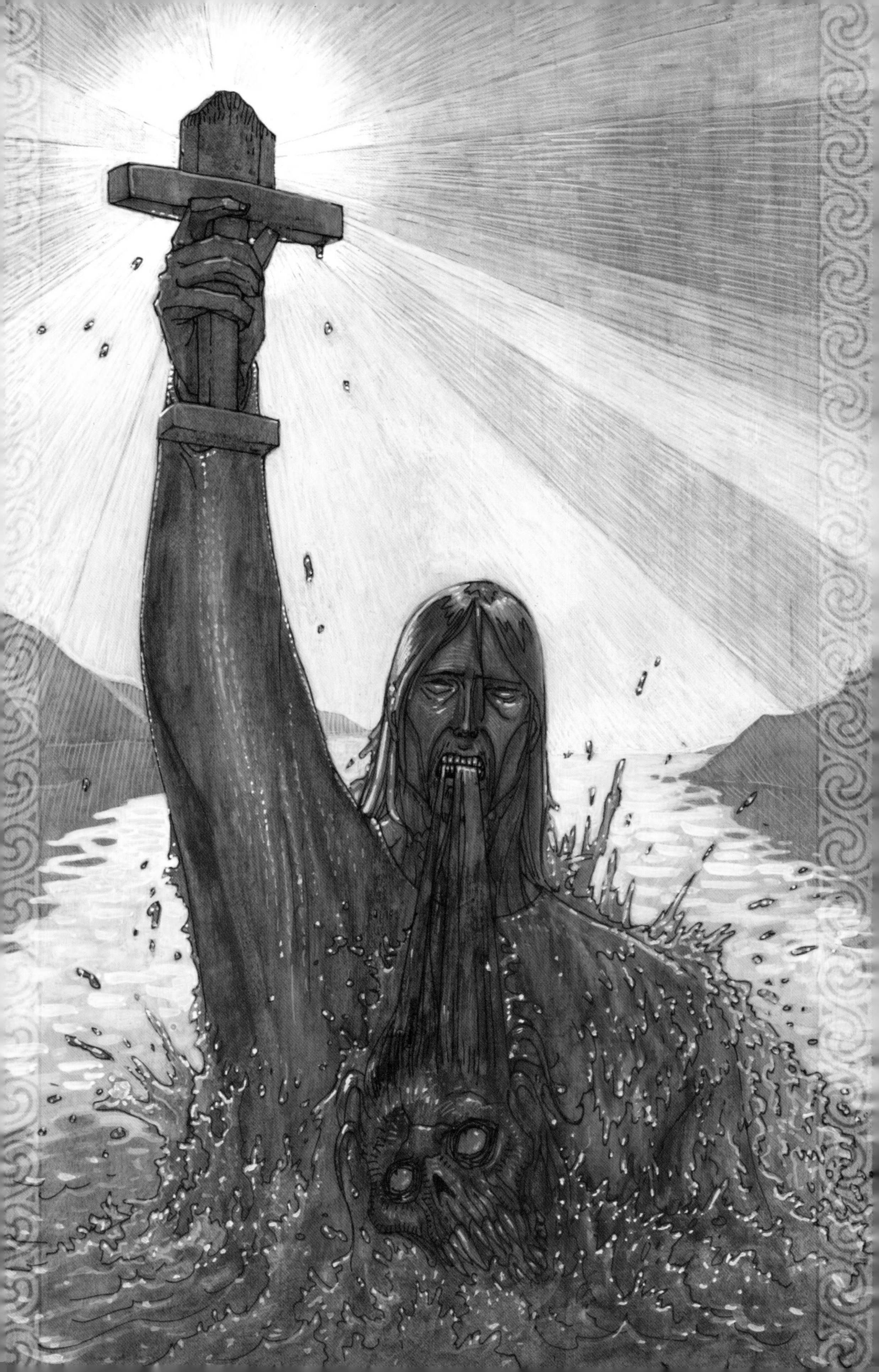

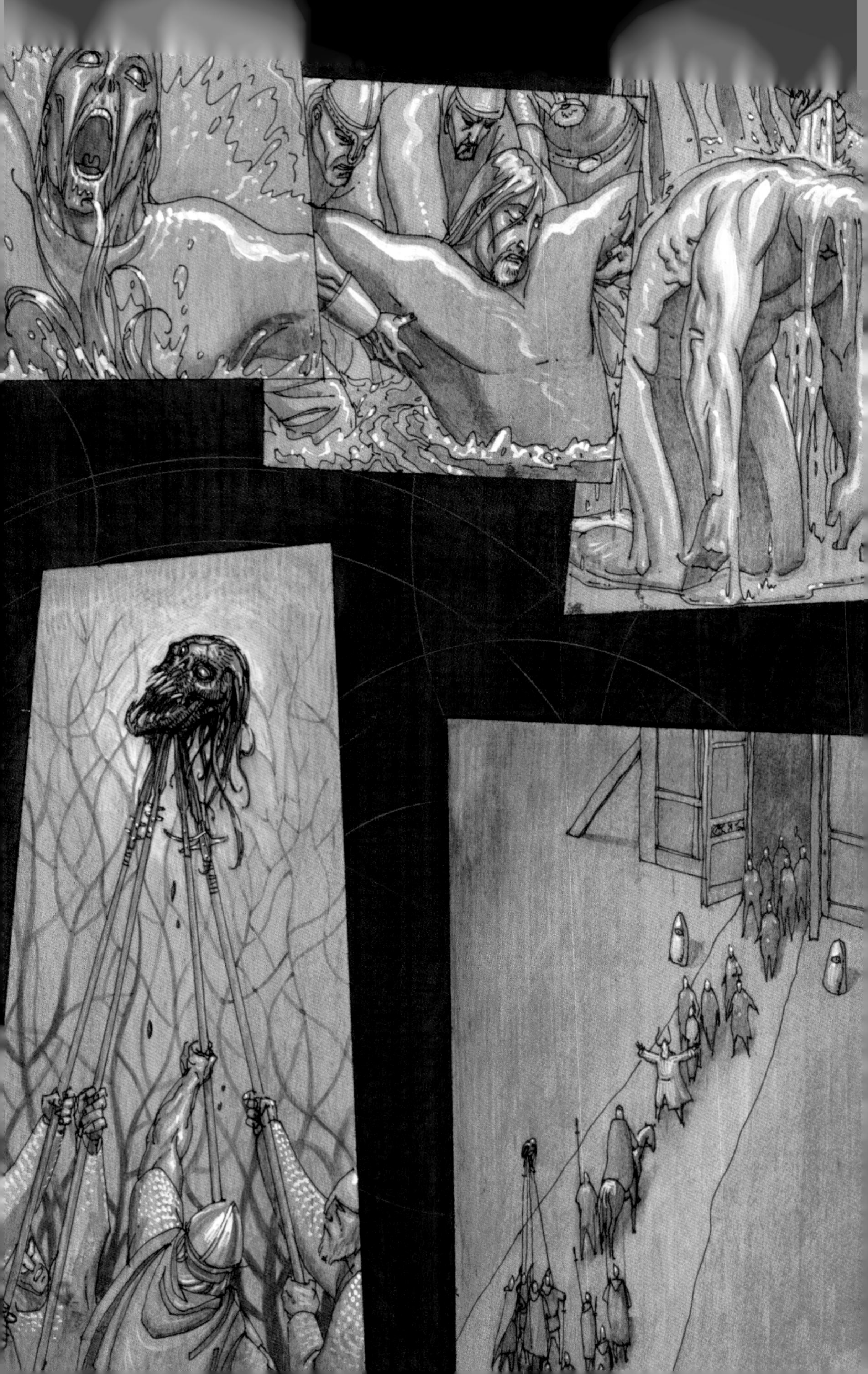

Beowulf soon delivered to Hrothgar the hilt of the giant-sword and the severed head of Grendel. The King rejoiced and all looked with awe upon the trophies. Then Hrothgar counseled the hero:

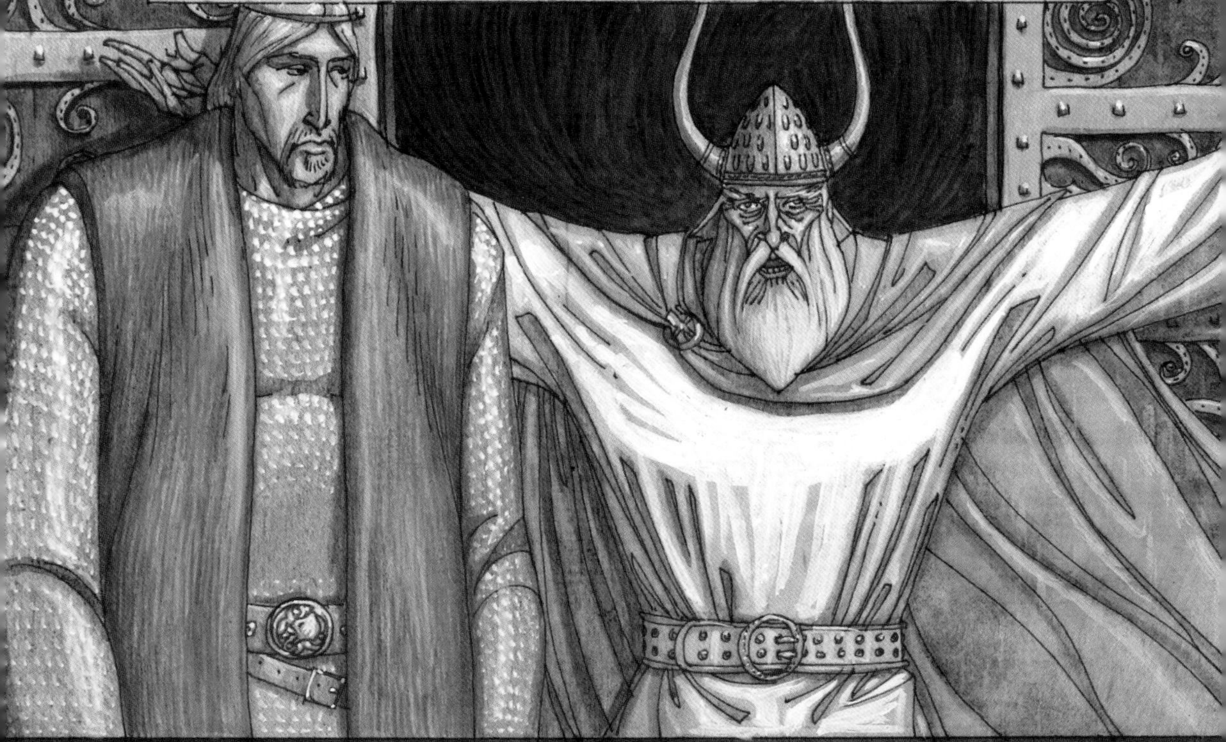

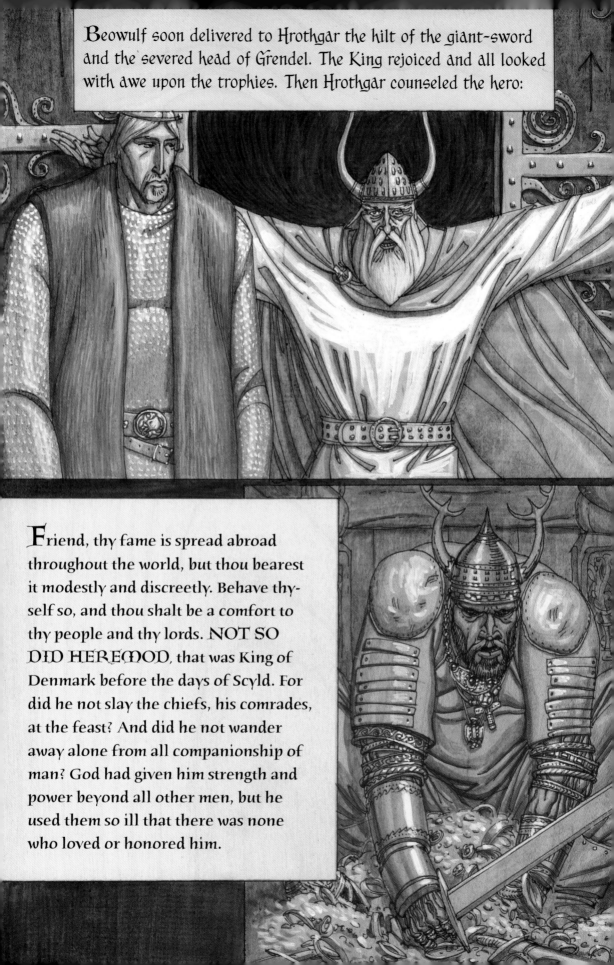

Friend, thy fame is spread abroad throughout the world, but thou bearest it modestly and discreetly. Behave thyself so, and thou shalt be a comfort to thy people and thy lords. NOT SO DID HEREMOD, that was King of Denmark before the days of Scyld. For did he not slay the chiefs, his comrades, at the feast? And did he not wander away alone from all companionship of man? God had given him strength and power beyond all other men, but he used them so ill that there was none who loved or honored him.

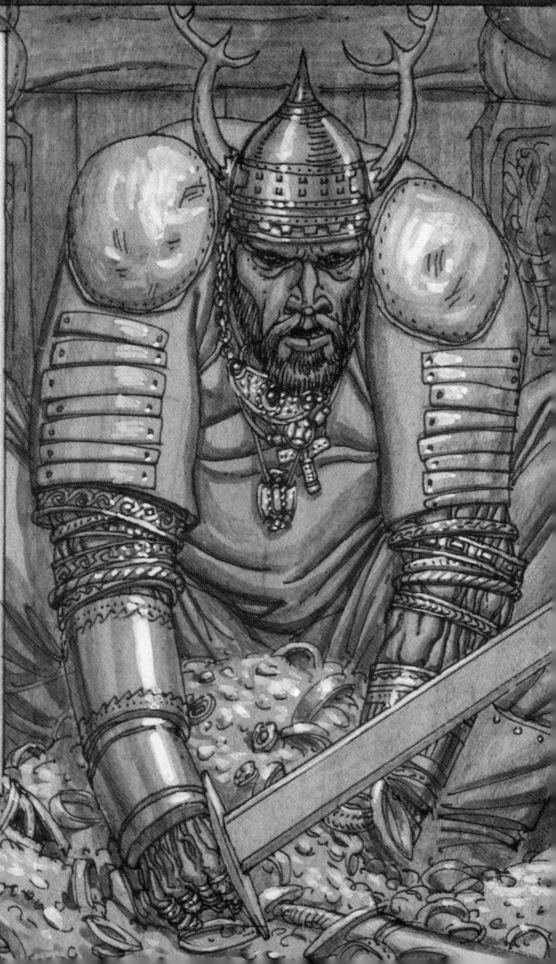

TAKE WARNING BY HIM, O BEOWULF.

Wondrous it seems when Almighty God gives a man fortune and fame and a wide dominion – power over great parts of the earth, an empire so ample that he can comprehend no end to it. But ever it comes that the frame of the body fragile yields, fated falls, and there follows another who joyously the jewels divides, the royal riches, and cares not for his predecessor.

Take thou, therefore, good heed, O Beowulf, against pride and arrogance. Choose the better path: profit eternal. Now, indeed, thou art in the pride of thy strength and the power of thy youth; but there will come of a surety, sooner or later, either sickness or the sword; fire shall consume thee or the floods swallow thee up. Be it bite of blade or brandished spear, or odious age, or the eyes' clear beam grown dull and leaden.

Come in what shape it may, death will subdue even thee, thou hero of war.

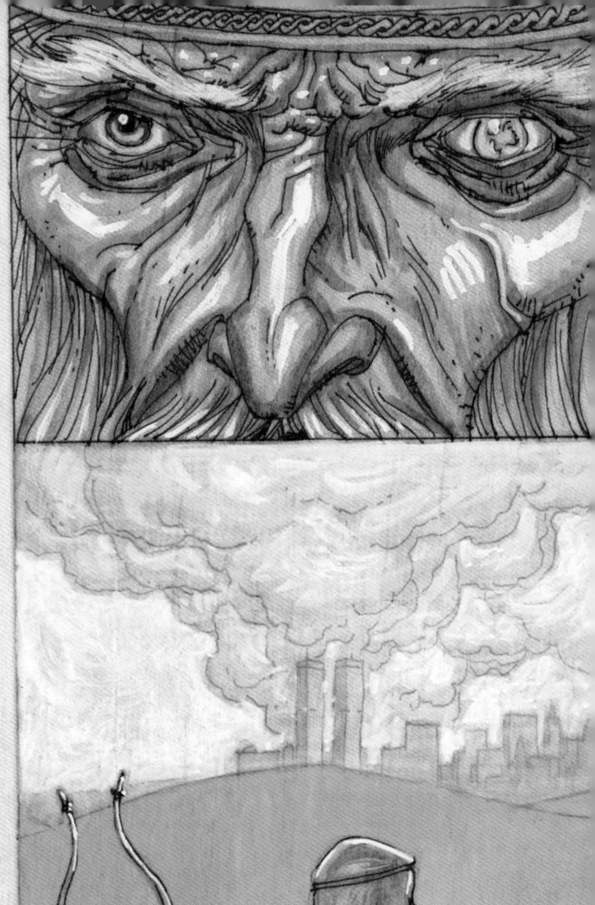

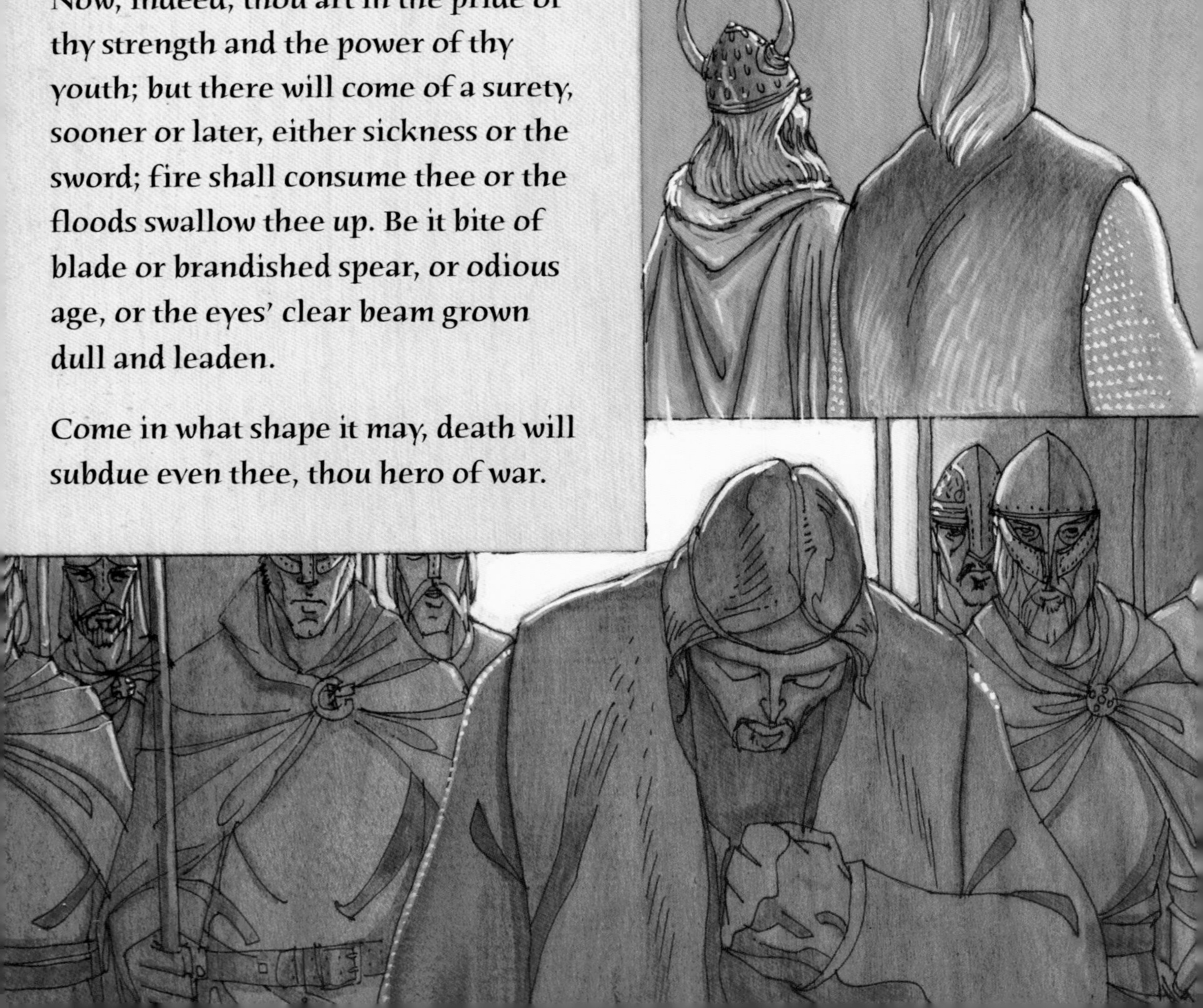

Then the King gave him jewels from his store, and after this, he threw his arms about the young man's neck, weeping the while, for he knew in his heart that he should see his face no more in Daneland. So Beowulf and his comrades rode down to the shore. Beowulf gave to the warden of the boat a sword bound with gold; high place did the man hold thenceforth among his fellows by reason of this gift. Then the Geats embarked upon their ship and set sail.

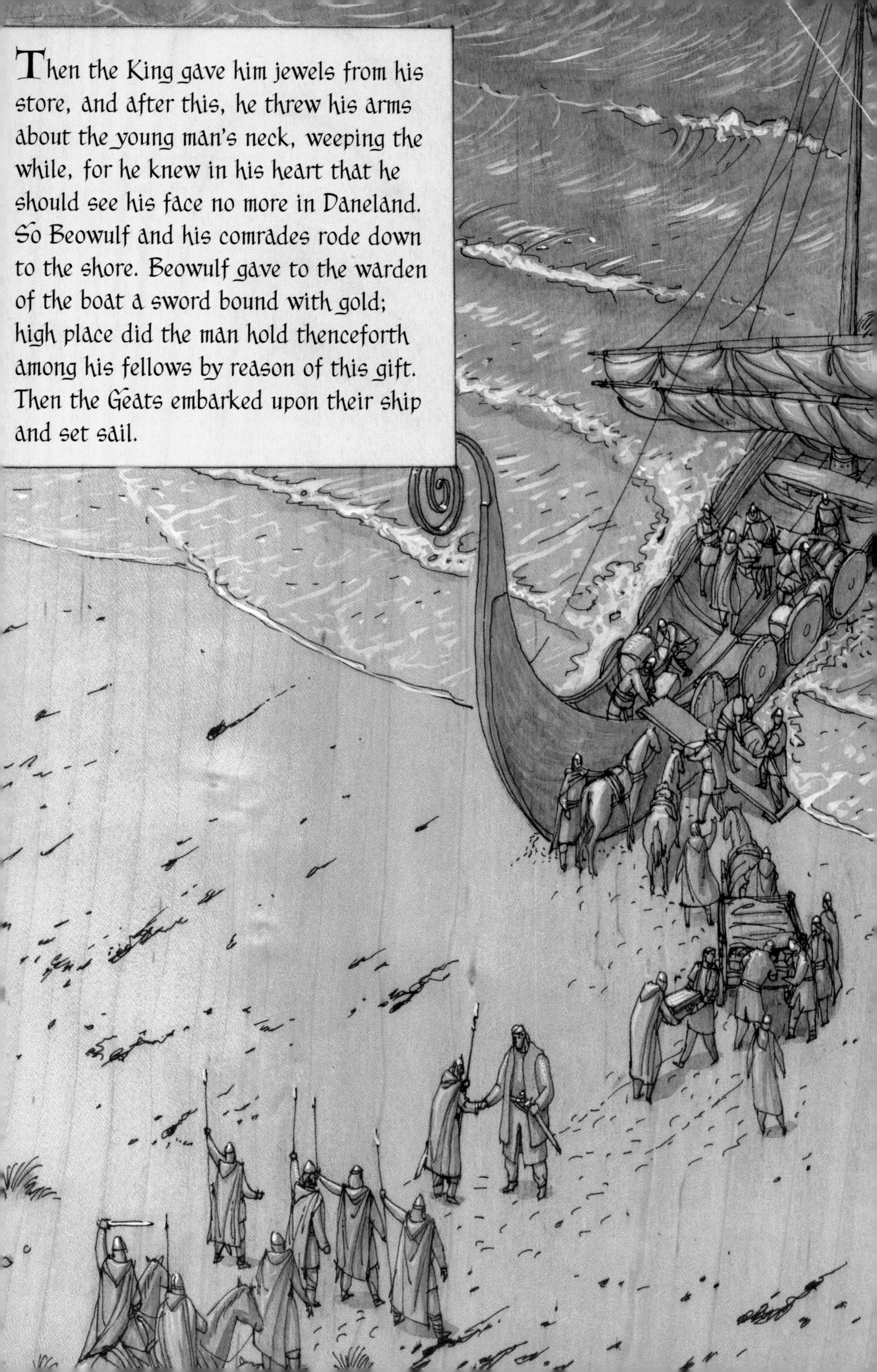

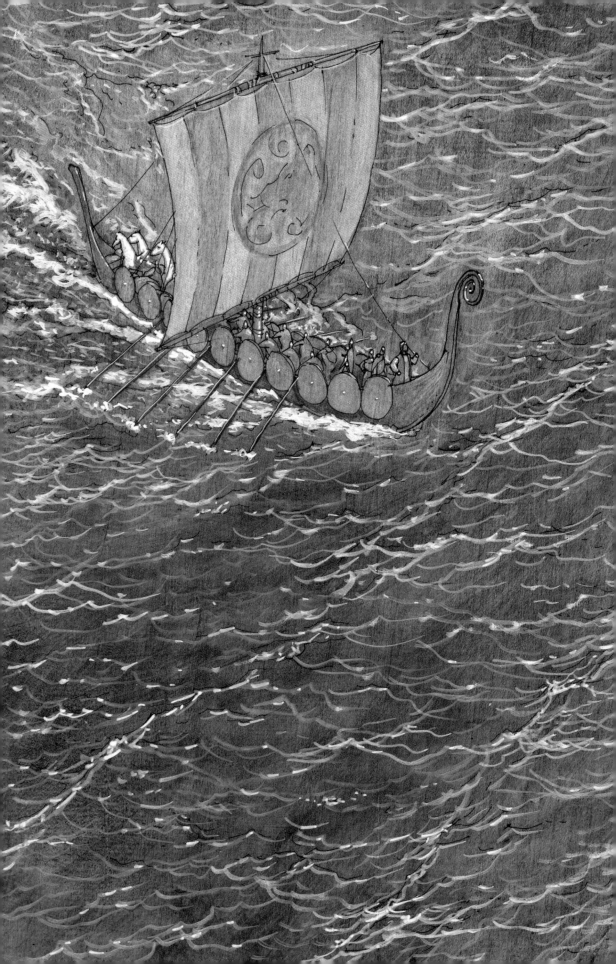

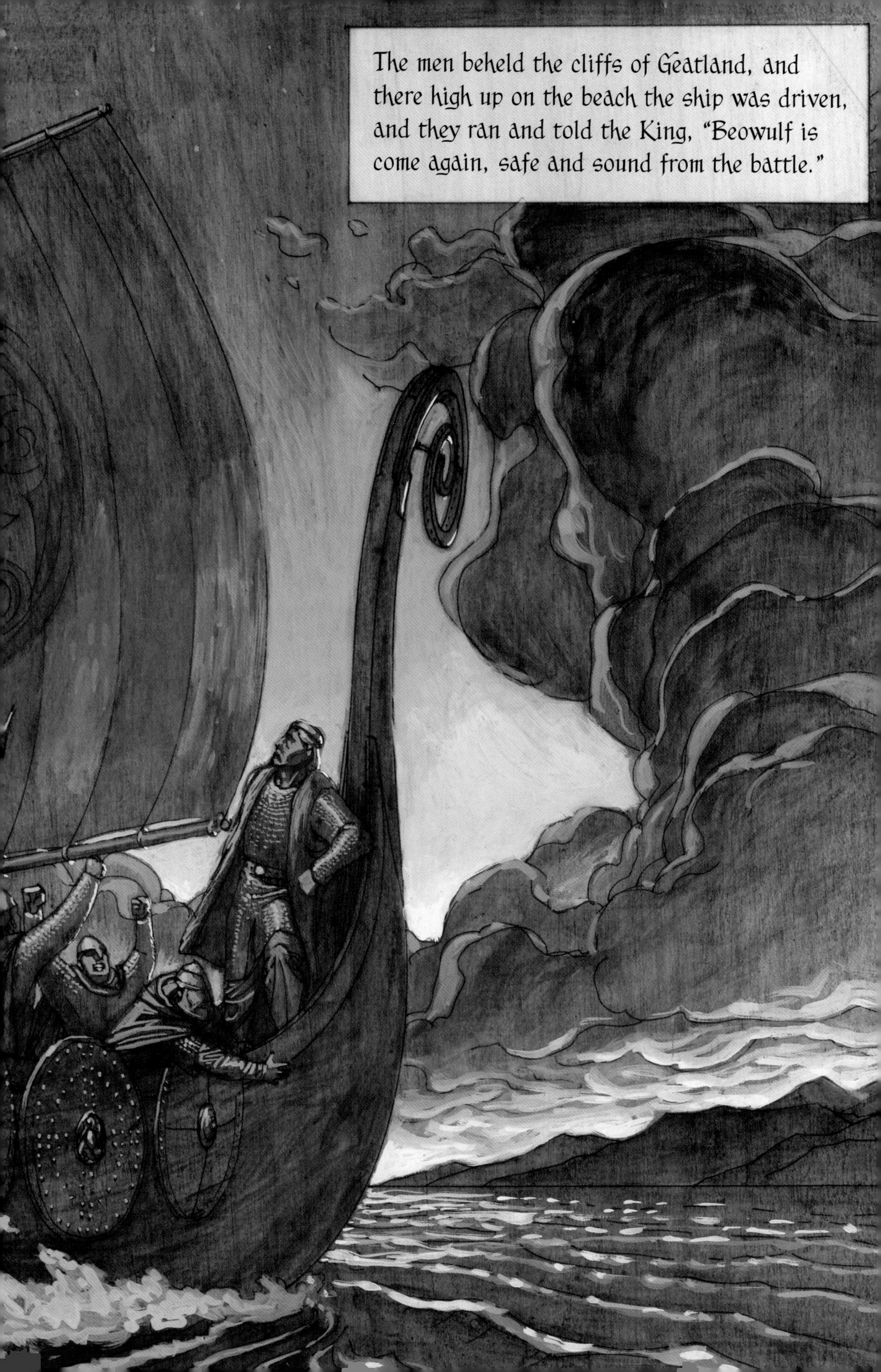
The men beheld the cliffs of Geatland, and there high up on the beach the ship was driven, and they ran and told the King, "Beowulf is come again, safe and sound from the battle."

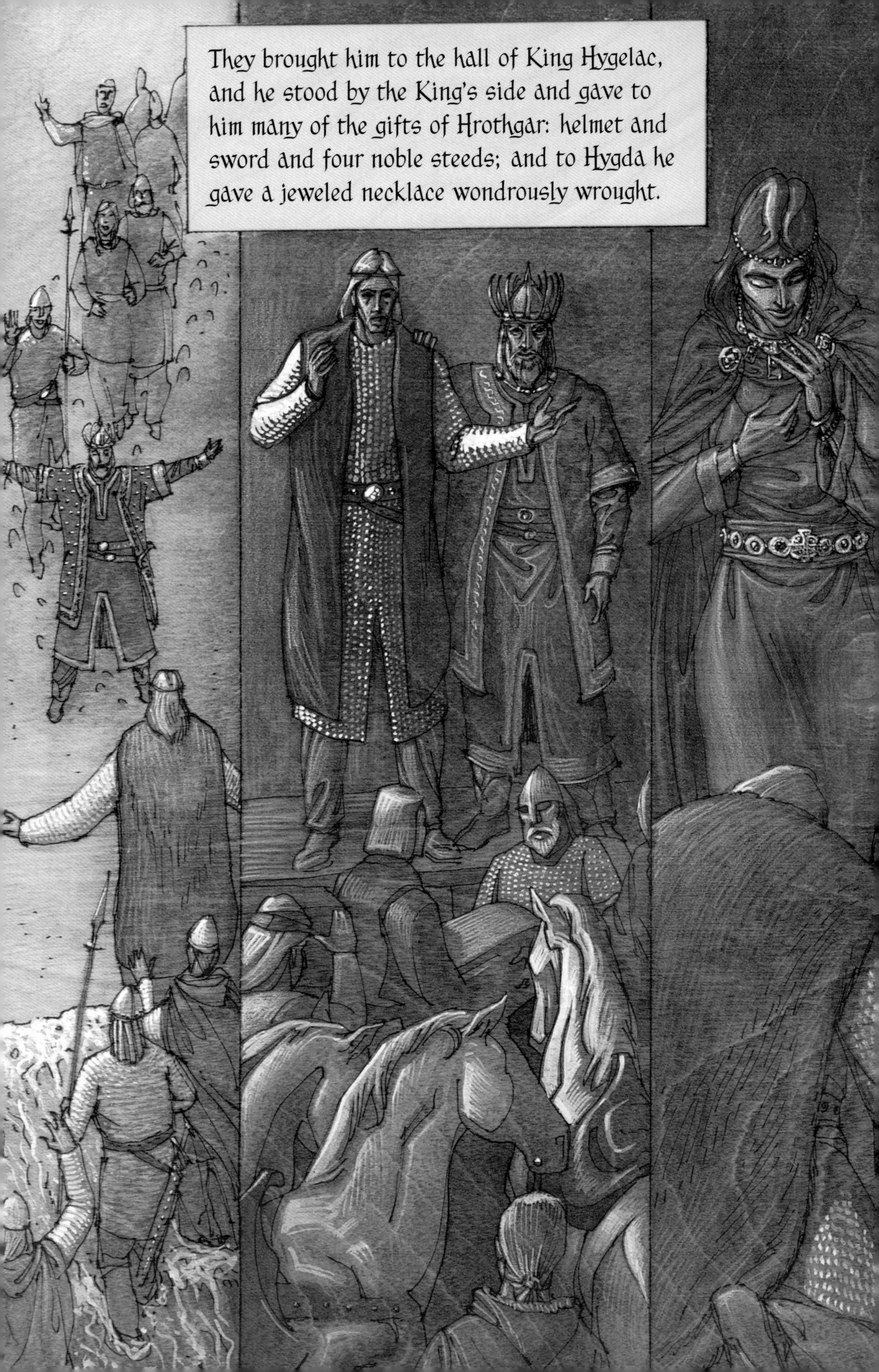
They brought him to the hall of King Hygelac, and he stood by the King's side and gave to him many of the gifts of Hrothgar: helmet and sword and four noble steeds; and to Hygda he gave a jeweled necklace wondrously wrought.

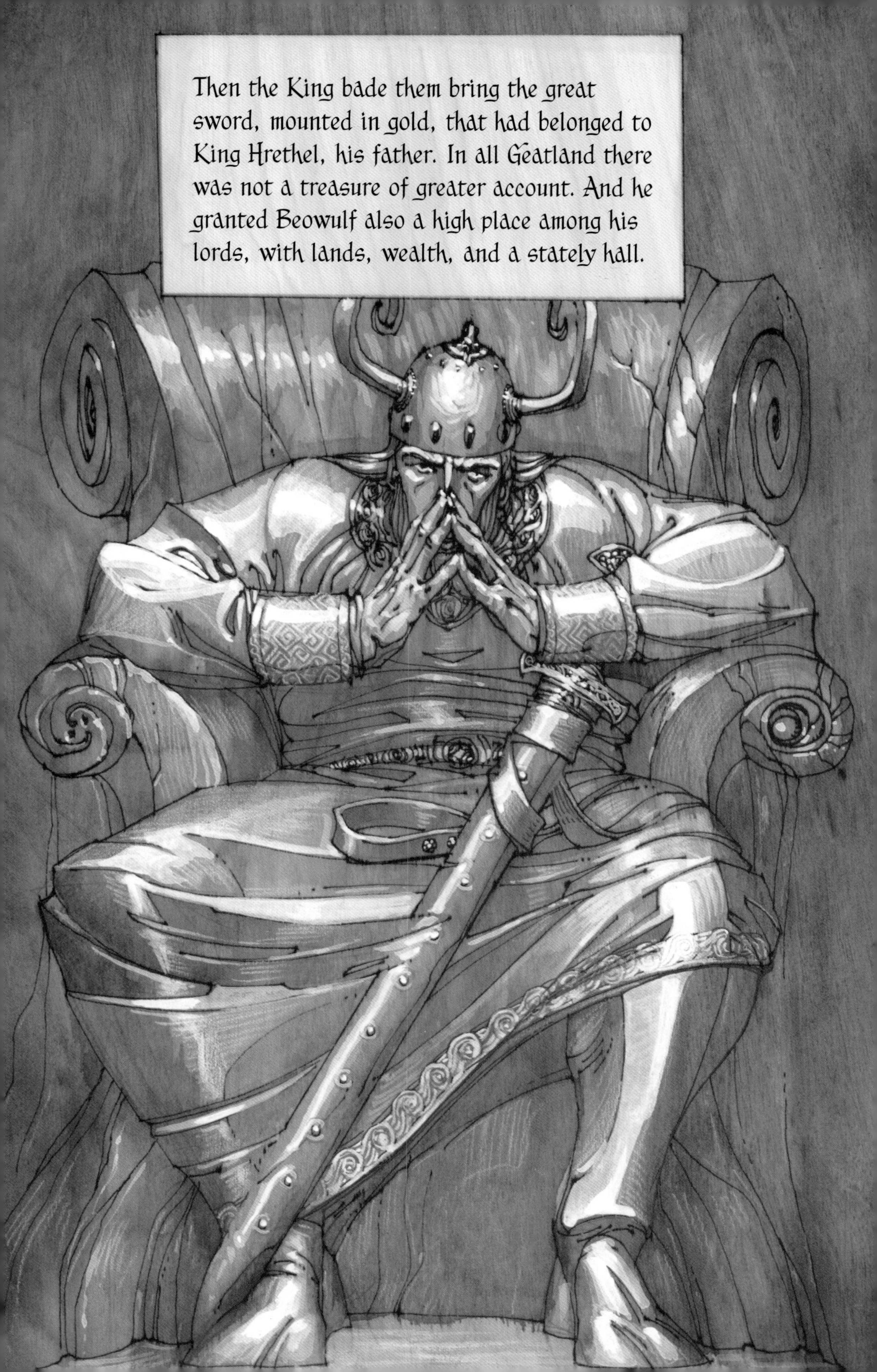
Then the King bade them bring the great sword, mounted in gold, that had belonged to King Hrethel, his father. In all Geatland there was not a treasure of greater account. And he granted Beowulf also a high place among his lords, with lands, wealth, and a stately hall.

BOOK THREE

Now it came to pass that King Hygelac made war against the men of Frisia, and he took with him a great host and many famous chiefs, but the King was slain and all his nobles with him, save Beowulf only. Then Beowulf took the kingdom upon himself, ruling its people prudently for fifty years, warding them well, until One began in the dark of night – a Dragon – to rage.

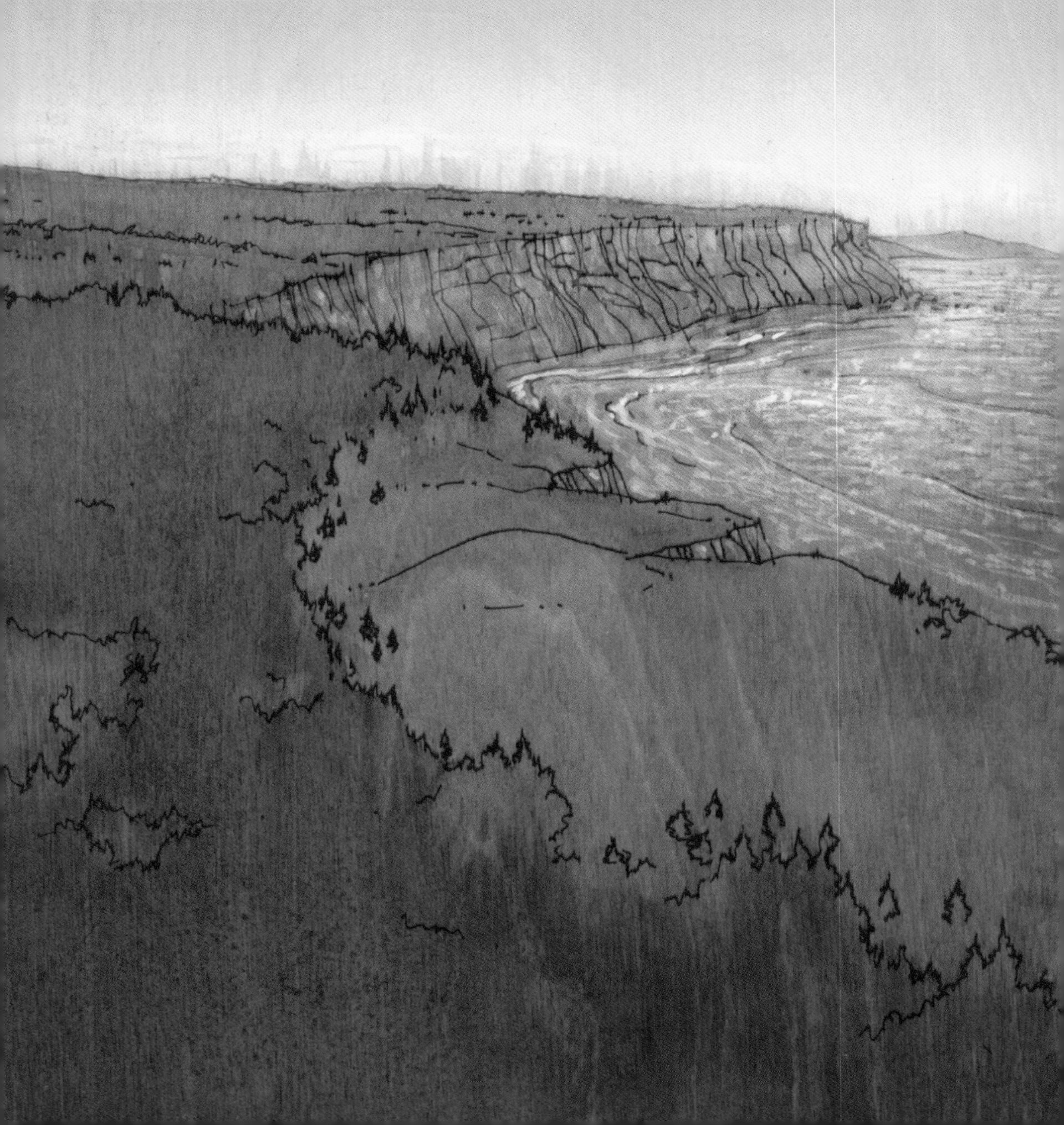

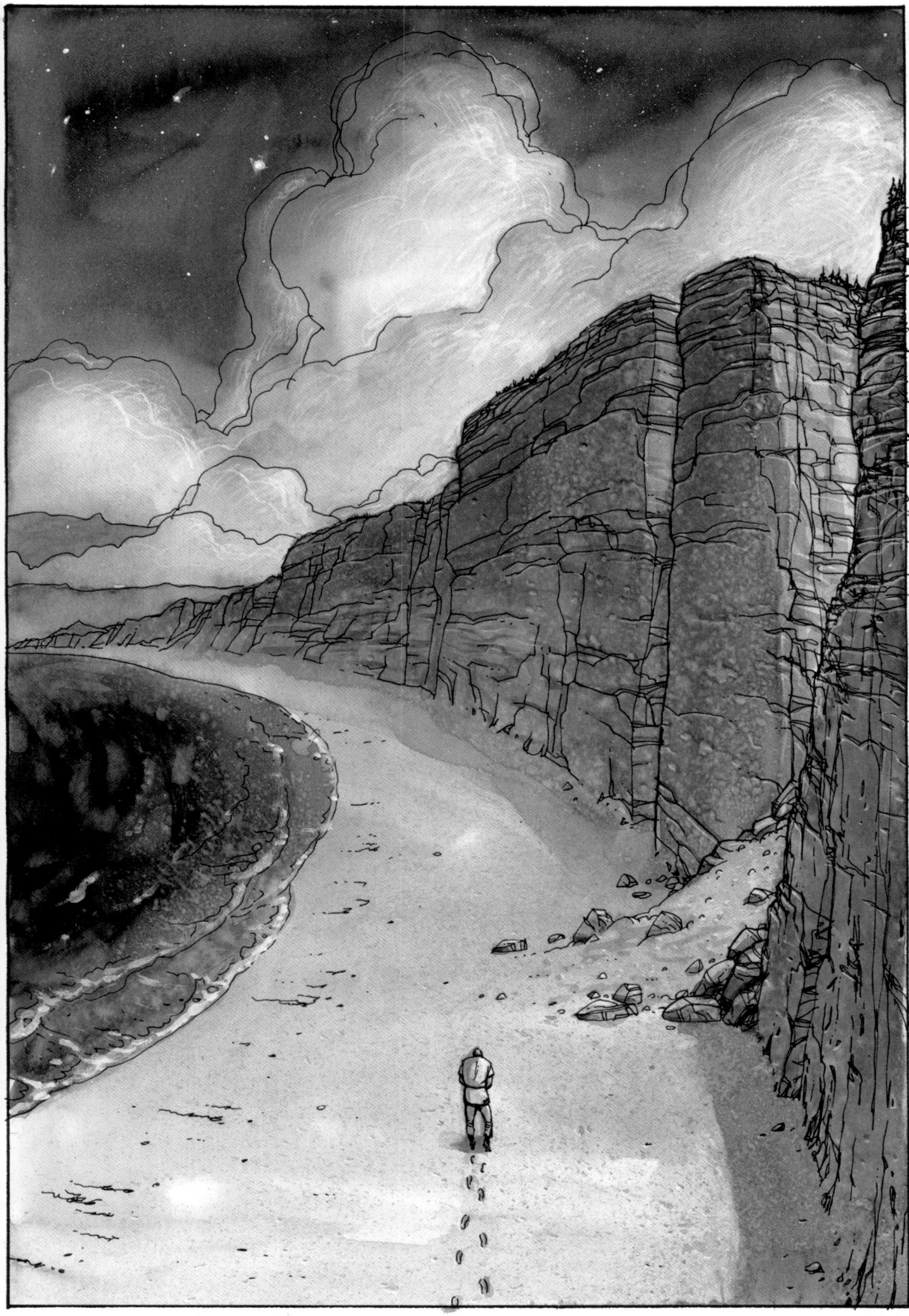

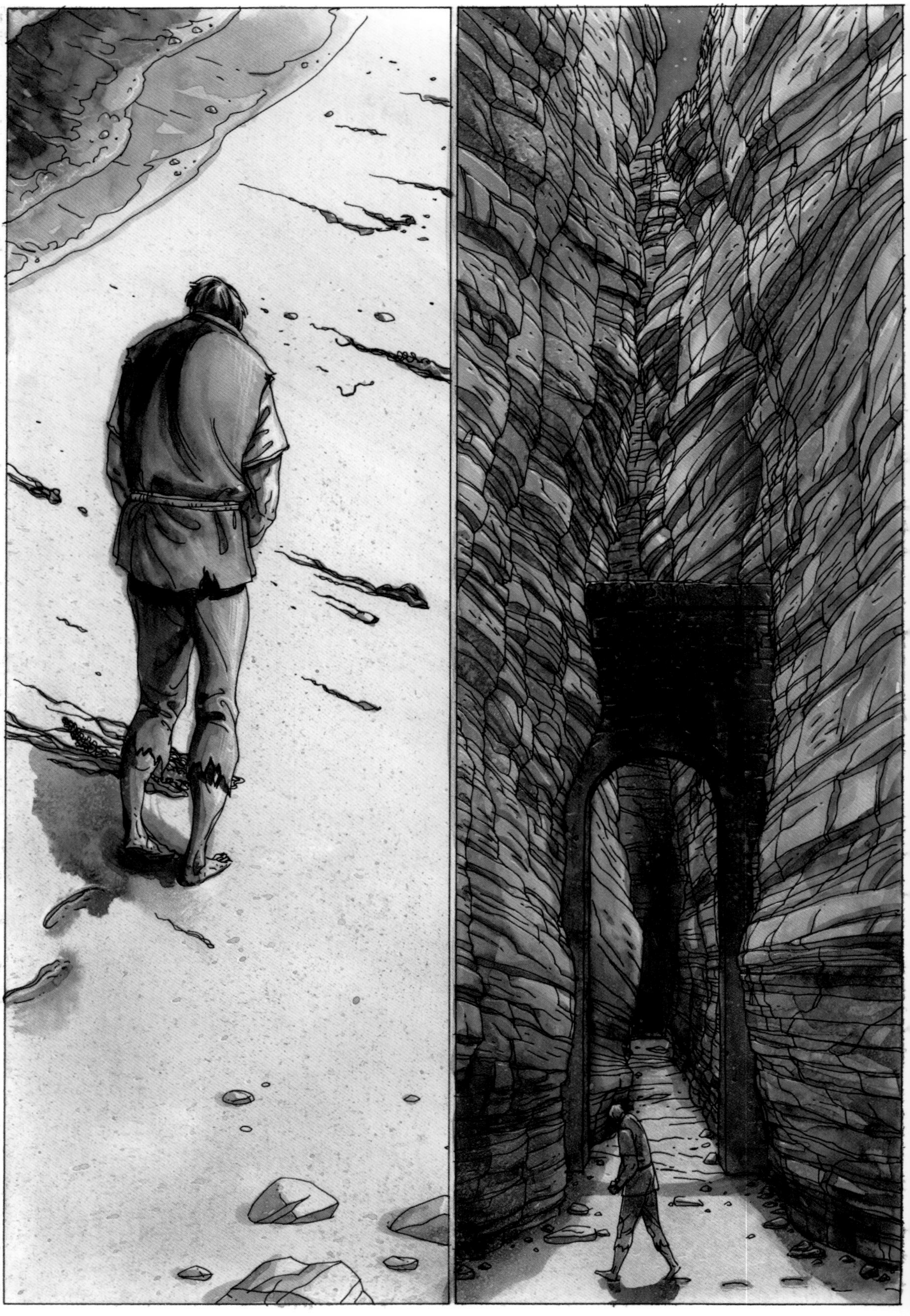

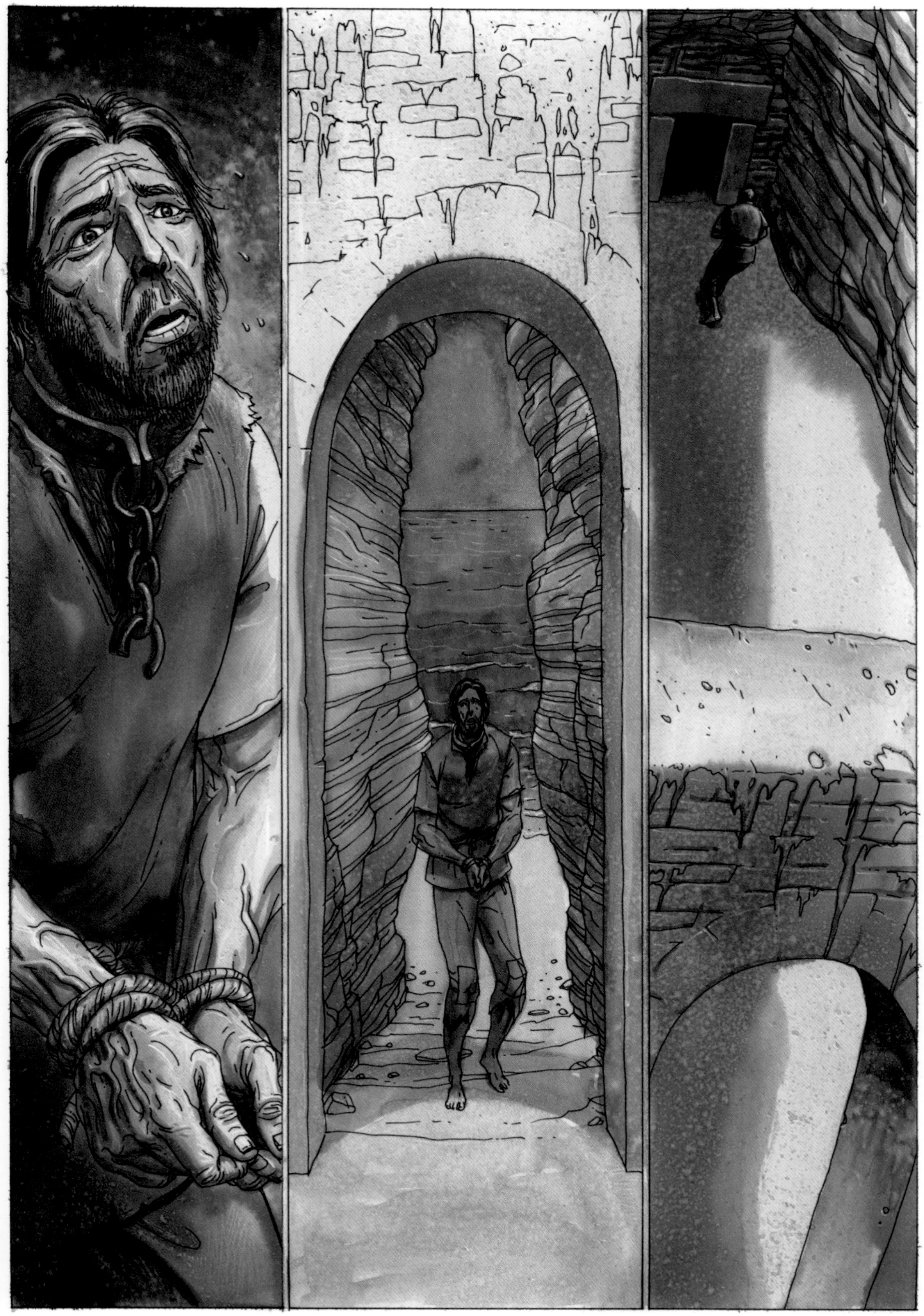

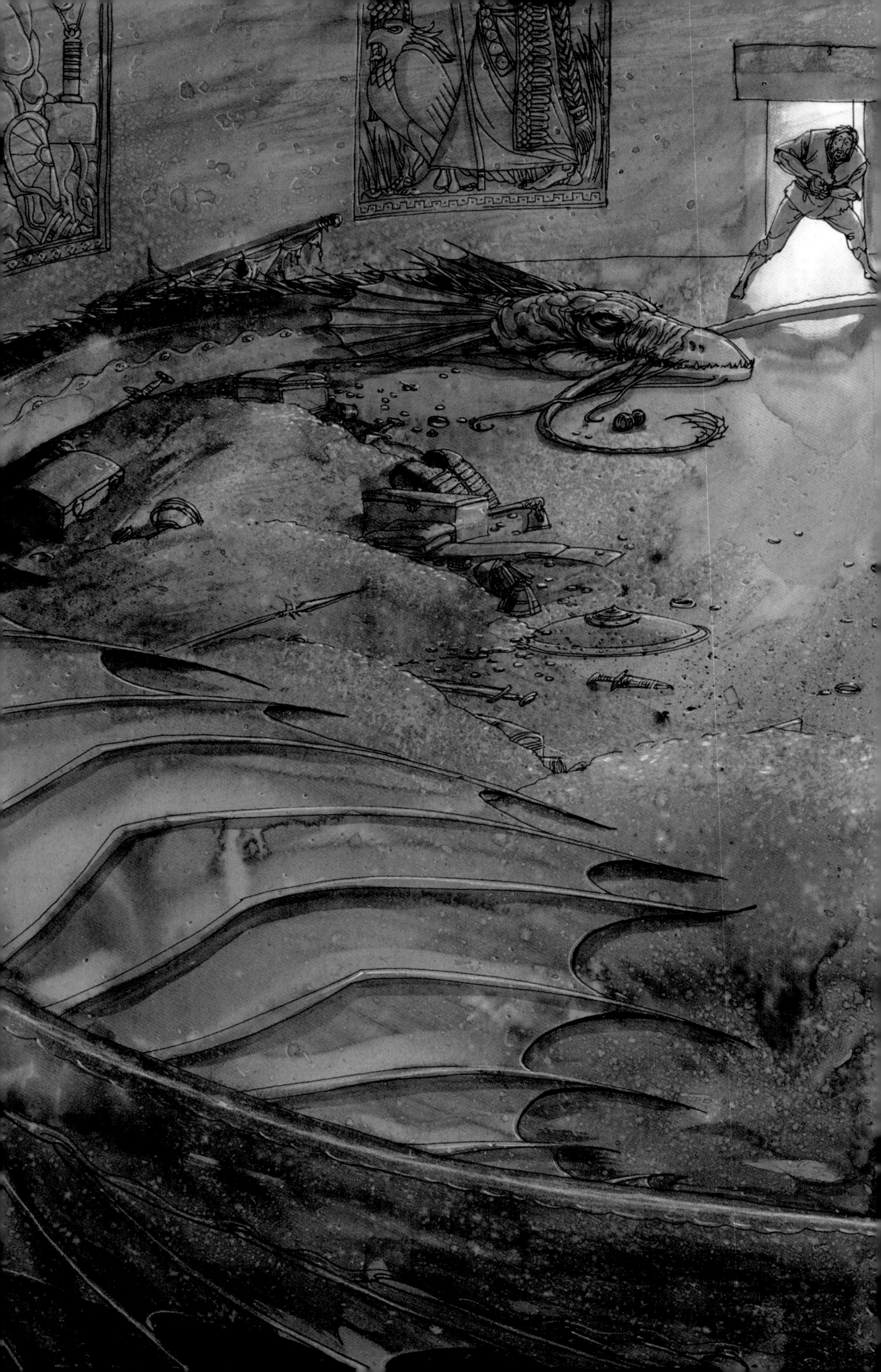

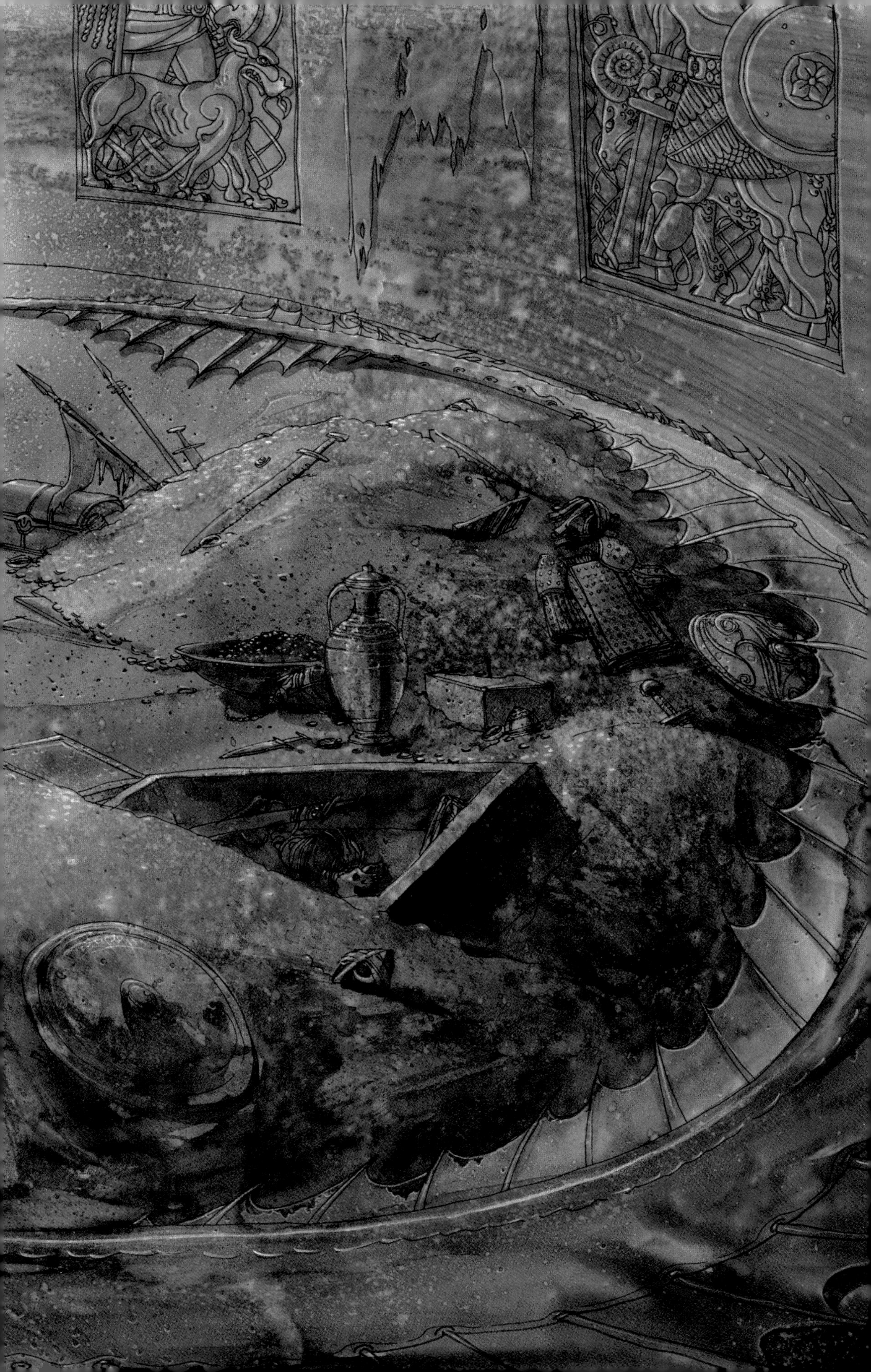

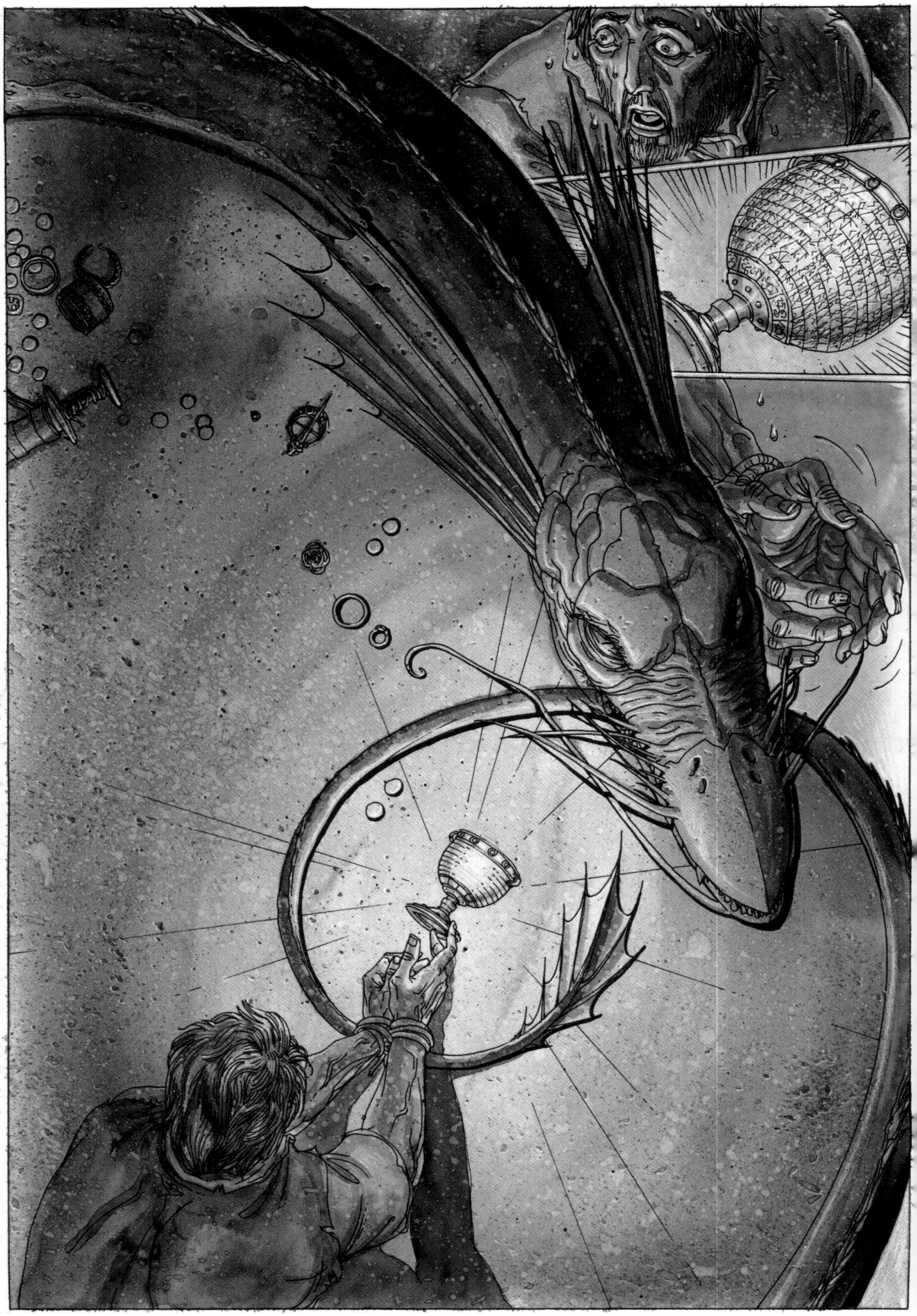

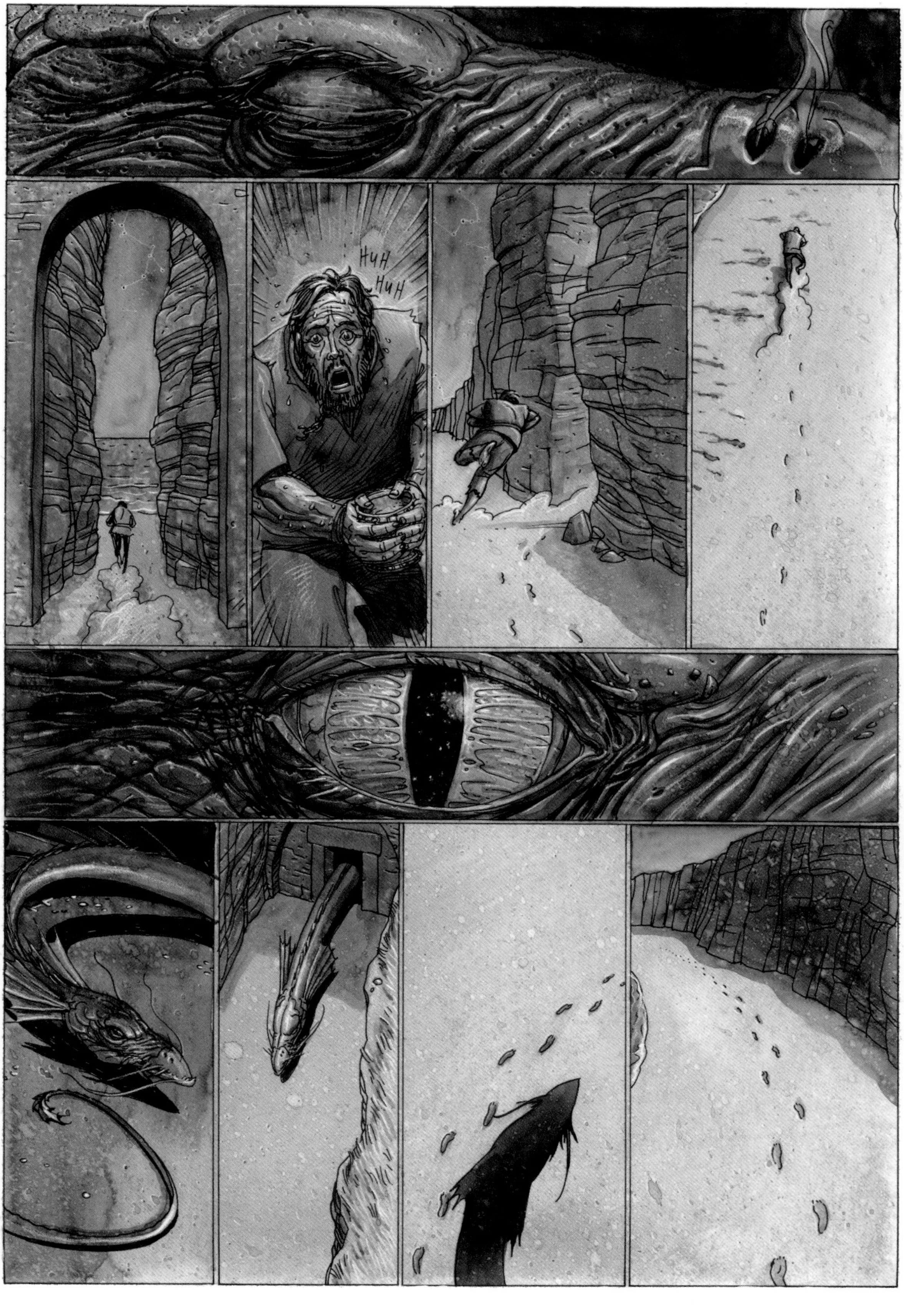
HUH
HUH

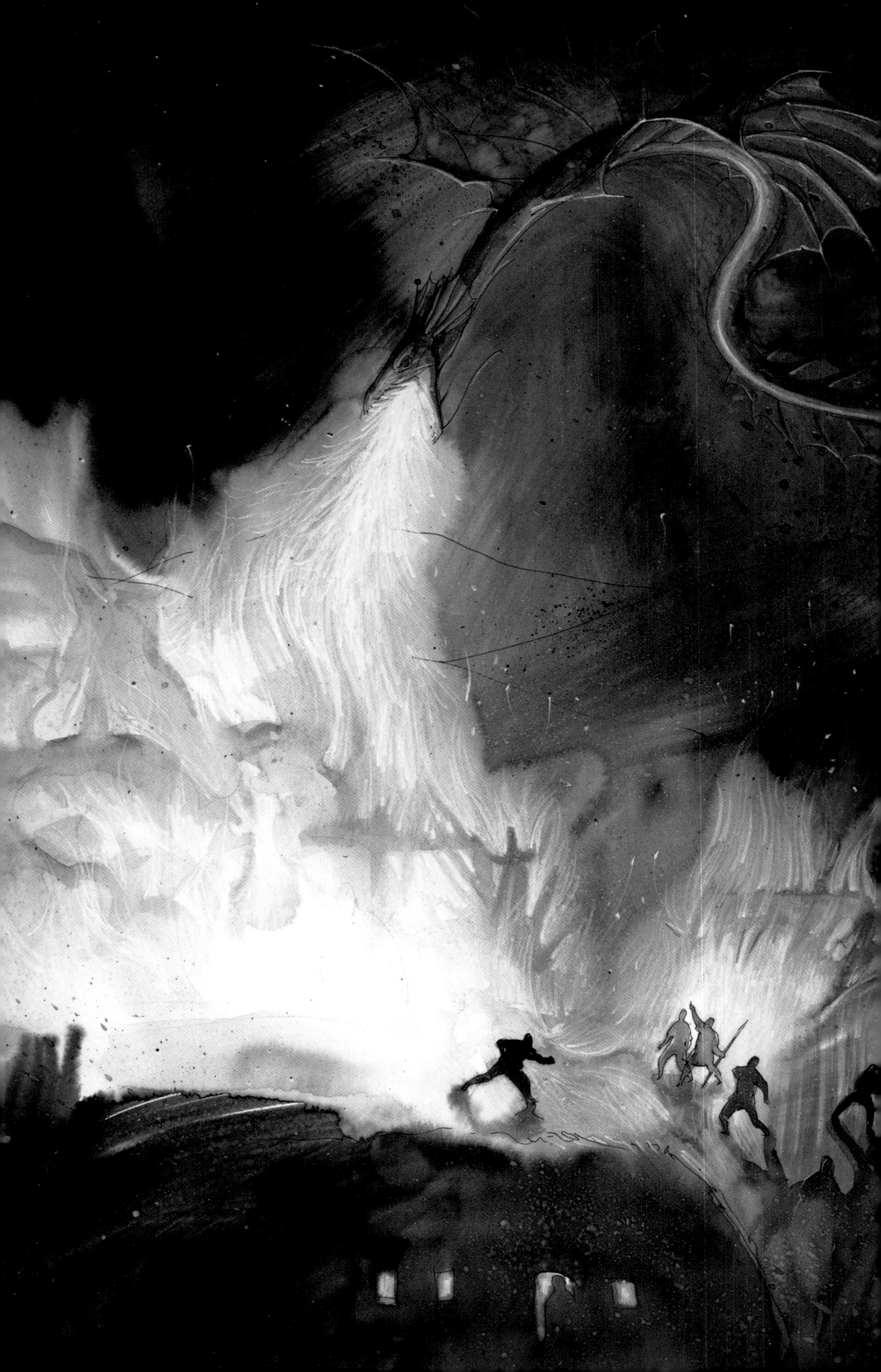

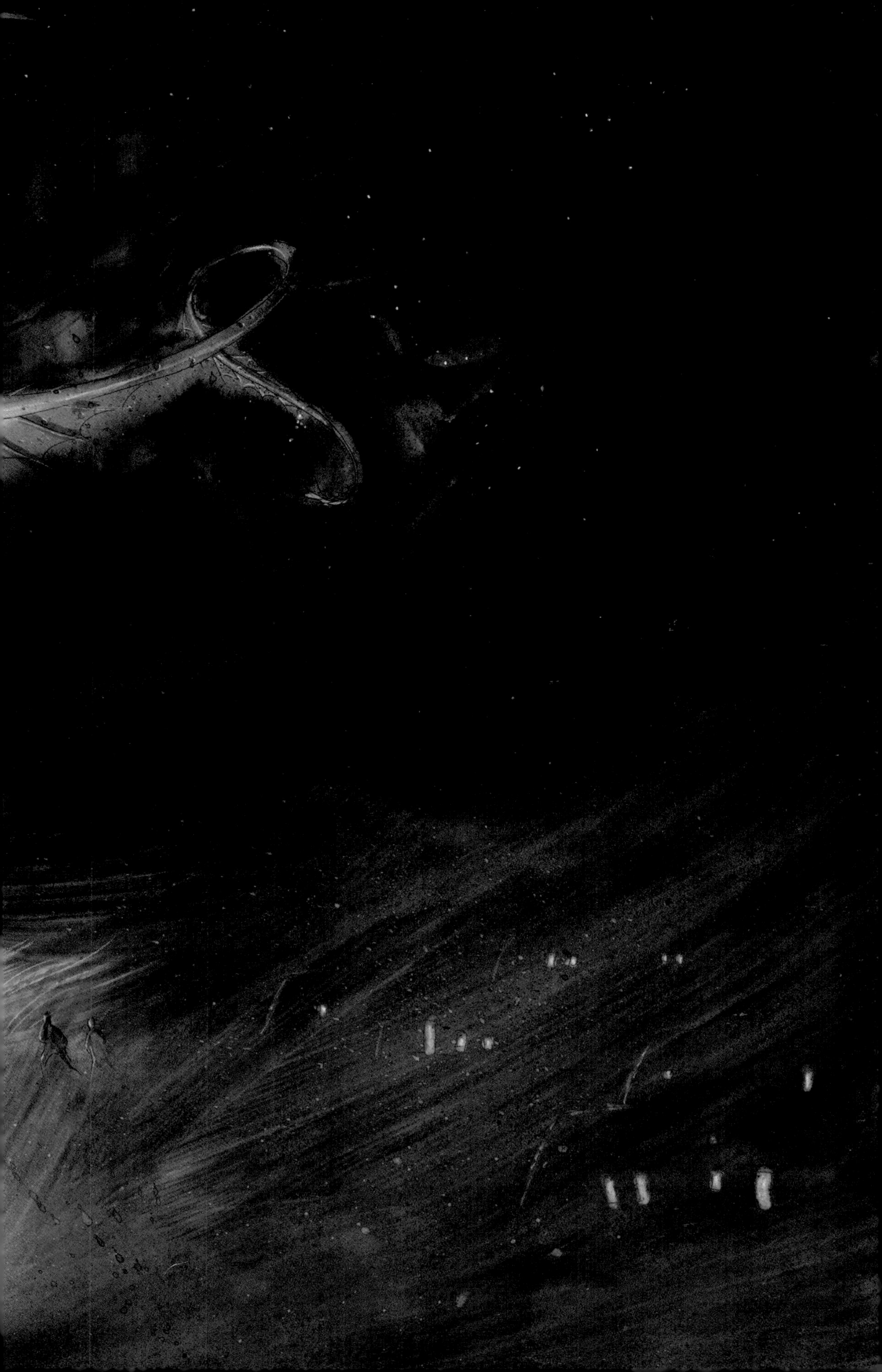

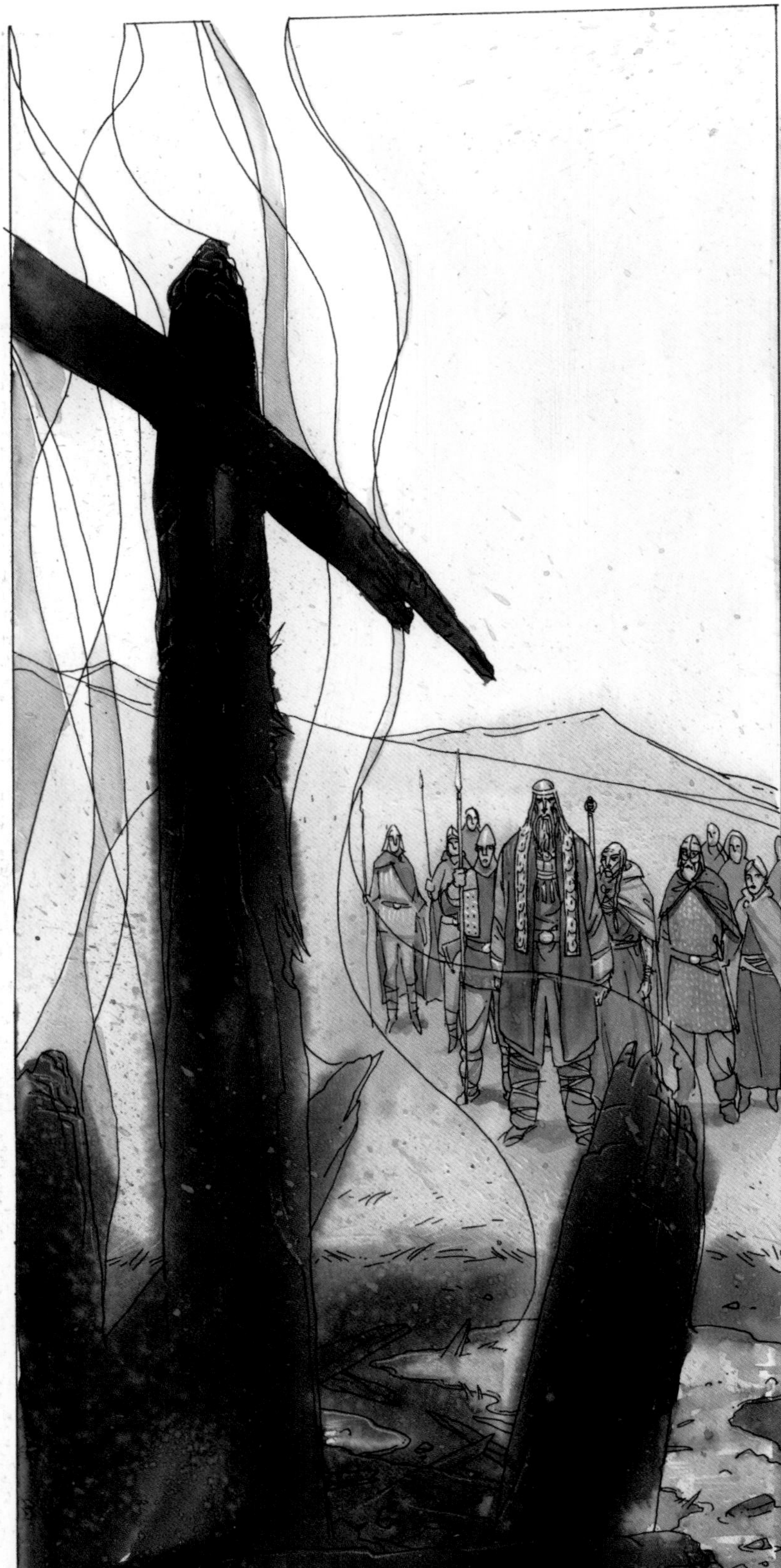

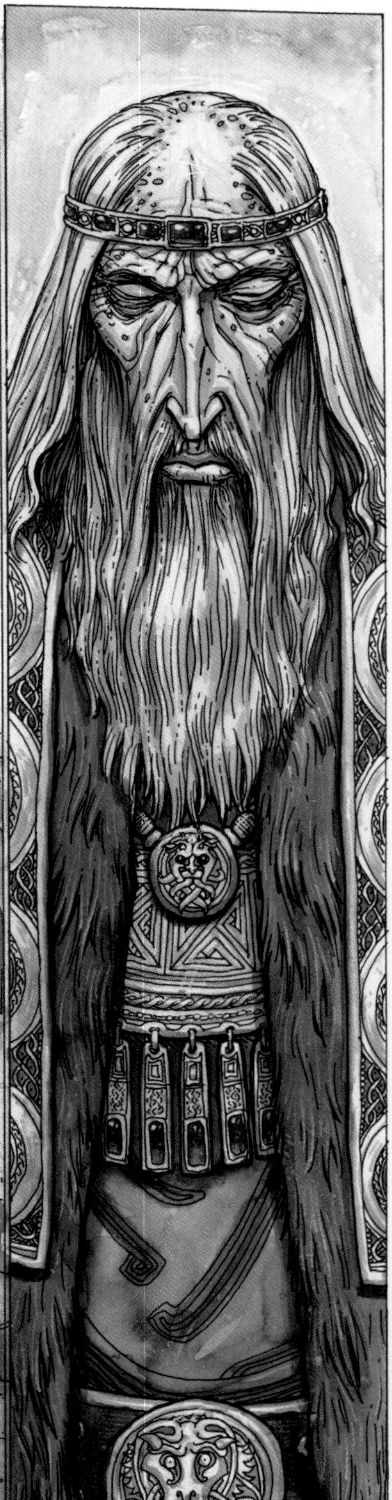

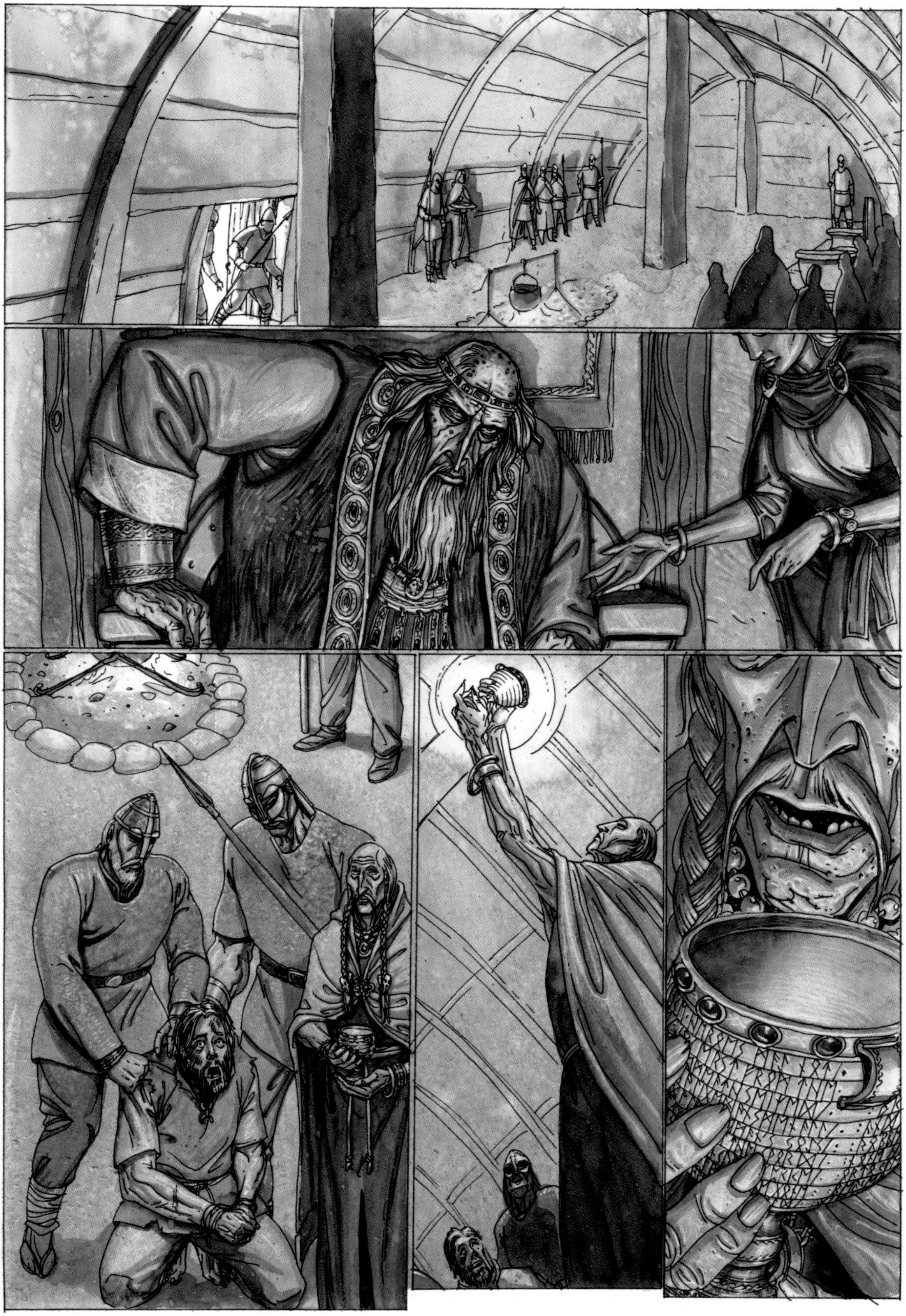

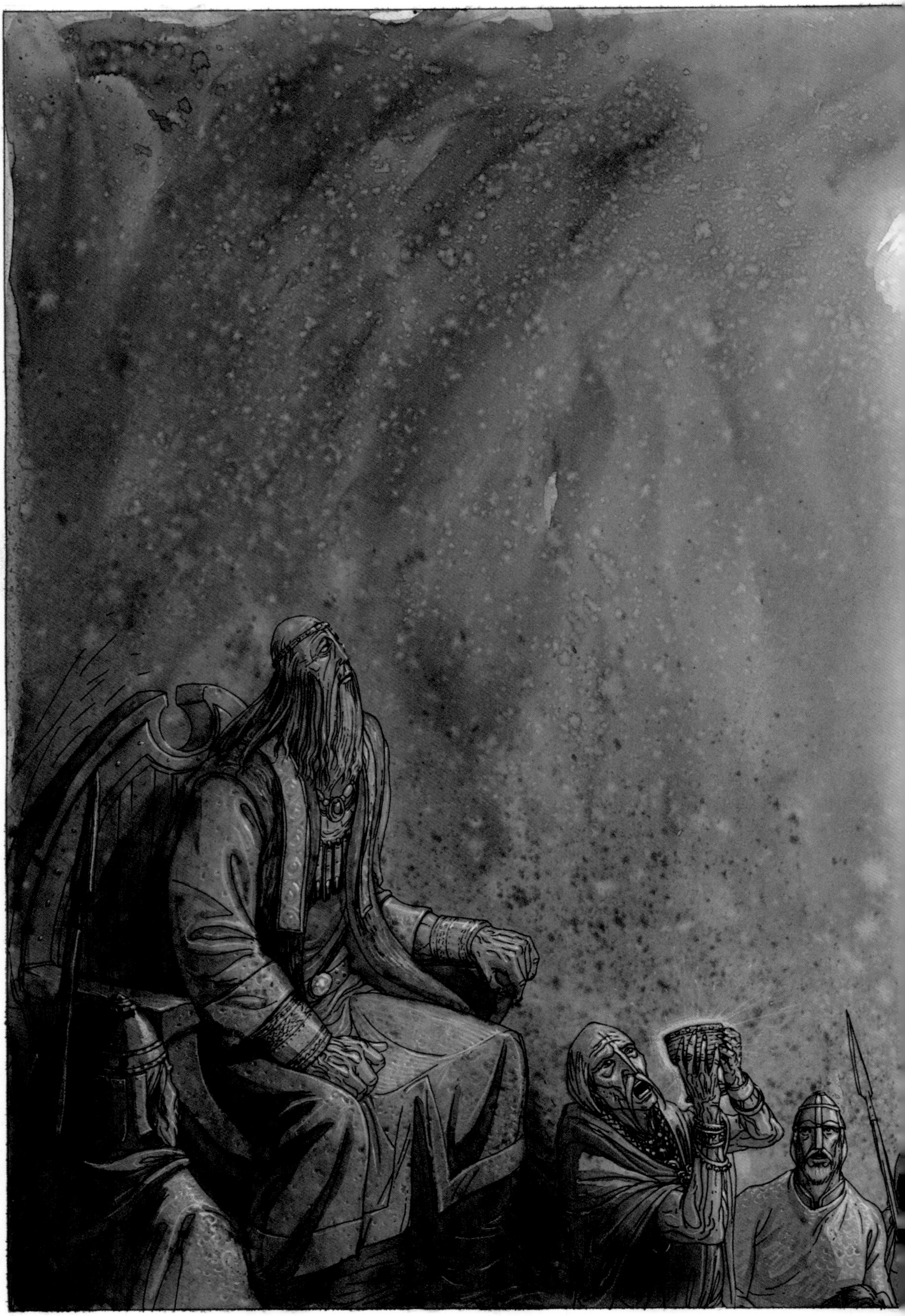

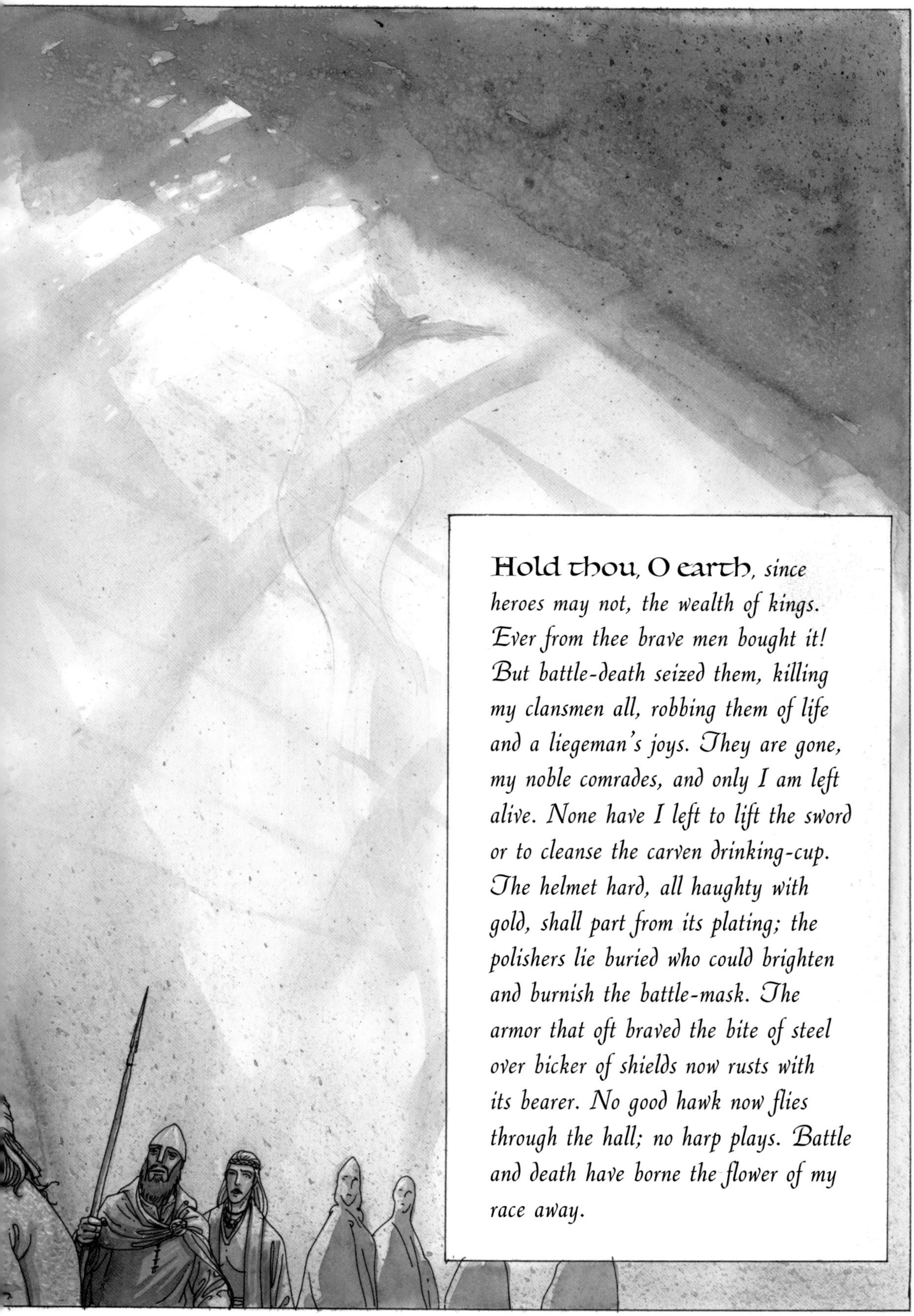

Hold thou, O earth, *since heroes may not, the wealth of kings. Ever from thee brave men bought it! But battle-death seized them, killing my clansmen all, robbing them of life and a liegeman's joys. They are gone, my noble comrades, and only I am left alive. None have I left to lift the sword or to cleanse the carven drinking-cup. The helmet hard, all haughty with gold, shall part from its plating; the polishers lie buried who could brighten and burnish the battle-mask. The armor that oft braved the bite of steel over bicker of shields now rusts with its bearer. No good hawk now flies through the hall; no harp plays. Battle and death have borne the flower of my race away.*

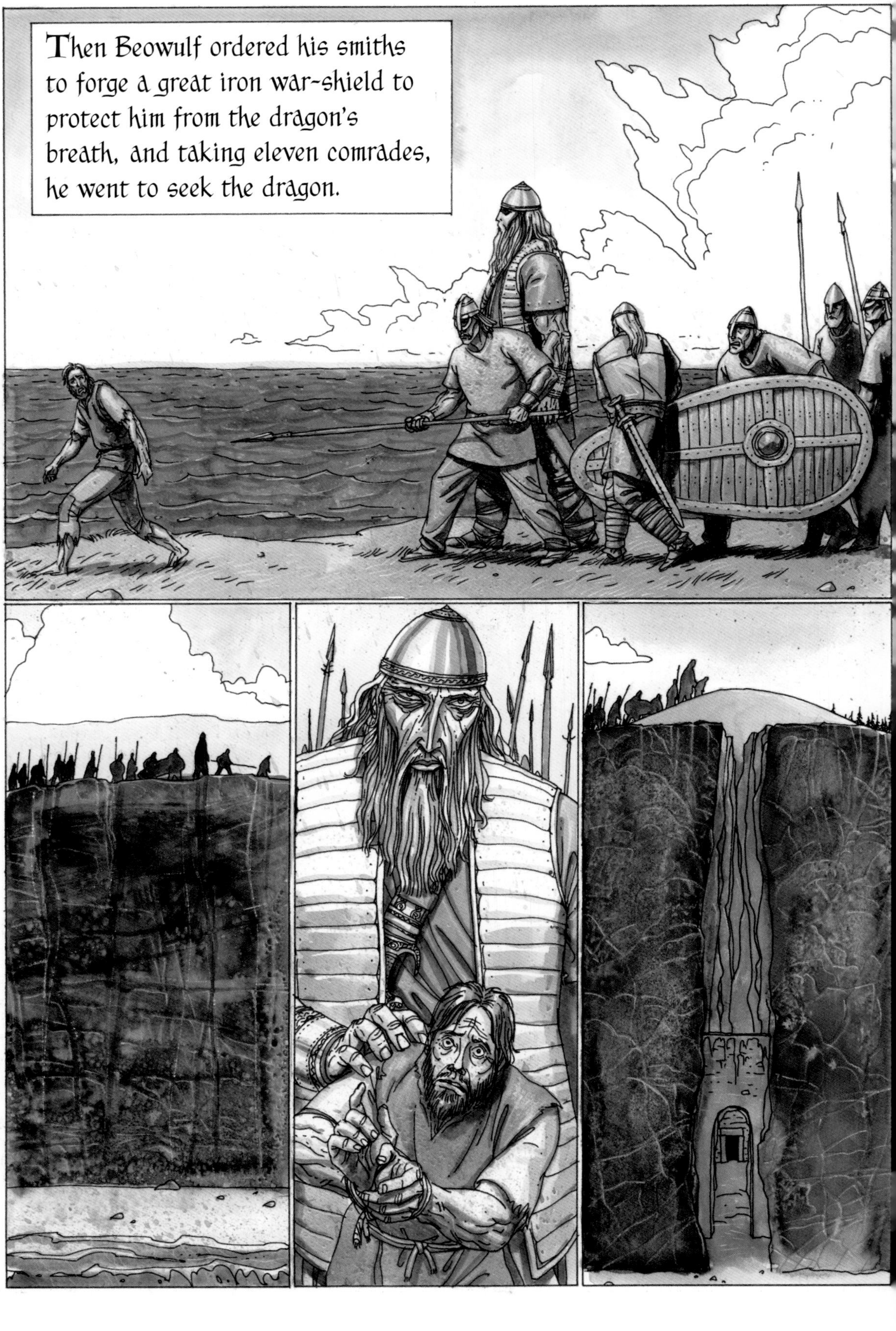
Then Beowulf ordered his smiths to forge a great iron war-shield to protect him from the dragon's breath, and taking eleven comrades, he went to seek the dragon.

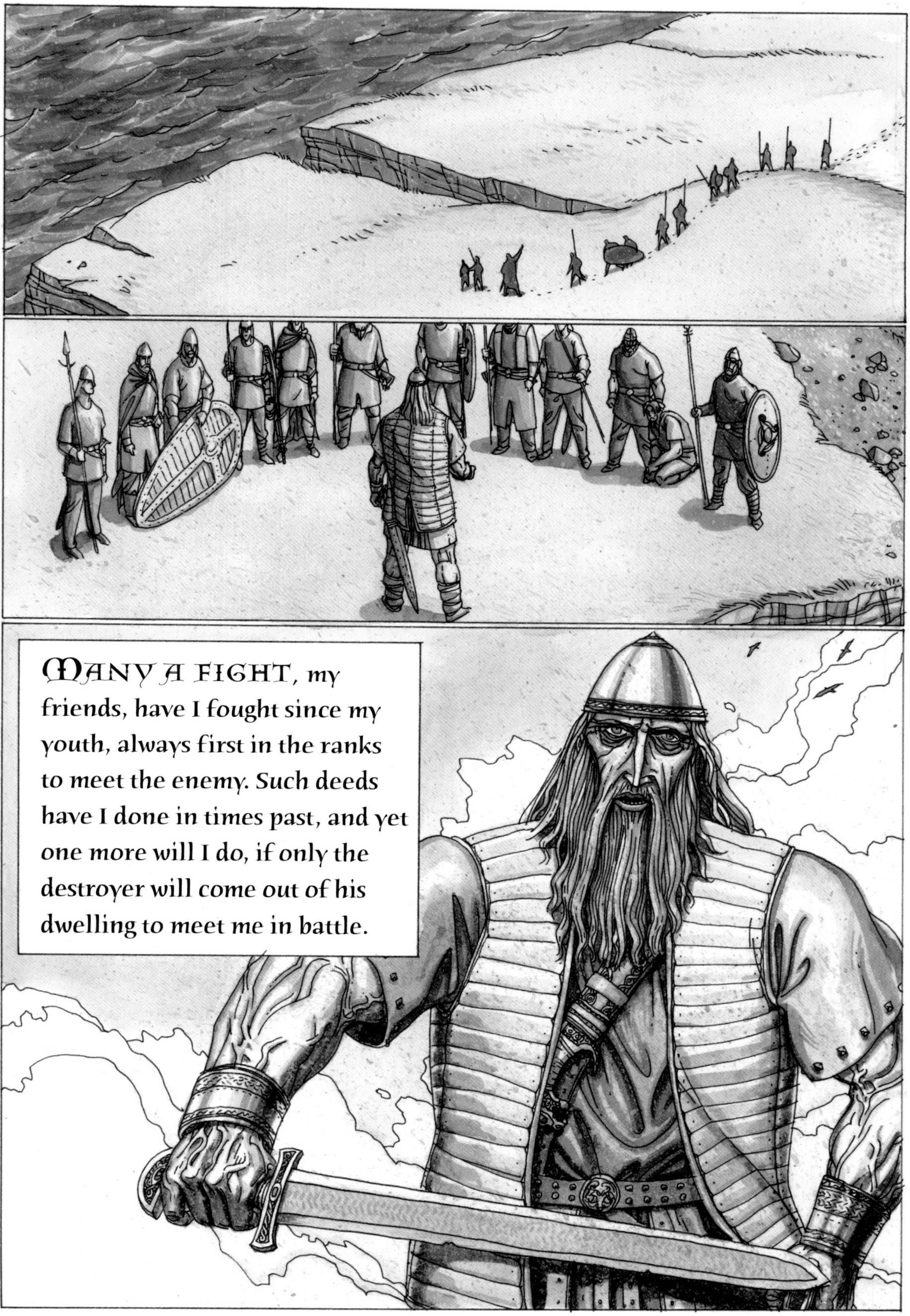
MANY A FIGHT, my friends, have I fought since my youth, always first in the ranks to meet the enemy. Such deeds have I done in times past, and yet one more will I do, if only the destroyer will come out of his dwelling to meet me in battle.

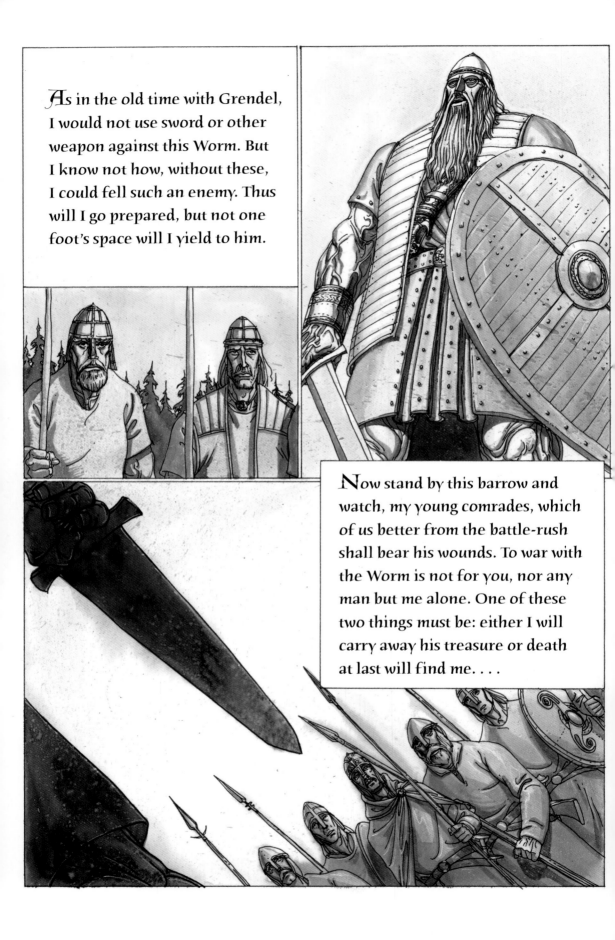

As in the old time with Grendel, I would not use sword or other weapon against this Worm. But I know not how, without these, I could fell such an enemy. Thus will I go prepared, but not one foot's space will I yield to him.

Now stand by this barrow and watch, my young comrades, which of us better from the battle-rush shall bear his wounds. To war with the Worm is not for you, nor any man but me alone. One of these two things must be: either I will carry away his treasure or death at last will find me. . . .

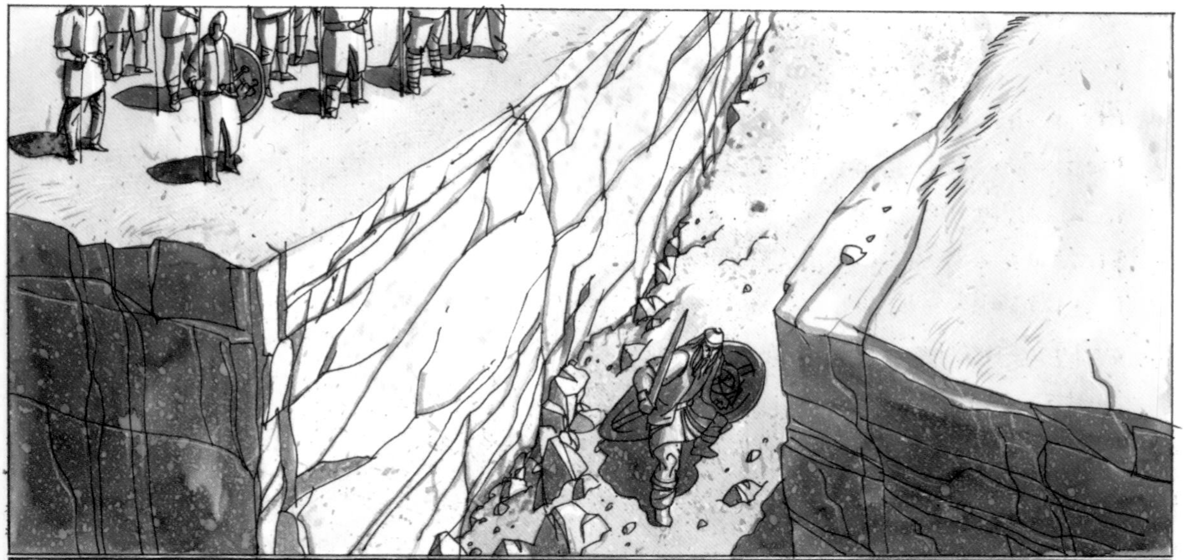

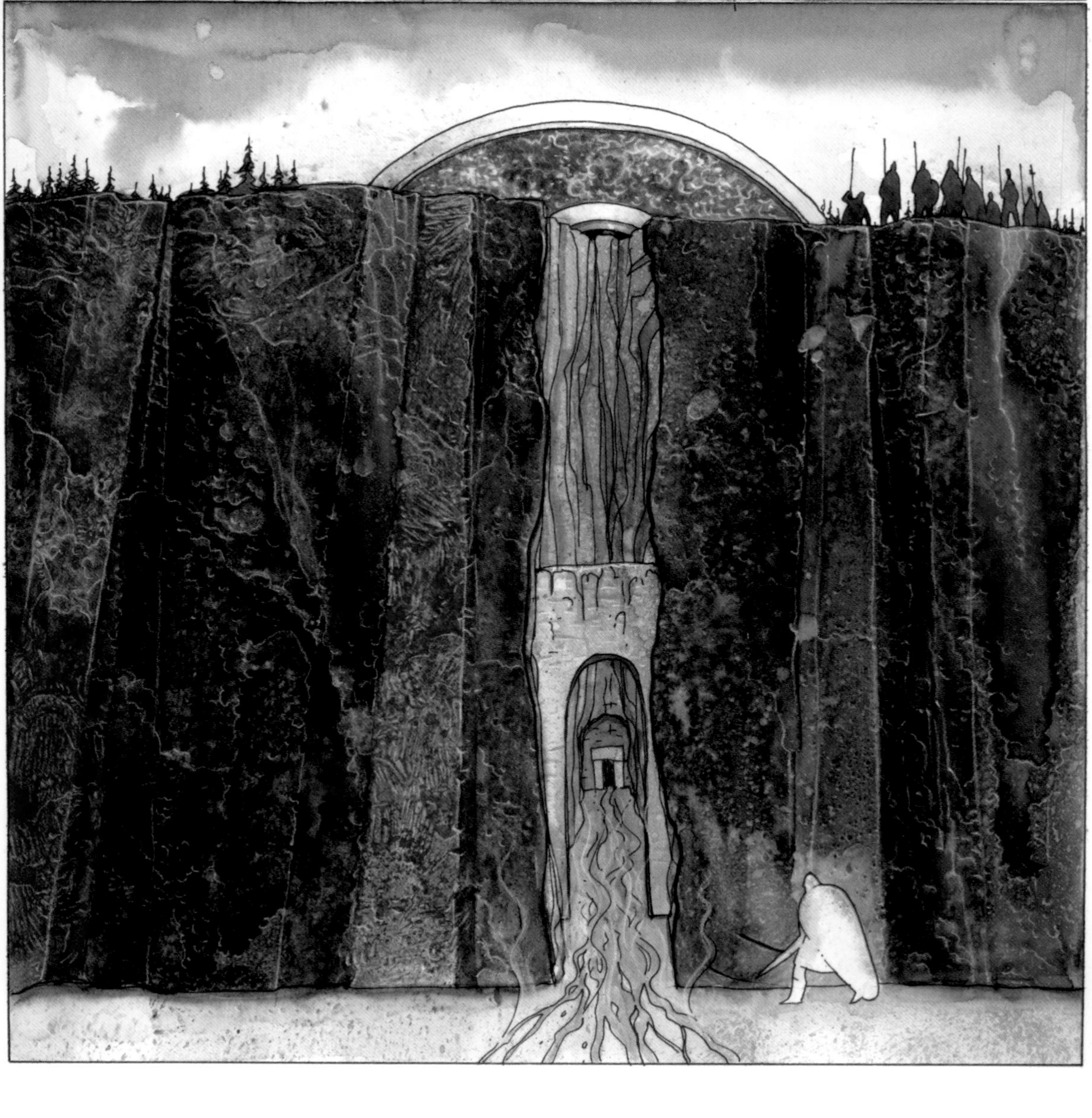

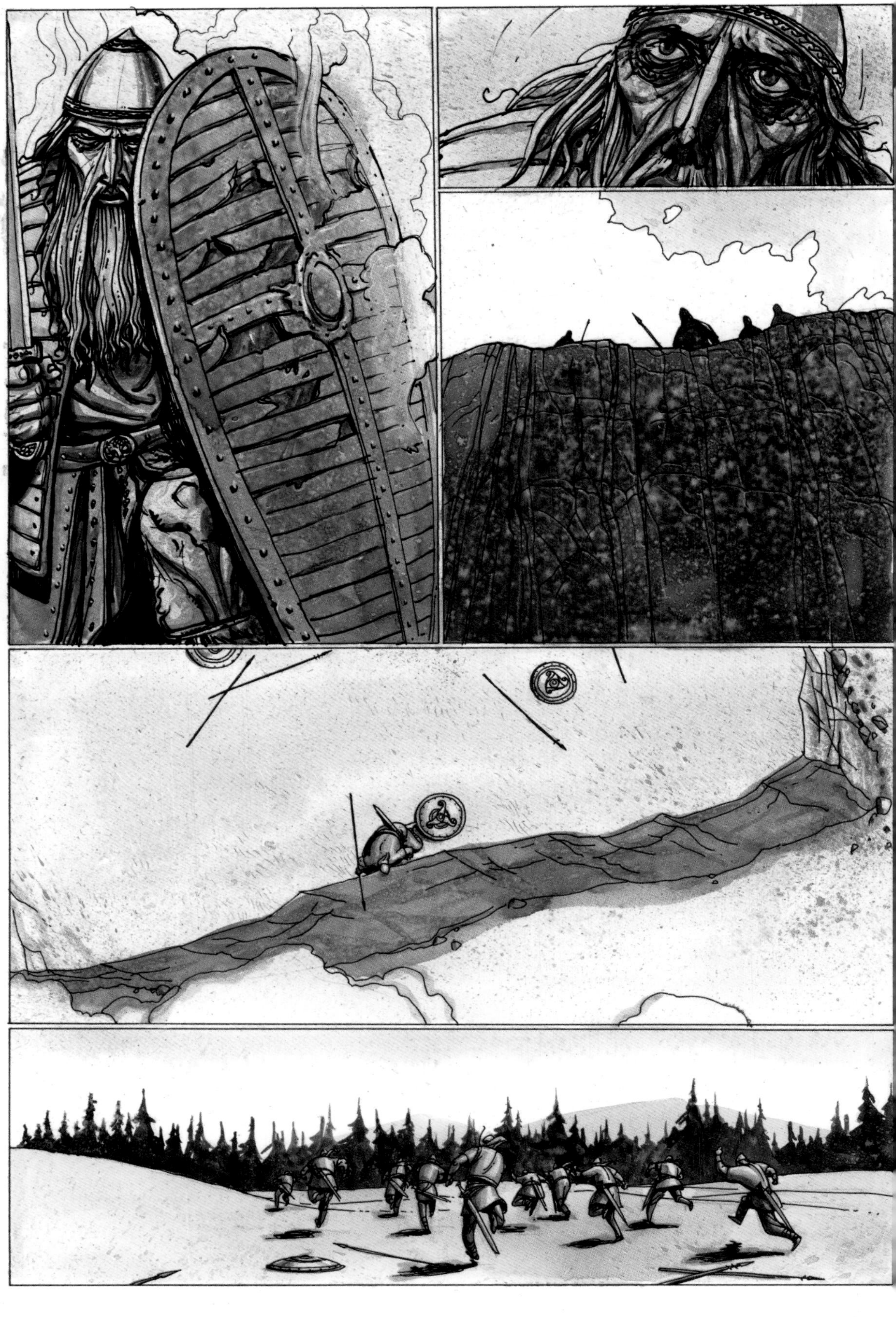

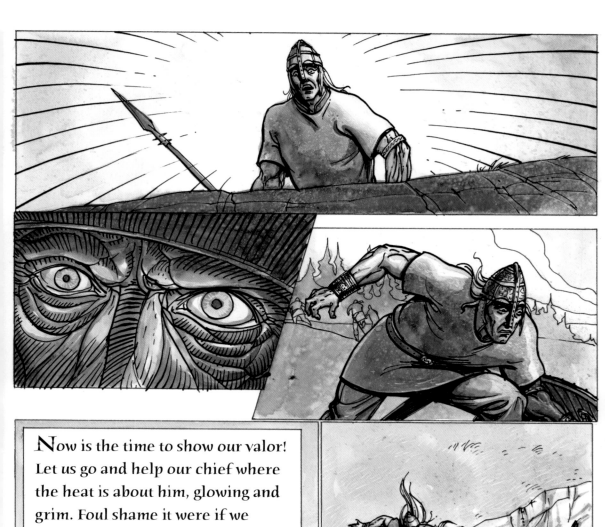

Now is the time to show our valor! Let us go and help our chief where the heat is about him, glowing and grim. Foul shame it were if we should carry back our shields to our home unless we can first destroy the enemy and save our King.

Beloved Beowulf, make good thy boast that never in life wouldst thou let thy glory wane! Use all thy strength, and fight for thy life; I will stand to help thee!

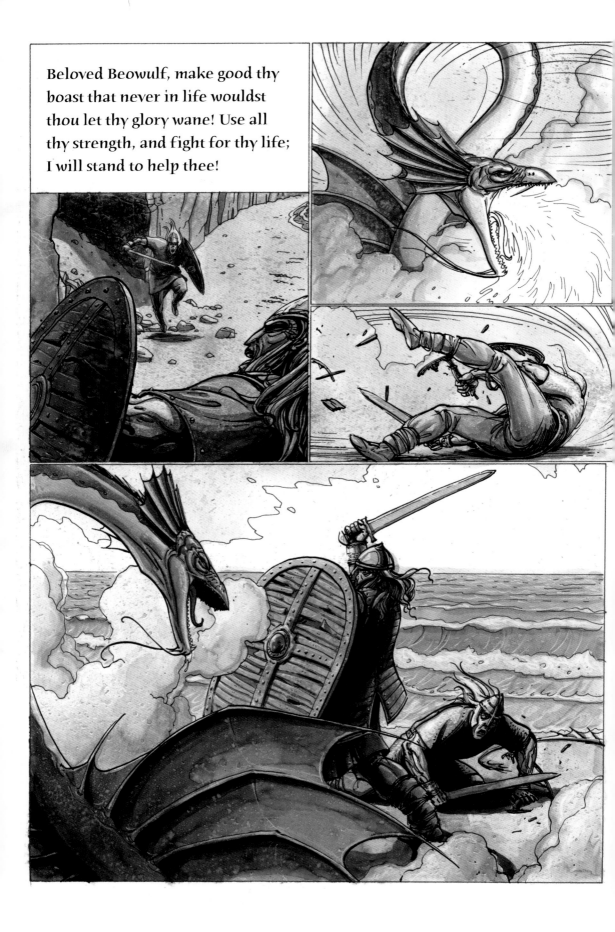

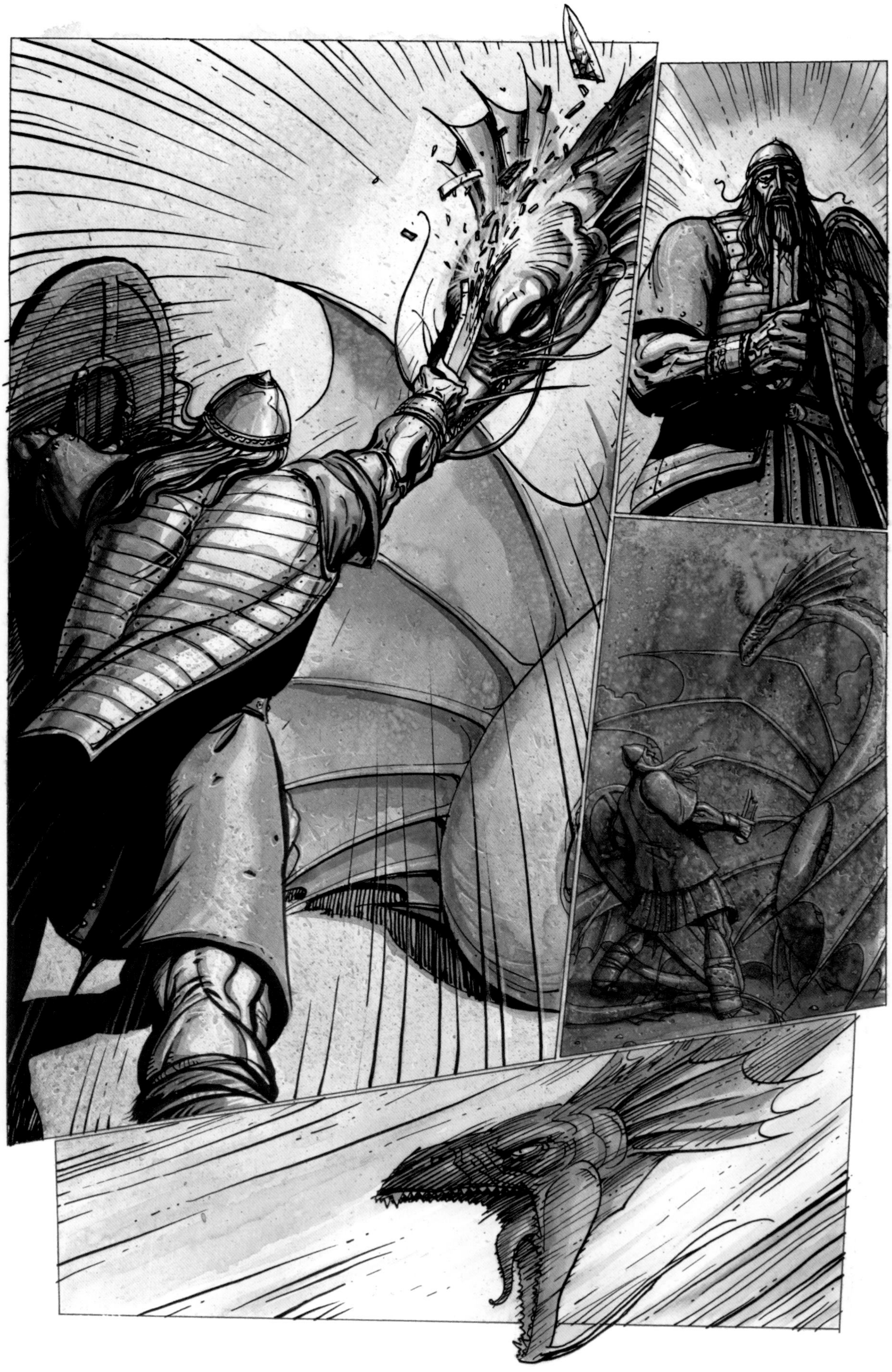

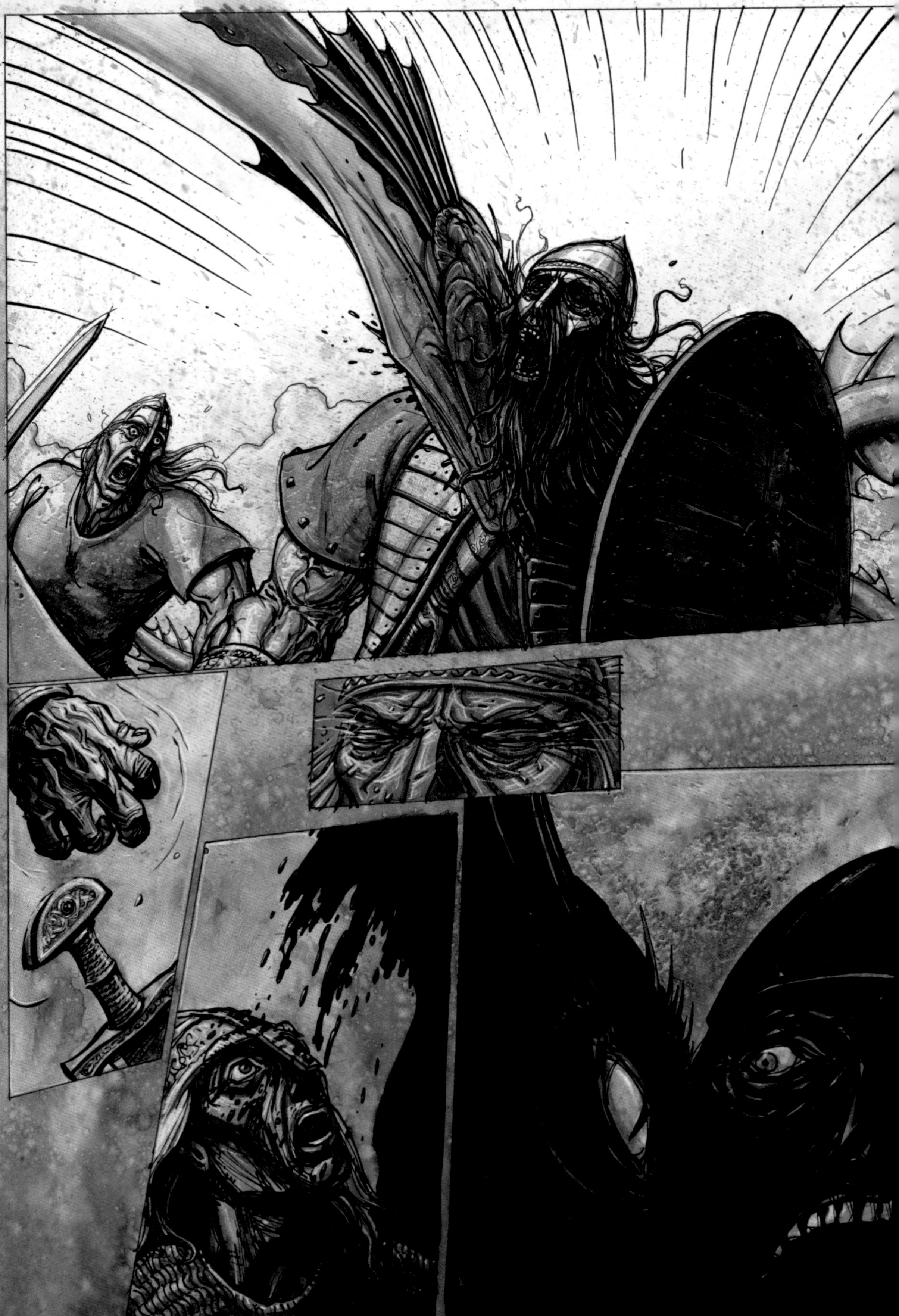

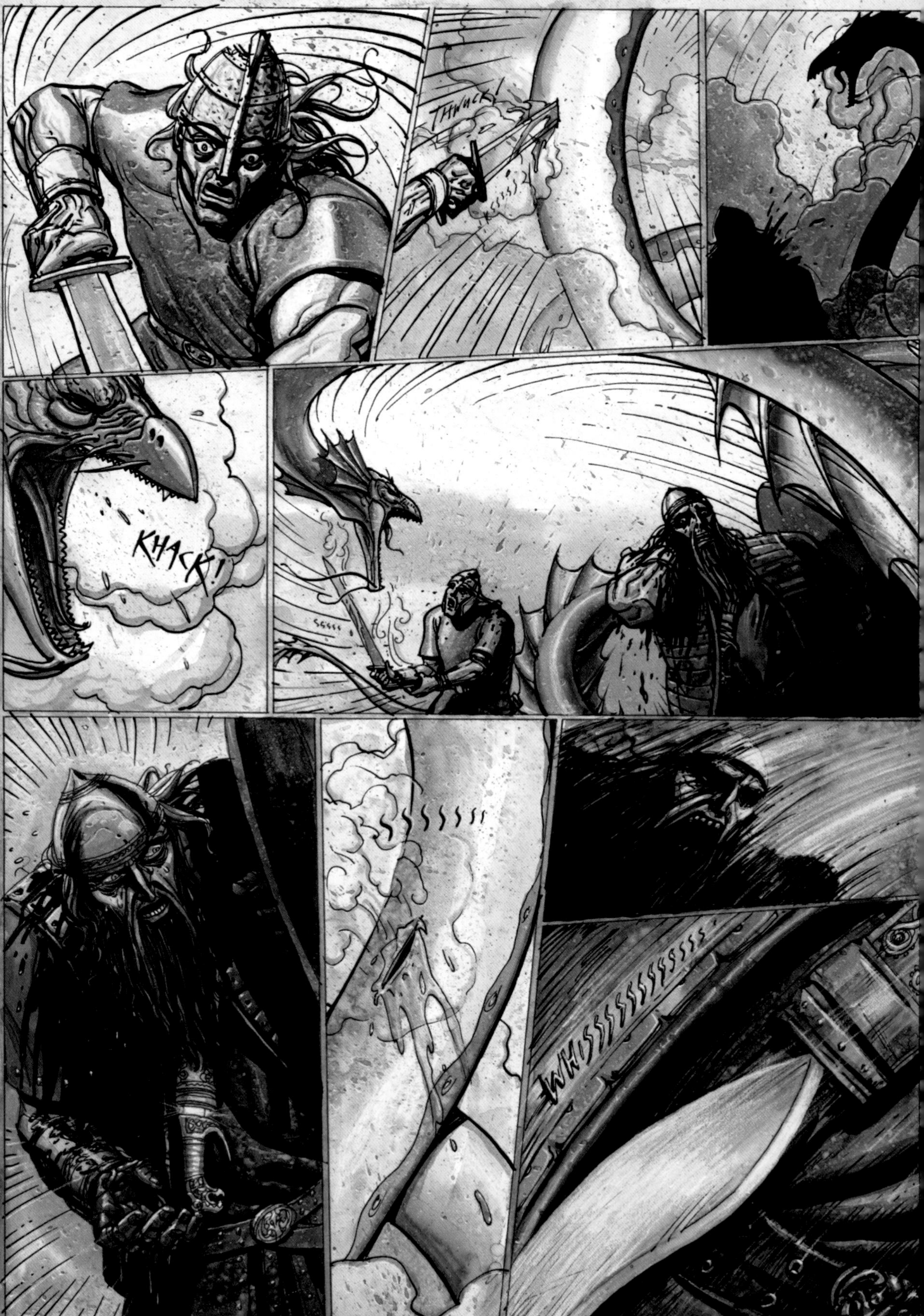
THWACK!
KSSSSS
KHACK!
SSSSS
SSSSSSS
WHISSSSSSSSSSSSS

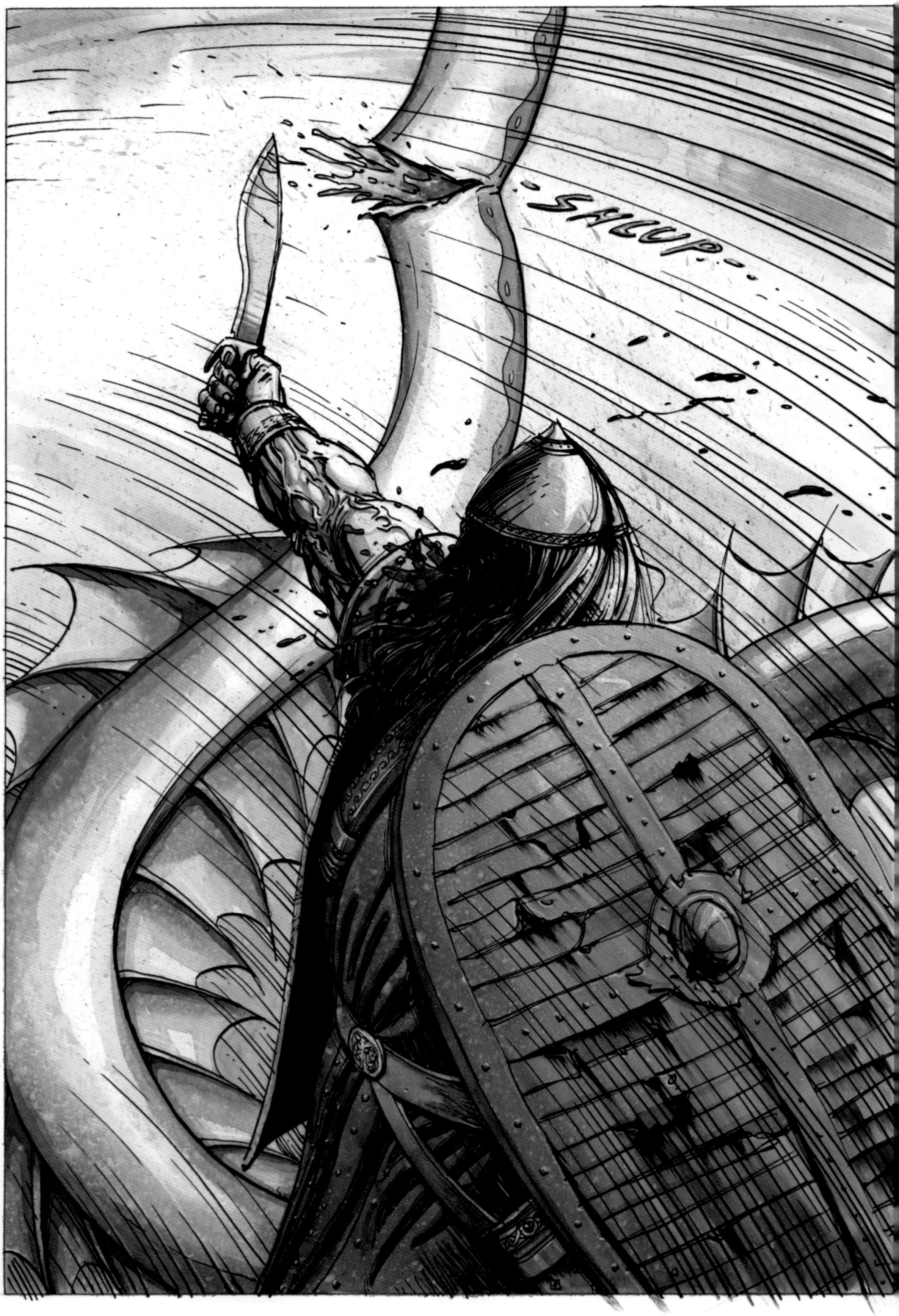
SHLUP

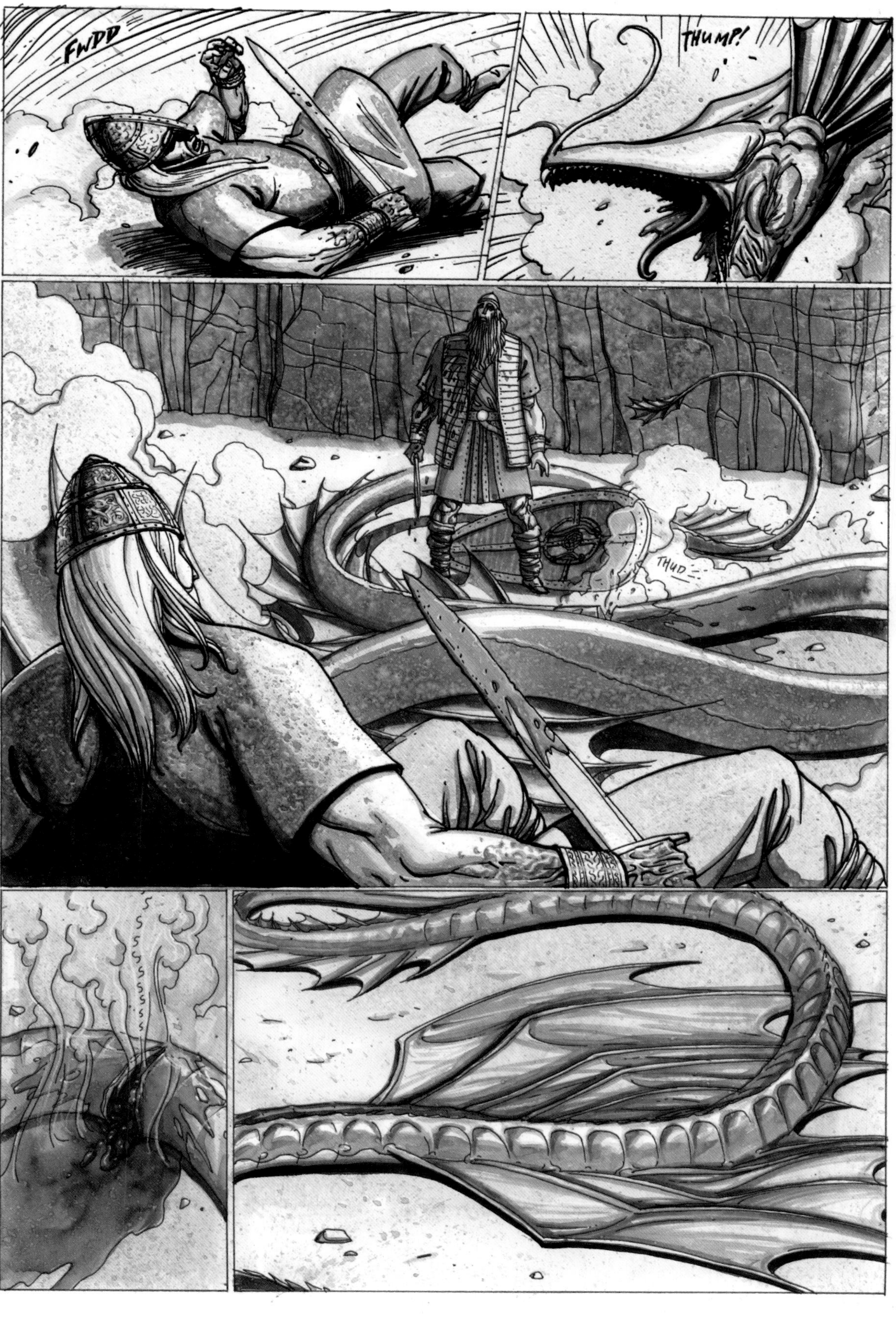
FWDD
THUMP!
THUD
SSSSSSS

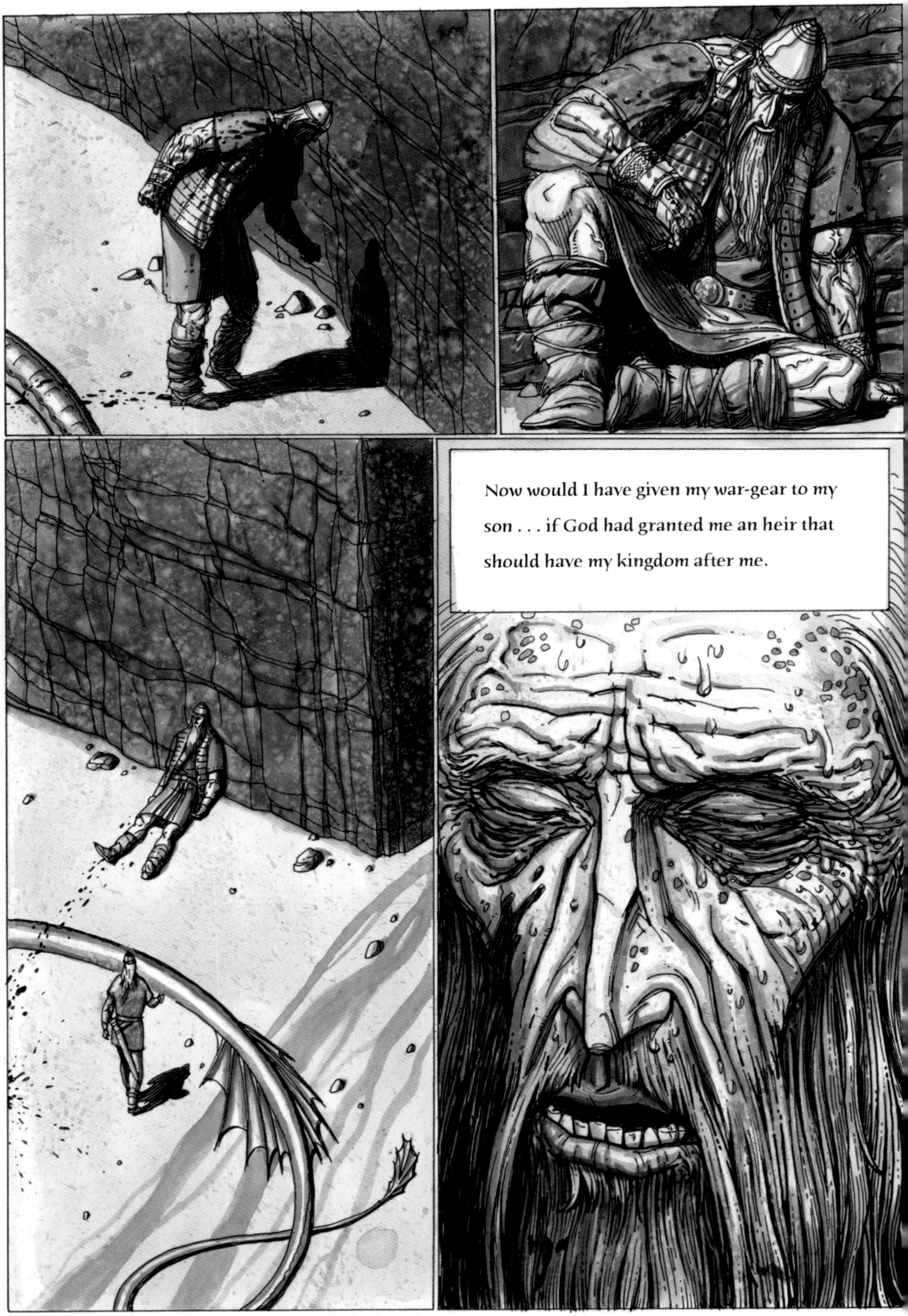
Now would I have given my war-gear to my son . . . if God had granted me an heir that should have my kingdom after me.

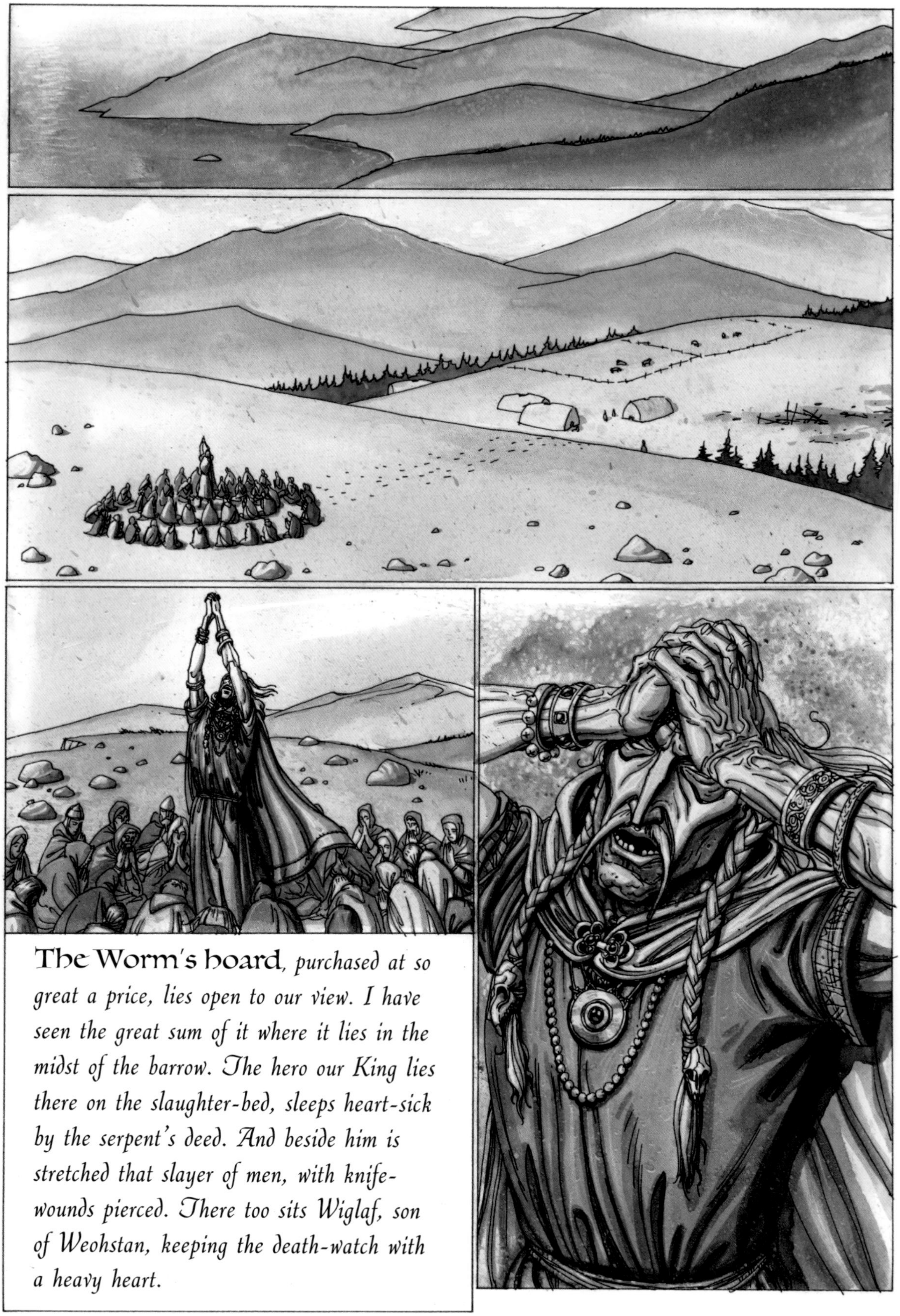
The Worm's hoard, purchased at so great a price, lies open to our view. I have seen the great sum of it where it lies in the midst of the barrow. The hero our King lies there on the slaughter-bed, sleeps heart-sick by the serpent's deed. And beside him is stretched that slayer of men, with knife-wounds pierced. There too sits Wiglaf, son of Weohstan, keeping the death-watch with a heavy heart.

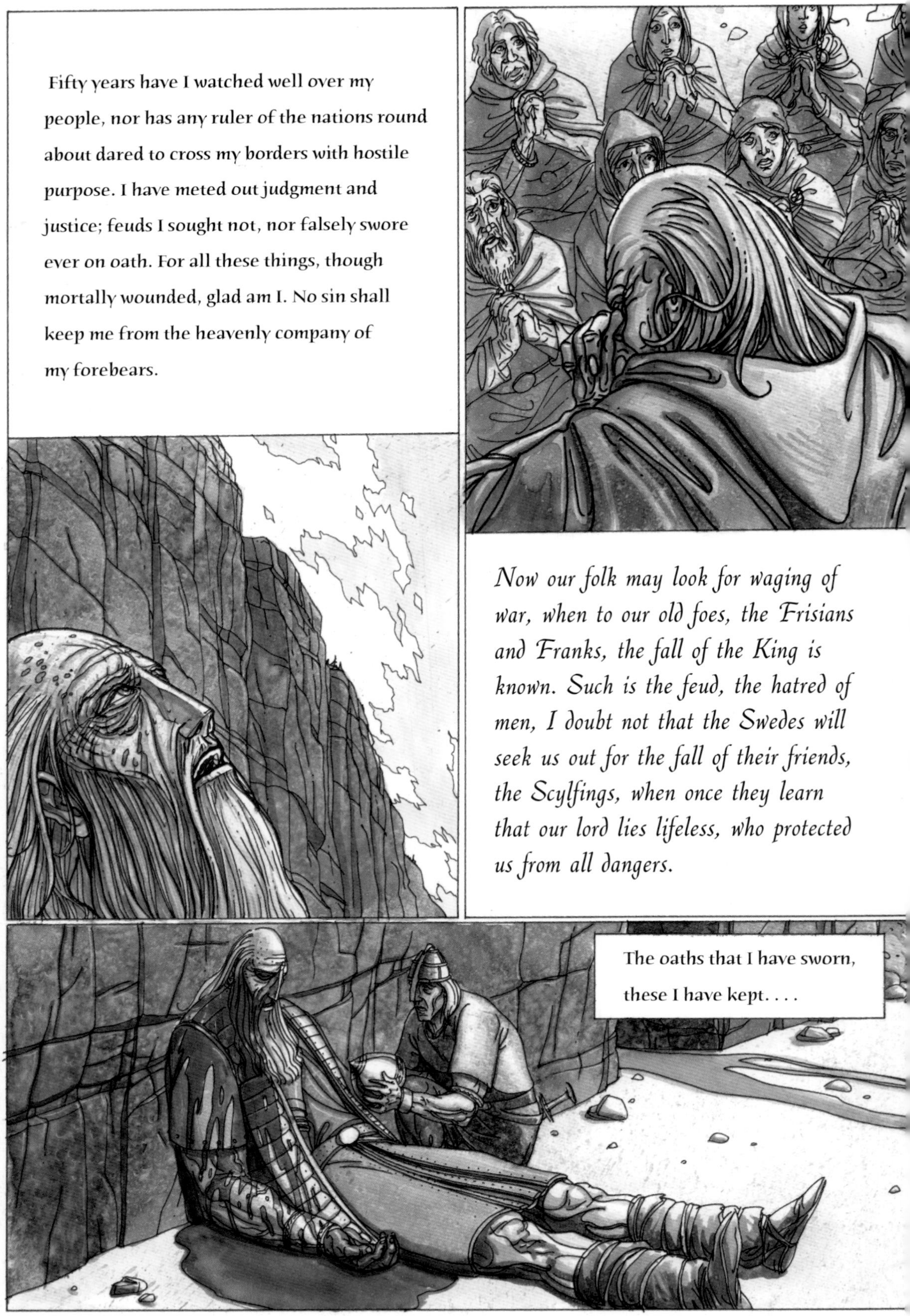
Fifty years have I watched well over my people, nor has any ruler of the nations round about dared to cross my borders with hostile purpose. I have meted out judgment and justice; feuds I sought not, nor falsely swore ever on oath. For all these things, though mortally wounded, glad am I. No sin shall keep me from the heavenly company of my forebears.
Now our folk may look for waging of war, when to our old foes, the Frisians and Franks, the fall of the King is known. Such is the feud, the hatred of men, I doubt not that the Swedes will seek us out for the fall of their friends, the Scylfings, when once they learn that our lord lies lifeless, who protected us from all dangers.
The oaths that I have sworn, these I have kept. . . .

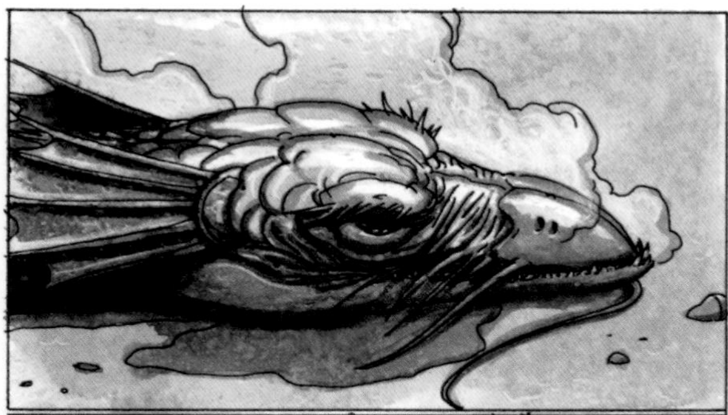

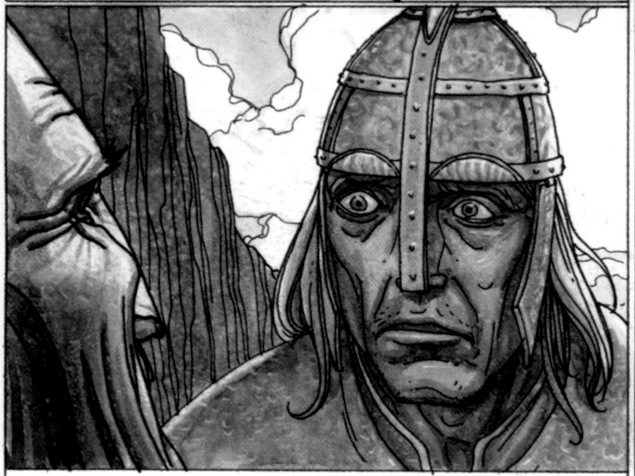

Now I pray thee, Wiglaf, go and gaze on the treasure. The Worm lies dead, and that which he guarded for many ages of man is his no more. Go quickly then, for I would fain see this treasure before I die. With better contentment shall I depart, knowing how great are the riches that I have won.

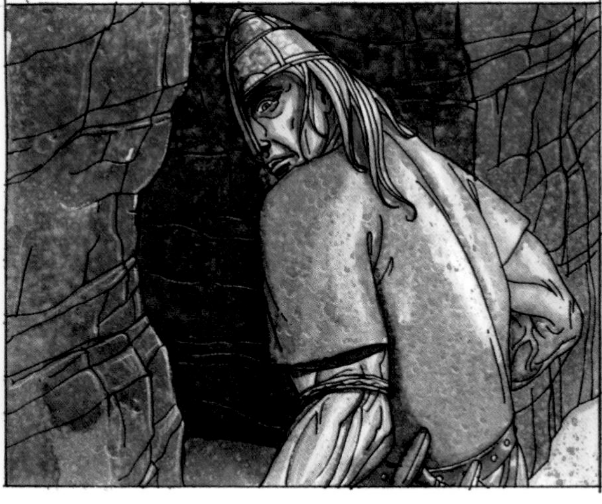

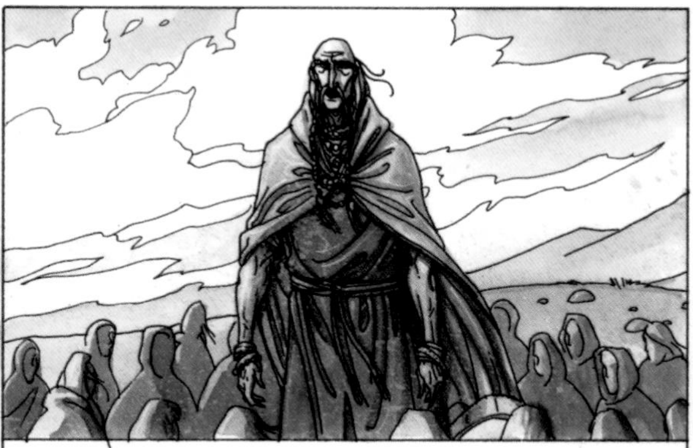

Now haste is best, that we go to gaze on our great lord and bear the hero to the funeral pyre. No tokens merely shall burn with him, but wealth of jewels, treasure at last with his life obtained — the flames shall eat it. No earl shall carry memorial jewel; no maiden fair shall wreathe her neck. Nay, sad in spirit and shorn of her gold, oft shall she pass o'er paths of exile, now that our lord all laughter has laid aside.

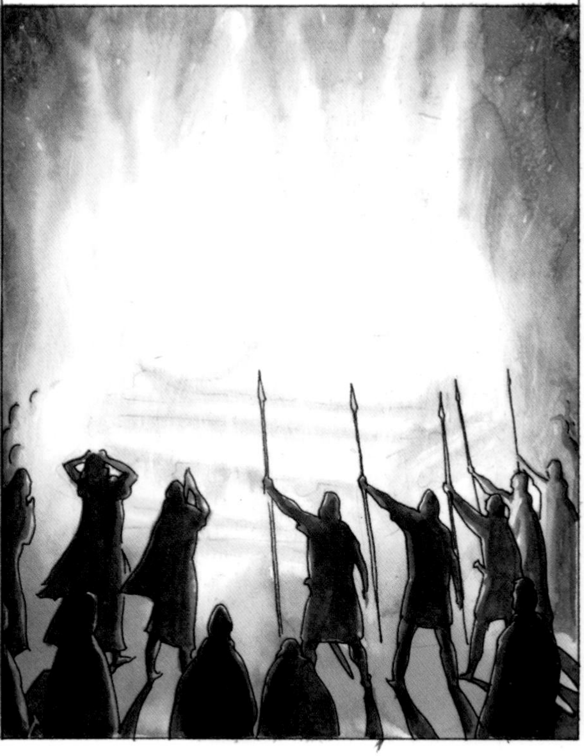

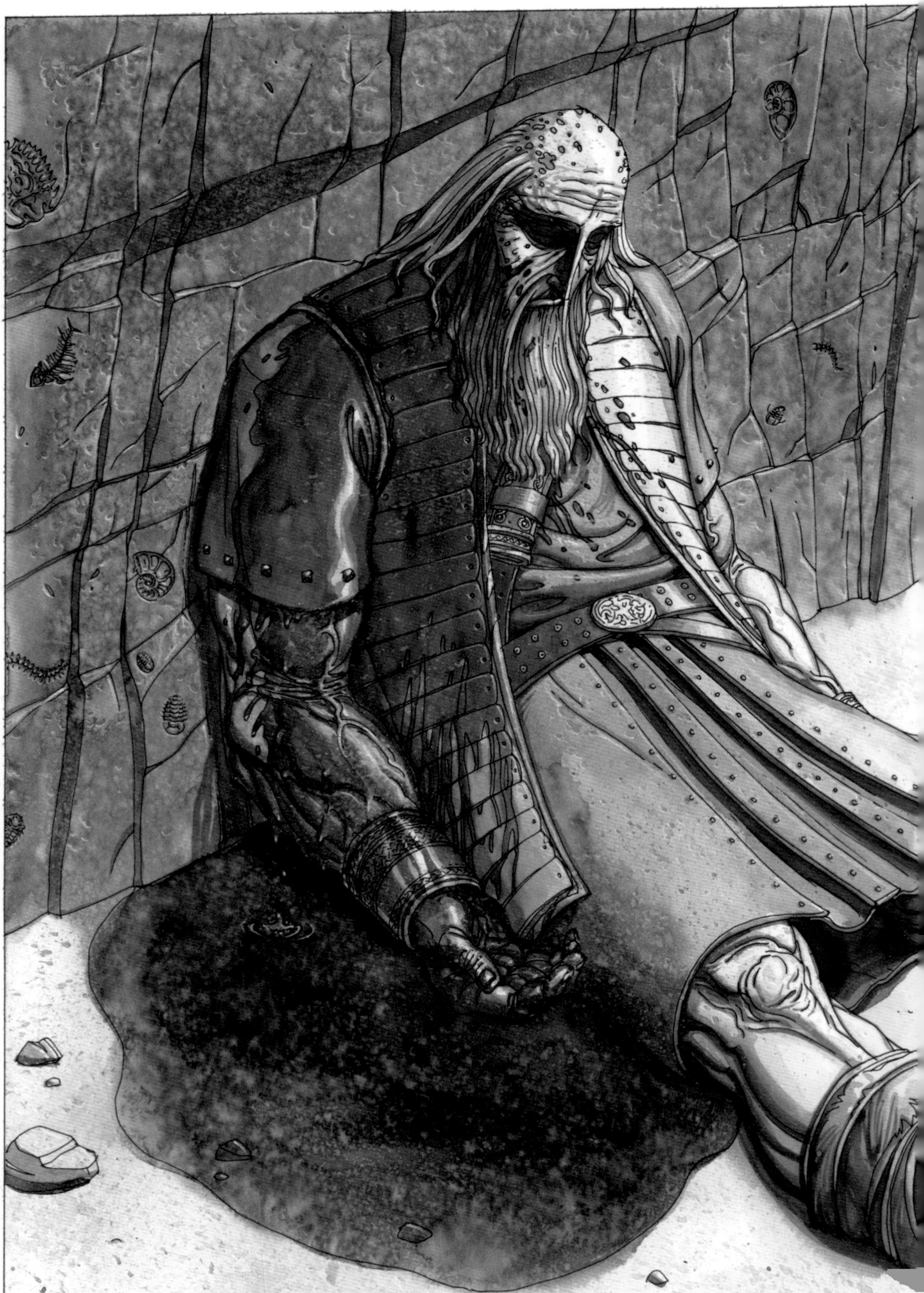

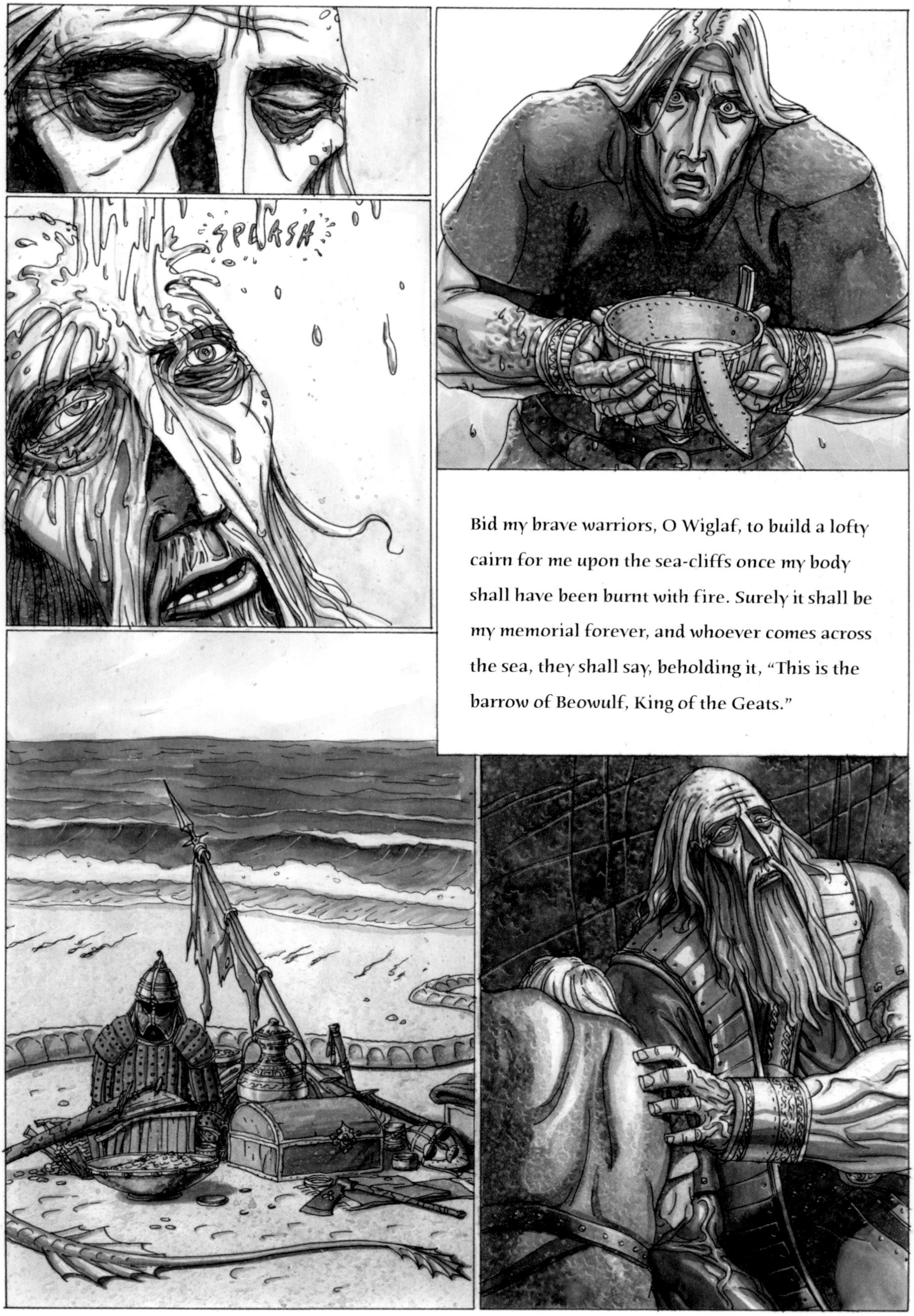
SPLASH
Bid my brave warriors, O Wiglaf, to build a lofty cairn for me upon the sea-cliffs once my body shall have been burnt with fire. Surely it shall be my memorial forever, and whoever comes across the sea, they shall say, beholding it, "This is the barrow of Beowulf, King of the Geats."

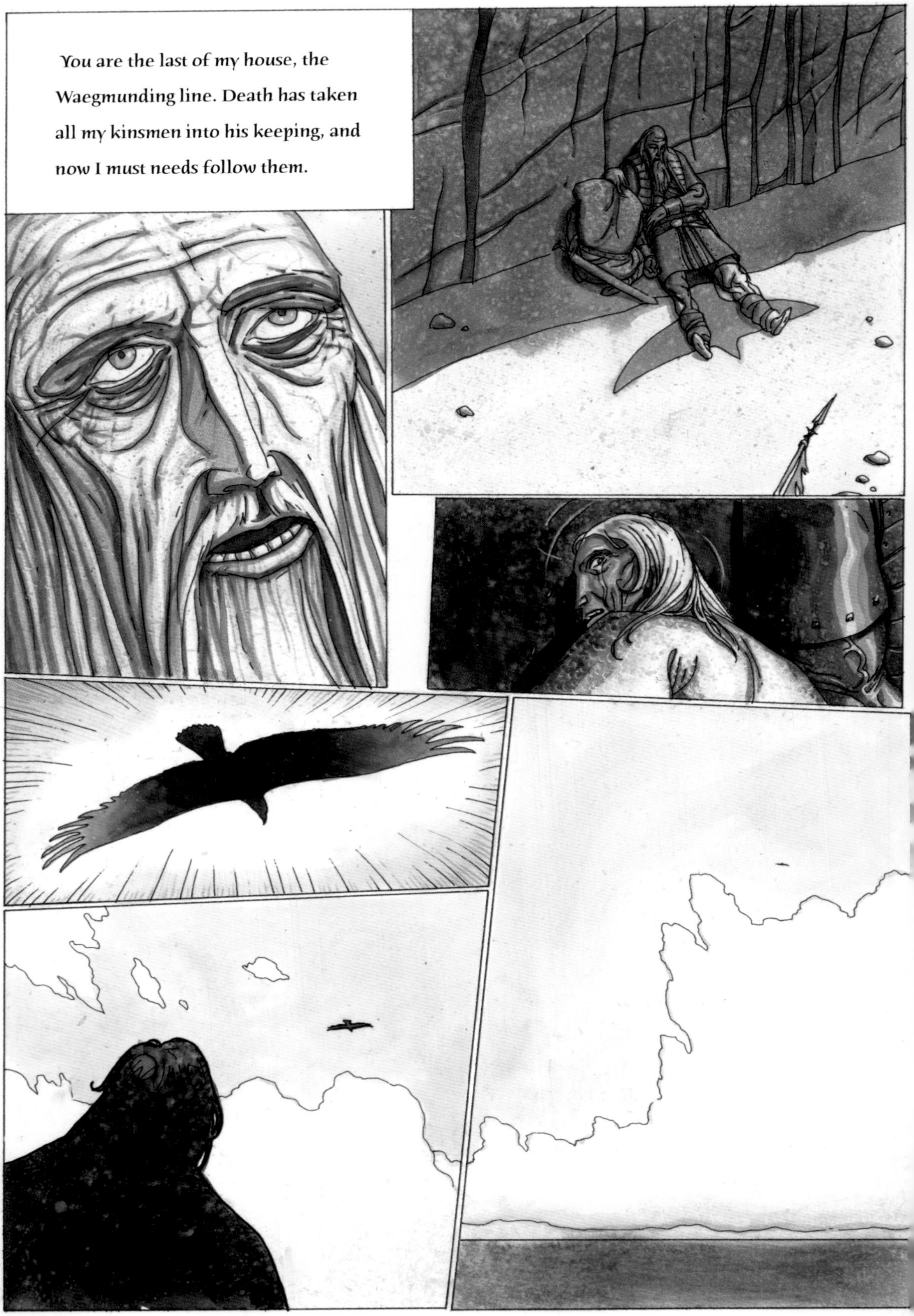
You are the last of my house, the Waegmunding line. Death has taken all my kinsmen into his keeping, and now I must needs follow them.

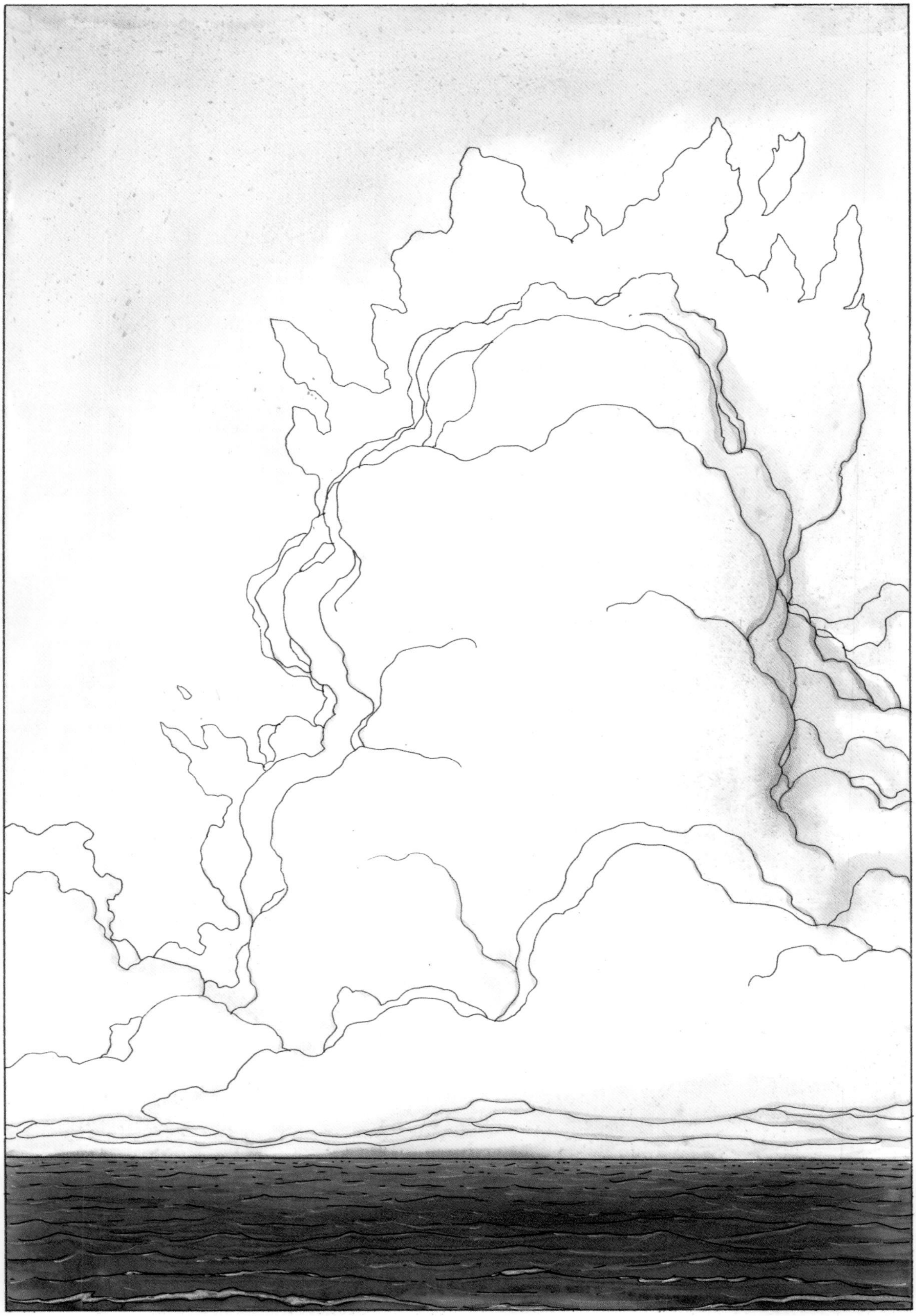

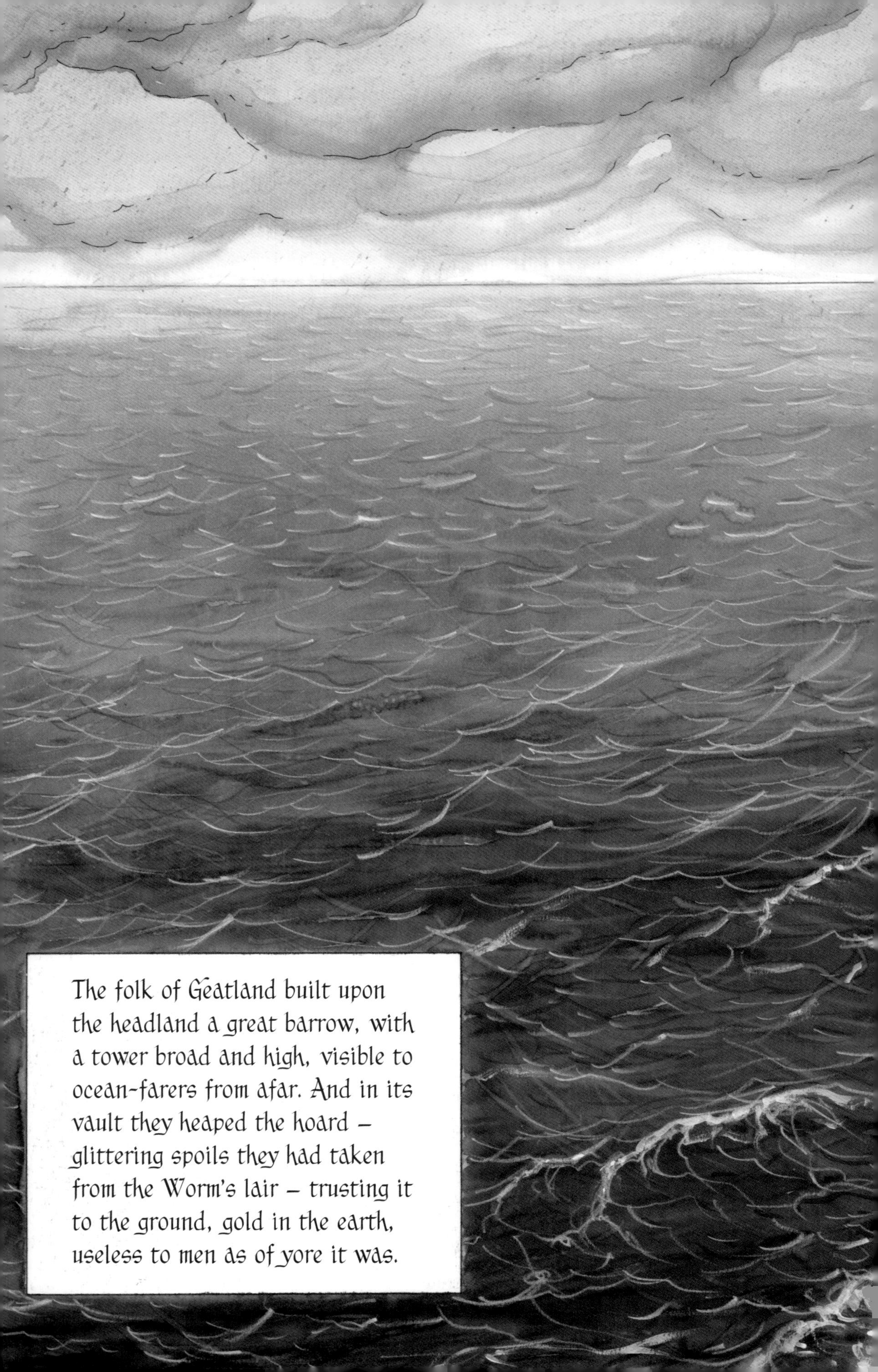
The folk of Geatland built upon the headland a great barrow, with a tower broad and high, visible to ocean-farers from afar. And in its vault they heaped the hoard – glittering spoils they had taken from the Worm's lair – trusting it to the ground, gold in the earth, useless to men as of yore it was.

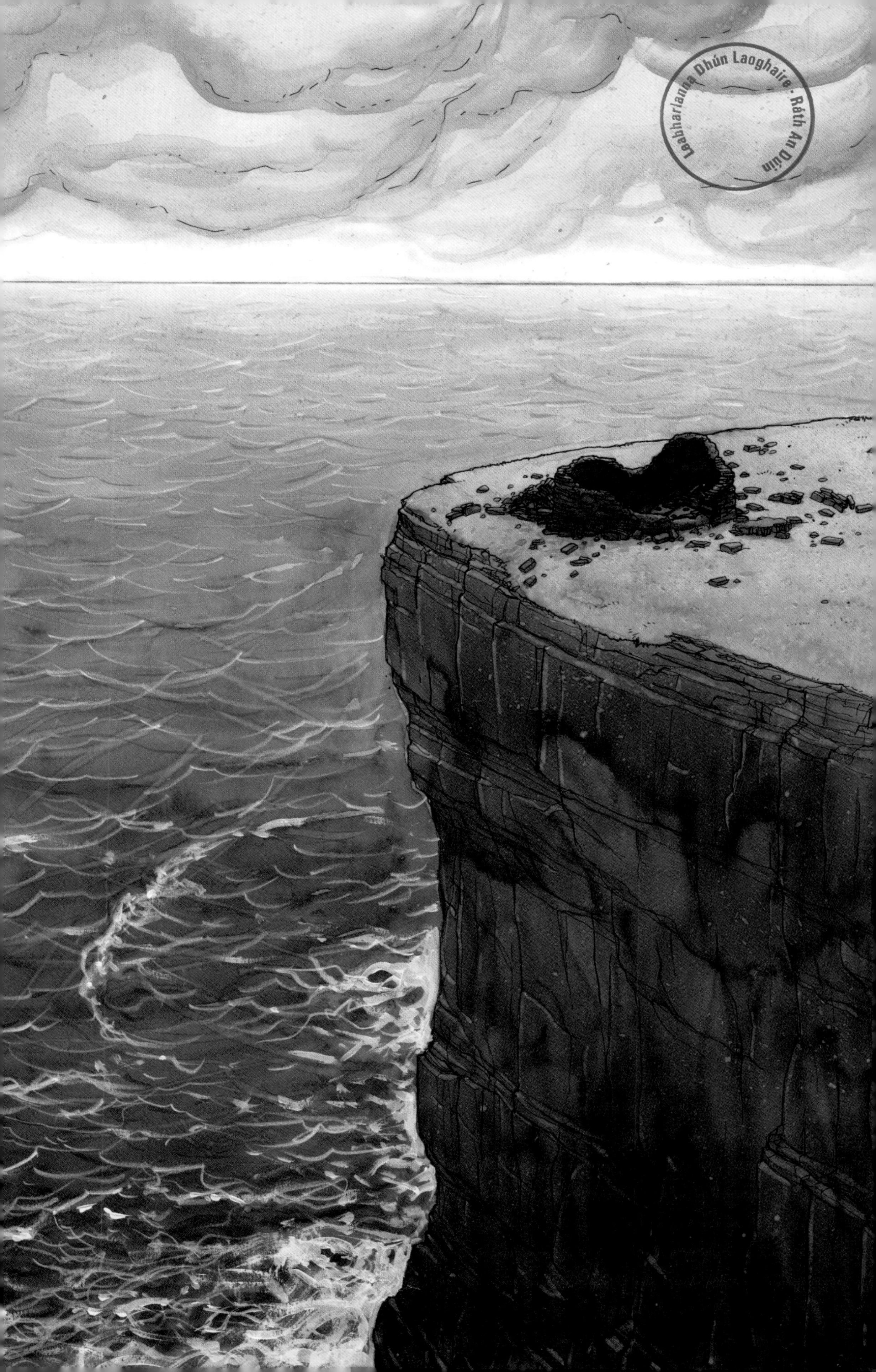

Historically, the grim prophecy of the seer probably came true. There was a long-standing feud between the Geats and the Swedes. The Geats occupied what we now know as southern Sweden, so it seems likely that they were killed or driven off. No further reference to them is found in history or legend after the burial of Beowulf. Some scholars believe that the Wuffing dynasty in Denmark was founded by exiled Geats, but nothing is known for sure.

ACKNOWLEDGMENTS

Project-specific contributions: Dan & Laurie Thron, David Cochary, Ben Hansford, Leslie Siddeley, Gretchen Laise, Dorian Hart, Rachel Ellis Adams, Timothy Weinmeister, Kristin Thalheimer, Stephen Krcmar, Patti Jones, Liz Bicknell, and Deb Wayshak. General: my folks, Joanne Greenberg, and the U-32 English Department.

Artistic mentors and instructors: there are too many; I'm sure I'll miss a few. But let's say foremost Dave Passalacqua and Warren Linn; but also Barbara Nessim, Les Kanturek, Sergio Baradat, Bob Siegelman, Donna Byars, Donna Romero, Pat Pritchett, Bob Cole, Susan Stillman, Luvon Sheppard, Alan Shepherd, John White, Diana Bryan, Julian Allen, Allen Barber, Nancy Van Goethem, Jim Kelso, C. Michael Dudash, Len Urso, Keener Bond, Wendy Popp, Lucinda Brogden, Gretchen, and my dad.

Self-publishing inspiration: Dave Sim and Ani DiFranco. An odd pair indeed. And the Xeric Foundation, for getting me started.

Since this is, after all, an action story, I'd like to thank my numerous martial arts mentors and instructors (in reverse chronological order): Bill Gleason, Joshua Grant, Yao Li, Joao Amaral, Robert Thomas, Ken Nissen, Ed DiMarco, Jean Duteau, Seleshe, Sarah Norton, Mike Carriveau, Dick Powell, and, collectively, everyone at Shobu Aikido, New England Aikikai, Boston Kung Fu Tai Chi Club, the Bond Street Dojo, Alan Lee's Chinese Kung Fu Wu Shu Association, the RIT Kung Fu Club, Burlington Aikikai, Two Rivers Aikikai, Aikido of Montpelier, the Montpelier Karate Club, and the Shiroishiku Sapporo Kendo Club.

This goes hand-in-hand with the above: I dedicate this book with my apologies to those people in my life who have suffered through my insensitivity -- particularly those whom, when I was younger, I physically bullied or picked on. You know who you are, but I want to offer particularly abject apologies to Jeff

First Candlewick Press edition 2007

Library of Congress Cataloging-in-Publication Data

Hinds, Gareth, date.
Beowulf / Gareth Hinds. – 1st Candlewick Press ed.
p. cm.
Graphic novel adaptation of the Old English epic poem, Beowulf.
ISBN: 978-0-7636-3022-5 (hardcover)
1. Graphic novels I. Beowulf. II. Title.

PN6727.H53B46 2007
741.5–dc22   2006049023

ISBN: 978-0-7636-3023-2 (paperback)

4 6 8 10 9 7 5 3

Printed in China

This book was typeset in Yuletide Log,
Humana Serif, and ATQuill.

Candlewick Press
2067 Massachusetts Avenue
Cambridge, MA 02140

visit us at www.candlewick.com

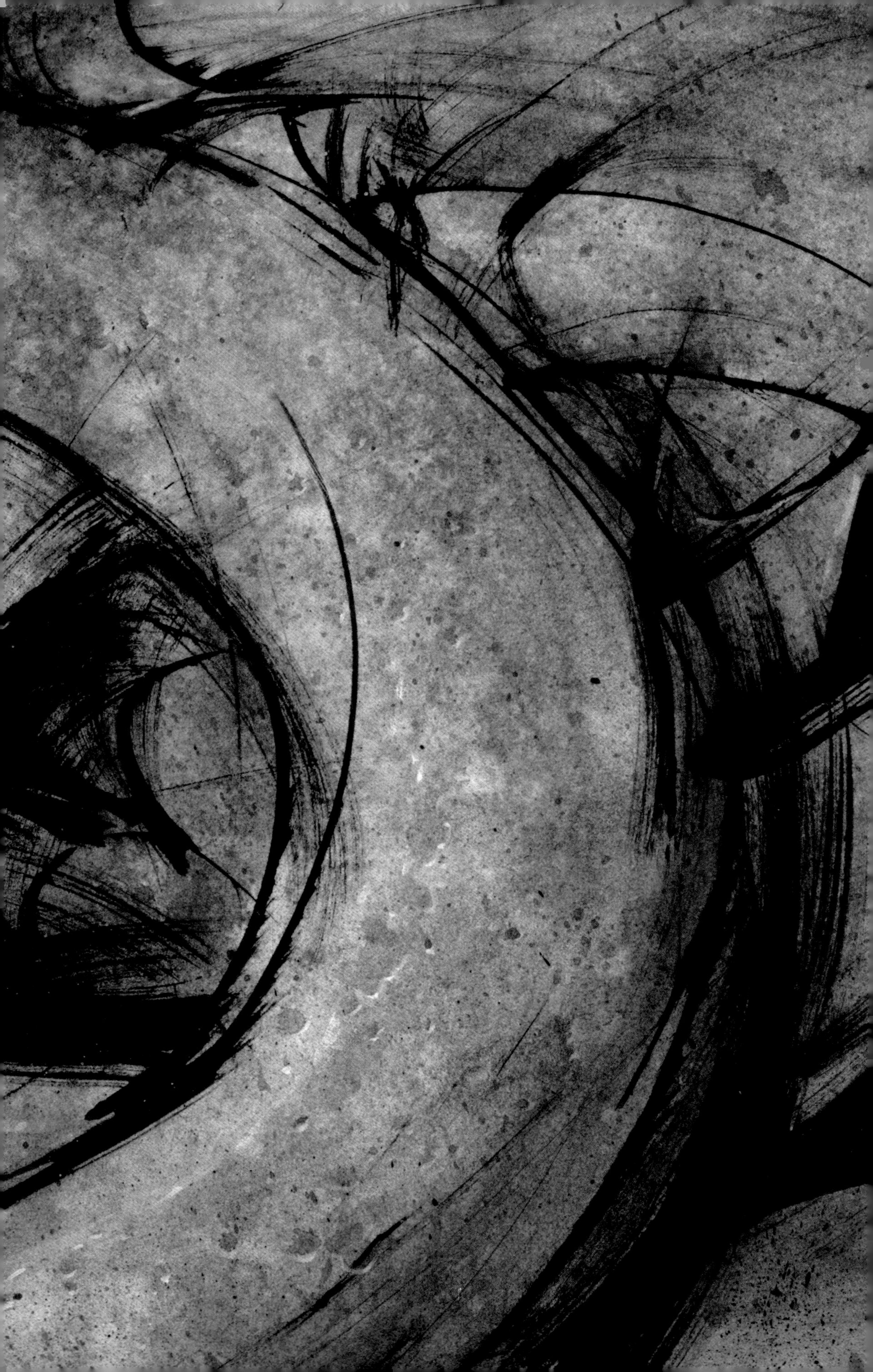

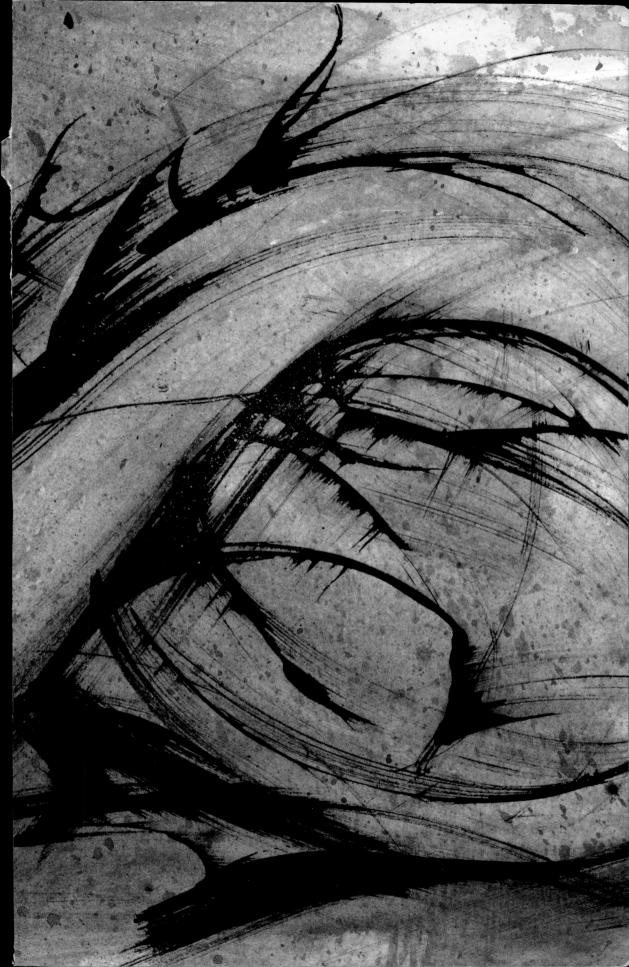